THE UNITED FEDERATION MARINE CORPS' LYSANDER TWINS

BOOK 5
BLOOD UNITED

Colonel Jonathan P. Brazee
USMC (Ret)

Semper Fi Press

D1227740

Acknowledgements:
I want to thank all those who took the time to pre-read this book, catching my mistakes in both content and typing. Thanks to Jim Caplan, my beta reader, and best_editor1 for her editing. And once again, a special shout out goes to my cover artist, the award-winning Jessica Tung Chi Lee. You can see more of her work at:

http://www.jessicatcl.com/news.html.

Original cover art by Jessica TC Lee

Cover graphics by Steven Novak

CORVALLIS

Prologue
Esther

The explosion shook the ground, sending smoke and debris into the air 50 meters to her left. Immediately, the avatars for three of Third Platoon's Marines grayed out, and four more shifted to light blue, indicating three KIA and four WIA. More pertinent to the company as a whole, the round had opened a gap in the line, and from the influx of data hitting her, it looked like the Amals were massing to prosecute the gap.

"Lieutenant Chambers, shift Second Squad left," Captain Esther Lysander, UFMC, shouted into her command net.

"Staff Sergeant Avalon, prepare to give me . . ." she started, then paused to pull up the mortar section's remaining rounds. "Prepare to give me eight rounds on three-oh-two and three-oh-eight."

"That will only leave me with eighteen, Skipper," the staff sergeant responded.

The mortar section leader, who'd been attached to Golf for three weeks now, had seemed to treat the section's combat load as his personal possessions, hoarding the rounds like a miser. Eighteen remaining rounds were nothing if it came to the FPF[1], so he had a point. But if the Amals were able to penetrate Golf's line, then they could roll up First Platoon easily, then turn and take on the rest of the company. It was imperative that they be stopped, therefore, even if they had to use up every last one of their remaining rounds.

---

[1] FPF: Final Protective Fire, the last flurry of intense fire designed to turn back an assault.

"Understood. My orders remain the same," she said curtly and leaving it at that.

She switched off the company command net and onto the battalion fire control net, asking, "Jerol, where we at? I really need that air."

"I'm trying, Esther," the harried battalion fire support coordinator told her. "Badger-One's still hard down, and Badger-Three's supporting the landing."

Esther didn't need to ask about Badger-Two. The Wasp had been shot down two hours ago supporting Bok Kim and India Company.

"I need something, Jerol. Things are getting puckering here. I'm down to 78%, and the Amals are massing. What about that armor?"

"I've got Beltzer with the landing force, trying to confirm that. No one knows if the armor landed or if it did, where it is."

"Come on, Jerol! That's bullshit! You can't just lose an armored column. Do your job and get me something! Adder-Six, out!" she passed, cutting the connection.

She was pissed, and she knew the Jerol Tympany was doing the best he could. At the moment, however, his best he wasn't good enough. Facing her 157 remaining effective Marines and sailors was something along the lines of 4-500 Amals who may not have the force-in-depth as the Navy-Marine task force, but were outfitted with the best that Amalgamation Sunset, Corp, could provide.

And that clusterfuck of a landing wasn't doing her any good, either.

It should have been much easier, she knew. This was the United Federation Navy and Marines doing what they were supposed to do best—land a fighting force on an enemy planet.

Not that Corvallis was technically an enemy planet. It was nominally neutral, and the Federation was not at war with the planetary government. The operation was a punitive raid against Amalgamation Sunset's vast holdings on the planet to drive the corporation to the negotiating table. It wasn't working out that way, though.

To make the lack of progress even worse, Esther's Second Battalion, Eleventh Marines had been on the planet for over a week now, landing on commercial liners, and bussed, for God's sake, to assembly areas in support of the coming landing. Esther's mission had been to secure the communications relay station on Bremmerton Peak, knocking out the Amals off-planet comms.

"We're not getting air," she passed to First Lieutenant Ogilvy, her XO, on the P2P.

"Shit. We need it, Skipper."

"It's not coming, and they don't know about the armor, either."

"They don't know?"

"Yeah, they lost a tank platoon."

"Mother and Child, how could this get any more screwed up?"

"Doesn't matter, Sam. Whatever their problems are, this is on our shoulders now. We need to fight our way out of it."

There was a fusillade of fire from the right side of the line. Esther paused, waiting for a report while pulling up her command display. No more Marines had been hit, and First Lieutenant Larry "Dispilly" Williams, the platoon commander, wasn't reporting in, so she shifted her mind to the problem at hand. She needed a sounding board, so she pulled up the first sergeant to join her and the XO.

"Tell me if I'm missing something.

"One: our mission was compromised, and we were ambushed by a battalion-sized unit that somehow escaped all of our vaunted Navy surveillance.

"Two: the landing force has been thrown into chaos by some yet unknown electronic countermeasures.

"Three: we are out on our own, out of artillery range, without air support, and with a tank platoon the LFC[2] graciously lifted out to us lost somewhere.

"Does that sum it up?"

---

[2] LFC: Landing Force Commander

"Yes, ma'am, but at least our position is pretty defensible," First Sergeant Lowell Watson said.

More by luck than anything else, Esther had to admit to herself.

When they'd been hit by the much larger force, Esther had ordered the company into a hasty defense, their backs against a butte that jutted up three klicks from the base of Bremerton Peak. By refusing their flanks, the company was able to focus their firepower to the front.

As if the Amals were listening in, a rocket shot across Second Platoon's lines to slam into the rock face of the butte, sending showers of debris down behind them. Esther barely noticed it. It was merely harassing fire, designed to keep the Marines' heads down while they maneuvered for the upcoming assault.

Looking at the AOR[3] readout as it played across her face shield, she thought that assault wouldn't be long in coming. Right at that moment, what looked to be a platoon-sized unit appeared 800 meters in front of Third Platoon's position.

"Shit," she heard the XO say over the P2P, and she knew he was monitoring the overall picture as well.

Not that the avatars were the ground truth. Electronic countermeasures and spoofing were in full force, and the display shifted from one minute to the next.

The Amal platoon, if it was even there and not a spoof, were in defilade, out of the reach of the company's direct fire weapons.

Not wanting to waste mortar rounds, she passed to First Lieutenant Stephen Cline, her Third Platoon commander, "Get someone to hit two-two-six with a couple of M505 rounds. Let's see if those are real bodies out there."

"Roger that," Cline responded.

Esther ached to initiate the coming assault. She was not temperamentally suited for sitting in the defense, giving the initiative to the enemy. As she tried to come up with an idea, however, nothing made tactical sense. They were outnumbered, and their position was about as good as could be hoped for. The

---

[3] AOR: Area of Responsibility

textbook solution was to let the assault be cut down by the disciplined firepower of the Marines.

The only problem with the textbook solution, though, was that it included air, naval gunfire, and arty, none of which she had at the moment.

The soft thunks of outgoing "Dunker" rounds reached her, and she paused her thoughts, mentally counting out the time to target. Her display blossomed with three hits, right in the middle of the Amal platoon—which didn't react. Either they were pretty well disciplined themselves, or the avatars were a spoof. A moment later, the avatars disappeared, either taken offline by the Amals or jammed by one of her ECM drones that hovered high overhead.

"Knew it," the XO said. There's no way they managed to get to that position undetected."

Unless they did and were cutting off their signatures to convince us they weren't real.

The punch and counterpunch were almost mentally overwhelming at times, and for a moment, Esther longed for the "clean" combat she experienced as a junior Marine. It was see the enemy, kill the enemy, and leave the chess game of the modern battlefield to the officers. Now, she was that officer, and it was up to her to put her Marines into position where they could prevail.

"I still don't like that blind spot by the spring," the first sergeant said. "I think I can take Porter and Jiminez and—"

The sound of concentrated fire from Second Platoon cut him off for a second. Esther switched to D-3, her Dragonfly III microdrone that overlooked the platoon's frontage. Two bodies 300 meters to the platoon's front were clearly visible, whatever countersurveillance the mercs had that had blocked their visibility now destroyed by Marine fire. There were flickers of movement retreating back through the dense brush, but nothing clear.

"Diane, what did that look like?" Esther asked her Second Platoon commander.

"Just a probe. We got two before they could duck back. I think they wanted to verify the gap," she passed.

Which was probably correct. While not technically a gap at the moment, it was painfully clear to Esther that it was thinly held.

But just as the Amals were trying to screw up the Marine's battlefield detection systems, so too were the Marines jamming and spoofing the Amals' systems. They knew where the Marines were, of course, but they probably couldn't be assured of each Marine's position. They tried to get real eyes on the lines and test the Marines' fields of fire, and that cost them two soldiers.

They probably now knew that the gap they'd created was at least partially covered. Esther wished she knew what how that knowledge would affect the decisions of her opposing commander.

"Skipper?" the first sergeant asked. "About that blind spot?"

"OK, take those two, but no hero stuff. Only if it's needed."

"Hell, Skipper, you know me. Mamma's favorite boy better come back home. I don't need no medals."

For someone with a Silver Star to his name, that was pure BS. Esther didn't want to let the first sergeant get too focused on a specific threat, though. He was there to keep the Marines operating at full efficiency and with maximum lethal intent, but he had a point about that small area by the spring, protected by an overhanging rock face. If an Amal sniper team got in there, for example, they could wreak havoc among Third Platoon. Esther was running thin on bodies, so she agreed to let the first sergeant assume that particular responsibility.

Esther's combat AI whistled a warning in her ears, and she dropped to the ground as a surge of power amped up her shielding. A split second later, the familiar half-whistle of the Amal Beta-Hawks reached her. These nasty little anti-personnel rockets had seeker scanners in their noses. If they passed within 10 or 12 meters of a Marine, the fuze oriented and fired a load of accelerated buckshot at him or her with enough power to penetrate the Marine's body armor. Their best defense was to overwhelm the Beta-Hawks' scanners with a concerted blast from their shielding projectors. The blast was power-hungry and could deplete each Marine's shielding system within 20-30 seconds, so the waves of Beta-Hawks could be intended to kill Marines—or to simply make them expend energy and leave them vulnerable to further assaults.

Esther held her breath as one of the rockets passed right over her, seemingly close enough that she could have reached up and grabbed it. Her shielding won the battle though, and the rocket continued on its way, looking for Marines where they were none. Five more Marines were not as fortunate, though.

Esther's power output dropped to normal, and she started to get up when the whistle sounded again. A second wave of over 50 more Beta-Hawks was on its way.

Shit, how many of the damned things do they have?

The rockets were not particularly expensive in comparison with other munitions, but still, they'd expended close to 400 so far, and they had to be reaching the end of their combat load.

None came close to her from this wave, but when the third wave was launched, Esther knew this was the real deal. The assault was on.

"This is it," she passed on the command net. "Heads up, and let's crush them."

"Staff Sergeant Avalon, get ready for those rounds," she passed to her mortar section leader. "The command's coming from Lieutenant Ogilvy or me. I'm going to want them on target as soon as they're called for."

"Roger that. But I've got a 17-second flight-time."

"Understood. You just fire on command."

Esther's position was behind a large rock behind and slightly to the right of her company lines and above them where she had a good view of the AOR. In medieval times, she might have a coterie of knights protecting her. In the 20th Century, Old Reckoning, she'd be with her radio operator and maybe some of her fire support personnel. In the modern Marine Corps, she was on her own.

She could watch the progress of the battle on her combat display, but that seemed to separate her from the battlefield, so she inched up until she could see the company's position. Explosions peppered the area, sending up gouts of dirt when the rounds landed, but her Marines were dug in pretty well, and no more avatars turned light blue or gray despite the incoming.

"You might want to keep your head down, Skipper," the first sergeant passed to her. "You're making a tempting target."

Esther turned to the left where she knew the first sergeant was. He, along with Corporal Porter and PFC Jiminez, was prone just behind a slight wrinkle in the terrain. Looking across the 200 meters of ground that separated him, he raised an arm, palm flat and down, and signaled for her to take cover.

"Can't see what's happening when I'm hiding, First Sergeant."

"That's why you have your combat display, Skipper," he replied before cutting the P2P.

She did slump down just a bit. She realized that she could be sniper bait, but unless they had some high-caliber weapons out there, she was still far enough back that her helmet should be protection enough from normal sniper rounds.

The Marines in Third Platoon opened up, the two M249's in the platoon's position spitting out their stream of death. Esther could see movement to the front as the Amals used fire and maneuver to advance.

"I need that air, Skipper," Lieutenant Cline passed.

"We don't have it," she replied before switching to the battalion fire support net.

"Jerol, tell me you've got something for me."

"That's a negative, Esther. I'm trying. Just hold on a little longer."

"I can't. They're into their assault now!"

Without waiting, she switched to the battalion command net, pulling up the commanding officer on the P2P.

"Colonel Rzeminski, this is it. The Amals are in full assault mode, and the numbers don't look good. I need fire support now, sir."

"I know, Esther," Lieutenant Colonel Peter Joseph Rzeminski, her battalion commander replied. "But I just don't have it. India's in it big time, and the port is still a cluster."

Esther had been following the battle between India and the Amal main force, and she knew the CO was right. India was down to around 90 effectives, last time she checked, and the company was facing close to 1,000 Amals. Golf was almost an afterthought to what was happening back there.

Not an afterthought to us, though!

"Look, I'll see what we can do, but you need to hang on." There was a pause, then he said in a quiet voice, "Protect what you can, Esther."

Which means surrender if I have to.

She understood the long-term strategic value of what he was saying. Despite the confusion the Amals had managed to sow over the spaceport, there wasn't any possible way that they could prevail over the long term. With fewer than 3,000 troops on the planet, they couldn't land reinforcements while the Marines could land an entire regiment, if they had to. If Esther surrendered her company, that would give the Amals some serious ammunition in negotiations, but it would also save Marine lives. The CO had essentially given her the OK to do that if she decided all hope was lost. In reality, it was her call, but he'd just reminded her of the option.

We're Federation Marines, damn it! We don't surrender.

She pulled up the XO and first sergeant, then said, "I just spoke with the CO. We're not getting any support. It's up to us."

"Typical shit," the first sergeant said.

"And, he basically authorized me to surrender—"

"Fuck that shit!" the first sergeant shouted into his mic at the same time as the XO said "No way!"

A Marine company was not a democracy, and Esther was going to be the one making the decisions, but still, she was gratified to hear that her two headquarters' senior staff agreed with her.

Surrendering might save some lives in the near term, but usually, the mere presence of Marines was enough to defuse a situation without rounds being fired. If the Marines started becoming known for surrendering when things got tough, then their presence would no longer be enough. There would be much more combat, and in the long run, more Marine deaths. The long-term price of surrendering was expensive, too expensive to contemplate.

The CO might have subtly given her permission to surrender, but the call was hers, and she intended to crush the Amals or make their victory so expensive that they wouldn't dare take Marines on again.

An Amal mortar round exploded ten meters in front of her rock, showering her with clods of dirt. She never flinched.

"My feelings exactly," she told the two. "If they really want to take on the Marines, let's make them pay."

She knew not every Marine would agree with her—and undoubtedly more family members of her Marines wouldn't agree. She already knew that the eleven families of the ten Marines and one Navy corpsmen who'd been lost past a reasonable chance at resurrection would have rather had her already surrender. But the Corps was a volunteer force, and every single one of them knew the risk of enlisting. That might sound trite and dismissive, but that didn't make it any less true.

"Ooh-fucking-rah, Skipper," the first sergeant said.

"Ooh-fucking-rah, First Sergeant" she replied. "Now, let's fight."

Esther looked over the company lines. She wished she had a rifle platoon in reserve, ready to react where needed, but her lines were too long for that. Weapons Platoon's had designated half of the Marines from the Meson-gun and Avalon's mortar section to help plug a gap or launch into a counterattack to take exploit an advantage, but that simply wasn't enough bodies to have much effect. Other than that glaring weakness, she was fairly confident as to the company's disposition. And under mounting pressure, she sure couldn't move Marines around now. The sheer amount of incoming fire could devastate any shift she tried to implement. No, she'd emplaced the company, and now it was bare-knuckle time.

A tiny blast from Second Platoon's line caught her attention, and she looked over just as a bright light exploded 400 meters up.

"Scratch one drone," Lieutenant Chambers passed.

"Good job, Diane," Esther passed, and she meant it.

The Amals had drones, and the Marines had drones, but not over each other's territories. Evidently, the Amals had managed to sneak one over Second Platoon's position, but not without being spotted. With one of their tiny Broebecks, the platoon had shot the drone out of the sky.

Her display was filling with data. Every round fired, every piece of gathered data, all helped develop what she knew of the battlefield. She'd gotten the hang of processing it all while still keeping her mind on the big picture, but that sometimes left some important items ignored until something happened to remind her of them. A blast hit the rock beside her face, sending rock fragments smashing against her face shield, one tiny particle managing to seeing-eye its way under the bottom of it and above her collar. She jumped back, hand reaching to her neck. Pulling it back down, she saw blood on her fingers; not much, but enough to remind her that a battlefield was a dangerous place, and she couldn't forget matters such as personal safety.

A moment later, five rounds detonated around her, one right on top of the rock at her back. She felt several hits that her helmet and bones absorbed, but nothing that had any effect.

"You OK, Ma'am?" the XO asked.

Lieutenant Ogilvy had the same battle command readout as she had, so he'd be able to see that her avatar was still a bright blue, but he must have been concerned at the volley of rounds targeting her.

"I guess I gave my position away, but I'm fine."

But I need to see what's happening.

She'd picked a secondary position 20 meters away, and she low-crawled to it as three more rounds landed back where she'd just left. Slowly, she raised her head just enough to look out over the lines, visually connecting what she was seeing with the sounds of battle that were reaching her.

It wasn't reassuring.

Second Platoon was taking the brunt of the incoming, just as Esther had figured. The question now was when to launch the FPF to take out as many of the enemy as possible before they could reach Marine lines. Luckily, the enemy seemed to be moving slowly enough that she felt she had time to react. A Marine attack force would be moving quicker, using momentum to magnify their impact. Evidently, the Amals were not so well trained.

But Intel said they were well-trained. Heck, most of those mercenaries had served in the military forces of the Confederation, the Alliance, the Brotherhood—and yes, even the Federation. They had to know that the longer they took, the more vulnerable they were to Marine fire. It didn't make sense.

Suddenly, she knew it did make sense.

"Sergeant Sri, give me a kamikaze at two-two-one ASAP!" she ordered Clark Sripituksakul, her dronemaster.

"Aye-aye, ma'am," the sergeant said immediately. "Sending D-4 now."

"What do you have, Skipper?" the XO asked as he monitored the command net.

She ignored him as she brought up D-4's feed. The little drone dove past the company's lines, heading right for a small swale 700 meters to the front of Third Platoon. The Amals had counter-mine measures, too, and within a moment, a tight finger of fire reached up to the Dragonfly. In kamikaze mode, D-4 didn't try to evade the missilette, and the tiny warhead easily took out the equally tiny drone—but not before it caught the signatures of several hundred Amals.

Two-two-one had been duly registered as a somewhat concealed position, but with a seemingly open avenue of approach to the Marine lines, Esther hadn't thought the Amals would attack from there, preferring the far better terrain in front of Second. Either the Amals felt the terrain wasn't as bad as Esther thought or they felt the surprise factor was worth it.

Or, more likely, they know the 90 mike-mike combat load of a Marine company, and are trying to make me expend it on a feint in front of Third.

The moment that thought hit her, she knew she was right, and that it had almost worked.

"Staff Sergeant Avalon, give me nine rounds on two-two-one, 25 meters grid," she ordered.

Nine rounds didn't leave her much for the FPF, but the Amals were massed closely together, and she needed to take the initiative.

"But there's nothing there, Captain," the staff sergeant started.

"Now, staff sergeant, or so help me God, I'll court martial your ass right in the middle of the battle!"

"Yes, ma'am!"

Staff Sergeant Avalon might be a pain in the ass, but he knew his mortars, and within ten seconds, she heard the reassuring thump of outgoing. The enemy commander had to know his or her plan had been revealed, and the Amal troops wouldn't just sit there as targets. The question was what they could do in the short amount of time they had. Esther cycled through her surveillance channels, trying to see what was happening at two-two-one, but the Amals' countersurveillance was up to the task. She almost sent in another kamikaze drone, but that would be a waste of resources. She'd know soon enough.

The first three rounds landed with loud blasts, dirt, smoke, and bits of vegetation shooting into the air from the target area. A moment later, three more rounds landed, followed by three more. From her position 900 meters away, the smoke and debris columns made an almost perfect box.

"Good shooting, Avalon," she passed as she scanned for a BDA.

It would take boots on the ground for an accurate Battle Damage Assessment, but while most of the attacking force's unit-sized countersurveillance capabilities would still be operational, seriously wounded or killed enemy troops would lose their personal shields, which depended on fighting suit integrity.

Numbers flashed on her display. Thirty-two Amal troopers had lost that integrity, and they, or their bodies, were now visible. There were undoubtedly more of them taken out of the fight but whose shields were still intact.

She couldn't have hoped for a more effective barrage. The Amals must have been packed in there like sardines. Part of her screamed to launch her own attack, to take advantage of the momentary swing of momentum while the enemy was discombobulated, but the fact of the matter was that she was still severely outnumbered. The Roman testudo, or "tortoise," was effective only when there were no breaks in the shield wall, and Esther couldn't launch an attack without making a break in her defensive line.

If she had the opportunity to bring the fight to the enemy, that was quickly lost. After a momentary pause, the Amal commander let loose his troops, ordering them forward. Sheets of fire reached out to the Marines.

"Two in three, hold your fire unless you have a confirmed target," she passed on the open circuit.

This has been part of her hasty operation order, given two hours prior, but it didn't hurt to remind her Marines of that. The company couldn't afford just to keep pumping rounds downrange, but the Marines also couldn't afford to simply give the assaulting force clear avenues of approach. Every third Marine, along with the attached sniper team, was to keep up a steady volume of fire. Meanwhile, the rest of the company, to include the crew-served weapons, were to remain quiet, both to conserve ammunition and to remain undetected. The riflemen could engage identified targets of opportunity as they acquired them, but not simply spray rounds downrange.

Contrary to Bollywood flicks, the vast majority of rounds fired in battle were not the well-aimed, single shots of lore. Except for possibly snipers, wide-spread one shot, one kill was a fantasy. Soldiers going back to Greek archers simply sent as many rounds downrange as possible, trusting the mass of fire to result in hits.

Golf Company was well-armed, especially with hypervelocity darts, but they had no method of resupply, so what they had was what they were bringing to the fight.

Esther's AI scanned the company's circuits, but not much was being passed. She knew her Marines were well-trained, and they were focusing on doing their jobs.

Esther's nerves were jangling—she still wasn't used to standing by while her Marines fought. She fired a string of rounds from her M90 carbine, more to get rid of her excess energy than in thinking she'd actually hit any of the Amals. She was supposed to be giving orders that would benefit the company, but with Third Platoon and part of Second engaged, the battle was now down to the individual rifleman.

For a moment, she considered ordering first to sweep right and attack the Amal flanks, but she knew the risk was too great. The attacking wave certainly was not the entire Amal force, and moving First would leave a huge gap in her lines. More than a few armies in history had been defeated by commanders who tried to get too fancy with maneuvering. At some point, a battle simply boiled down to whoever wanted it more.

A crack of ionized air finally reached out to the advancing forces. Corvallis had a thicker atmosphere that Earth Standard, so the range on her M303 meson cannons were more limited. The Amals had come within that range, however, and Sergeant Tennison had opened fire with one of his two cannons. The Amal soldiers had shielding, of course, but the big gun probed the attackers, seeking to deplete that shielding or find a crack through it. Two more Amals popped up on her display—whether they'd fallen to the cannon or not, Esther couldn't tell.

But not enough of the Amals were falling. Her Marines should be taking out more, even given the professional fire and maneuver being shown by the enemy.

"Any word on supporting arms, Skipper? We've got a shitload of bad guys advancing on us right now," Lieutenant Cline asked.

"That's a negative, Steve. Just keep on mowing them down."

Esther had to hand it to the enemy commander. Faced with dug-in Marines, he or she had double feinted. The first feint had been the fake troops at two-two-one. The second had been the massing of troops in front of Second Platoon's lines, which seemed reasonable once the "troops" at two-two-one were discovered to be spoofed. But then, the real assault, which was advancing to Third Platoon's position, had been put into play.

Esther had been correct in predicting that the enemy commander would want to attack over the more favorable terrain in front of Third, but the feints had put that into doubt until now.

Unless this is yet another feint, she reminded herself.

"Where are we with that armor?" she passed back to Jerol.

"Still trying to find it."

"Not good enough," Esther shouted into her mic. "We're getting hammered."

At that moment, two more Marine avatars grayed out, something Esther knew Jerol would be able to see on his own monitors.

"I need something now!" she said before cutting the connection.

"Are we getting to FPF time?" the XO asked.

Another Marine avatar switched to light blue. Esther zoomed her display so she could see the FPF kill zone. There were enemy soldiers maneuvering through it, but not enough.

"Not yet," she responded, then on the company net, "Weapons free."

Immediately, the outgoing fire increased as all Marines were free to fire as they identified targets. More and more Amal avatars started appearing on her display as their shielding was either penetrated or was compromised by Marine fire.

And there were an awful lot of red avatars.

A large-caliber round hit her shoulder with a loud smack.

"Son of a bitch!" she exclaimed, rotating her arm.

Her bones had stopped the round, but still, there had been quite a bit of kinetic energy to absorb, and it hurt like hell. Her STF[4] bone inserts could stop most small arms fire, but that meant stopping the penetration. A large enough caliber round could still act like an old-fashioned mace or warclub, breaking bones. Marines had lost limbs or had broken necks from rounds that never actually penetrated the armor inserts.

She didn't know who had shot her, or if she was being specifically targeted, but she guessed it was by someone not too far away.

"Sergeant Tennison," she passed, trying to ignore the pain, "What's your effectiveness right now?"

"Not great, ma'am. We're taking a few down, but there's still too much beam dissipation."

In space, energy weapons were the de rigueur. In atmospheres, they were far less effective, needing larger and more powerful energy sources. An M1 Davis had such a powerpack, but the small, man-ported M303 meson cannon simply didn't have the power to punch through that much atmosphere. Against infantry with modern body armor, the max effective range was around 600

---

[4] STF: Shear Thickening Fluid. A gel-like substance that hardened into armor upon impact.

meters at Earth Standard atmosphere. Her two cannons were right at 500 meters from the FPF kill zone,

"When we fire the FPF, I want you to range in and cover the lines."

She had just cut the range from 500 meters to around 400 or less, which would make the cannon all the more effective.

"Roger that. I'm entering the firing data now."

Esther was counting on the M303 to help turn back the Amals. Even when the energy weapons were not killing the bad guys, it took an awful lot of discipline to keep advancing when shielding was being degraded.

But they're showing they might have that discipline.

The enemy incoming suddenly increased, and Esther's display reset as the battle AIs took in the new data. There was one glaring problem that immediately demanded all of her attention.

Hell!

"Jerol, I need something, anything on three-one-four, like now!"

"I still don't have anything to give you, Esther."

"You'd better shit something, or we're sunk."

"Skipper, we've got a Karzai firing at us," Lieutenant Chambers passed, overriding her circuit with battalion.

"I'm working on it!"

"Did she say they've got a Karzai?" Jerrol asked.

"A nineteen-oh-one," she answered.

"Let me see what I can spring loose."

A Karzai 1901 was an old, but very capable armored gamma gun. With an effective range of possibly 1200 meters in this atmosphere, it could stand off and pound the Marines, its electro-fusion generator able to supply continuous power. Each type of energy weapon had a specific signature, and by firing, Esther's AI had identified the Karzai. Esther quickly ran through its capabilities and vulnerabilities.

The main gun was a brute, and already, Marines were being taken out of action, their personal armor no match for the megajoules being fired at them. The Karzai's weakness was in its chassis. It wasn't very maneuverable, and using the old gap-plate armor, it was vulnerable to modern anti-armor weapons. The gun was undoubtedly dug in, but if she could get her Marines close enough, they had any number of weapons that could knock the gun offline. A simple airstrike would render the Karzai as so much junk.

"Avalon, do you have any two-forty-threes?" she asked her mortar section leader.

"Negative. Only two-oh-twos left."

The M243 mortar rounds had some armor-penetrating capability, more than enough for a Karzai, but the M202 round was anti-personnel, which would have no effect on the gun.

"Colonel, I've got a Karzai taking us under fire. I need air, now!" she passed on the battalion command net.

"We're working on it, trying to get the last Wasp back up. Hold on," the CO replied.

I can't hold on. We're getting shredded!

Esther's AI gave her a warning as her shielding increased for a moment. She'd been hit with a sidelobe of the Karzai's fire. Just that touch had degraded her personal shielding to 64%. Marines on the lines were getting hit harder, and outgoing fire was diminishing as Marines were taking cover inside their fighting holes.

But the red avatars of the enemy had stopped their advance. A gamma gun didn't know friend from foe, so as long as the Karzai was firing, the Amal infantry had to hold in place.

And suddenly, Esther knew what she had to do. She pushed the ramifications of that out of her mind and connected to Lieutenant Williams.

"Dispilly, I need a squad to take out the Karzai. You should be able to range it from here," she passed, flagging a small rise 600 meters from second platoon's lines.

What she didn't have to say was that was a long, long 600 meters for Marines to cover under fire. They might not be vulnerable to the Karzai until they reached the rise, but they'd be fish in a barrel to the Amal infantry arrayed in front of the company.

"I'm shifting fires to give whoever you send some cover, but it won't be enough. You've got to get your Marines to haul ass."

First Platoon had taken the least amount of fire and had the fewest casualties, and Esther hoped that meant the area to their front had the fewest Amals. That had impacted her decision, but the terrain in front of the platoon put them in defilade to the Karzai up to the rise she designated. Once the assault team passed about 50 meters, the Karzai couldn't fire upon them. Infantry, yes; Karzai, no.

Defilade or not to the gamma gun, they would be under constant fire from the infantry. Esther had to mitigate that.

She quickly designated several targets, then passed them to Staff Sergeant Avalon before giving her orders to the rest of the company. They were going to attempt to clear the way for the team from First.

Just before she gave the order, firing sounded from First's far left flank.

Shit! Can't they give me a chance to kick this off first?

"Scratch one sniper team," First Sergeant Watson said. "Caught them sneaking in and zeroed them."

Thank God for that. If they'd gotten into position . . .

If they had, they could have targeted the assault team all the way out.

"Are you ready, Dispilly?" she asked her platoon commander.

"Roger that, Skipper. The team is ready."

"Go when the mortars hit."

"All hands, when the mortars hit, I want every single swinging dick to put rounds downrange."

With the Karzai still firing, Marines were hugging the bottom of their fighting holes. She needed them engaging the Amal infantry.

"Fire, Avalon," she passed.

Soft thunks of outgoing signaled that the first three rounds were fired. He'd wait five seconds before the second set, then another five before the third. Hopefully, that would be enough to get the assault team on their way without being cut down at their lines.

Esther counted down the flight time, squeezing the pistol grip of her M90, the pain in her shoulder forgotten.

When the first crump reached her, she shouted out "Open fire!" over the net and jumped up to add her own rounds to the effort. She didn't stop to aim, but sprayed the AO. The shear volume of Marine fire interrupted the Amal incoming as the soldiers took cover.

Dropping her magazine and inserting another, Esther glanced at her display. Thirteen Marines were moving rapidly down into the depression, already beyond the reach of the Karzai. Not beyond the reach of the infantry, though. One Marine faltered and stopped, his avatar the light blue of WIA. Esther couldn't take the time to worry about individual Marines in the middle of a battle, but she was only human. She instructed her AI to display individuals. The wounded Marine was PFC Lin Justice—and leading the assault was First Lieutenant Larry Williams, she saw.

"Dispilly, I said a squad!"

"Roger that, Skipper," he said, his breath coming in heavily as he ran. "I've got a squad here, and if you don't mind, I need to focus."

Shit, shit, shit!

Staff Sergeant Tor was a good man, but Esther wasn't convinced as to his ability to lead. With Williams leading the charge, and with only two squads left on the line, Esther wanted someone else there. She was about to order the XO to go take over, but the Karzai hadn't let up, and that was a long way for him to cover.

"First Sergeant, leave Porter and Jiminez and get your ass to First. Tor's got the platoon, but I want some adult supervision with him."

There was a pause, then the first sergeant said, "Hell, the lieutenant's leading the assault. Not surprising at all. I'm on my way."

Not surprising? Should I have foreseen that?

Esther fired off another magazine. Marines were falling to the Karzai, but she couldn't get caught up in the casualties. They had to cover Williams and his assault. He lost two more Marines as his team sprinted ahead.

Esther had to monitor the entire battlefield, but she couldn't resist taking Lieutenant Williams' feed and popping it in the upper right-hand side of her face shield display. It was jerky as he ran over the terrain. He grunted as he was hit by a round, but kept going.

Six hundred meters is a long ways to advance under fire, and several times, the squad had to slow down to return fire. Still, five minutes later, five of the original thirteen reached the near side of the small hill only to be hit from fire to their right.

"First Platoon, open fire on the Target F," Esther passed, painting a bright red "F" that corresponded from where Williams was taking fire. She could have used anything to designate the target, but the "F" was the first thing that came to mind.

"Corporal Bamburger, take Dilbert and Prielli and give me some cover," Williams ordered, which Esther overheard from streaming his feed. "OK, Ceasar. This is it. Do you have the location?"

"Yes, sir. I've got it."

"Then do it."

Esther, through the lieutenant's feed, watched as Lance Corporal Kleinmaster put one Hatchet on the ground beside him, readied another, then stood up to fire, only to receive the full blast of the Karzai. He faltered a moment, flinching, and that was all the Amal gunner needed. Kleinmaster's shielding collapsed, and the Marine fell back, his upper body cooked.

"They're waiting for you," Esther passed, stating the obvious.

Lieutenant Williams crabbed sideways to Kleinmaster's body and shoved it aside, revealing the second Hatchet. The first would have had the electronics fried, but the second, behind the crest of the rise, should still be functional.

"Displace, Dispilly. Don't pop up right there again," Esther ordered him.

Williams looked to his right, and Esther could see over his feed the approaching Amals. Bamberger and Dilbert were KIA, and Prielli was engaging, but despite the rest of the platoon's support, it was obvious their position was untenable.

"No time for that, ma'am."

He looked down at the Hatchet, setting the flight pattern for pop-up. Esther knew what he was going to do. If he fired in direct-fire mode, the same beam that would reach out to him would fry the warhead. He had to immediately acquire the Karzai, fire the Hatchet within the target cone, and do it quick enough for the missile to rise above where the gamma beam would be fired.

He grunted again, as two rounds slammed into him. His vitals remained steady, so neither round had penetrated, but they were reminders that he had no time left.

"Mother Mary, grant me strength," he muttered, then with one fluid motion, stood and hit the firing stud on the launcher.

He started to drop back down when he was struck by the gamma beam, and his feed cut off.

Hell, Dispilly, Esther thought, deflated.

A moment later, there was a small explosion in the direction of the Karzai. Esther didn't know if the Hatchet had hit the gun, and if it did, had it had taken it out. There was only one way to find out—if they took incoming, Lieutenant Williams had missed. If the Karzai was silenced, he'd hit it.

"Here they come," Lieutenant Cline passed.

Esther looked down at the past the FEBA, the Forward Edge of the Battle Area. Past this, except for possibly PFC Prielli, there were no Marines, only bad guys. She didn't need her display to see them come. They were moving, and moving quickly.

Esther knew right then that the Karzai had been knocked out. The Amal commander was trying to regain the initiative and strike before the Marines could react.

Back on Earth, there had been a battle in the American Civil War outside of a village called Gettysburg. All Marine officers studied this battle, and while Esther hadn't actually made the pilgrimage to the site, she was intimately familiar it. While the Amals weren't exactly advancing shoulder to shoulder as Pickett's soldiers were, she could imagine the Union's Colonel Joshua Chamberlain, on top of Little Roundtop, looking down upon the the attacking force.

A big difference, however, was that Chamberlain had the strength of the Union artillery behind him. Esther had nine rounds of 90mm mortar.

And 101 Marines. I've still got a fighting force.

"Get ready with your rounds, Staff Sergeant," she told Avalon. "As soon as you fire, I want you up on the lines. Things are about to get dicey here."

Esther checked the disposition of her Marines, but there wasn't anything she could do that would make a difference. The battle was closing, and it was going to be a toe-to-toe slugfest.

Esther brought up her M90, sighted on some of the closest Amals, and fired. The distance was a little far for the carbine, but not extraordinarily so. She didn't know if she hit anyone, but it was better than doing nothing.

Her AI chimed for her attention. The concentration of enemy in her FPF kill zone was reaching a probable high point.

"Fire the FPF," Esther passed.

Immediately, she heard the outgoing thunks of her remaining rounds, and the crescendo of fire from the Marines momentarily stopped the Amals as they took cover. The mortar rounds were set to detonate 15 meters above the deck, spewing death downwards, and the prone Amals had no chance. Sixty, maybe more, were taken out by the six rounds, far more than could normally be expected.

When the rounds detonated, the Amal immediate action, just as would be the Marines, was to get up and through the kill zone. The surviving Amals rushed forward, only to be cut down by Marine fire.

But Marines were being cut down as well. Enemy fire, both mortar and small arms, was taking a toll. Esther watched her display tick down: 90 effectives, 85, then 80. They couldn't hold out much longer.

"We've got Amals within the line," First Sergeant Watson passed.

Esther immediately pulled up his feed just as he grappled with a tall Amal. Esther couldn't make out what was happening, but suddenly the Amal was down, and the first sergeant was looking up as three more Amals appeared.

Hand-to-friggin-hand? Give me a break.

She pulled up the XO, but over on the left side of the line, he was too far away to help.

"XO, you've got the company," then "Avalon, get off your asses and follow me," she passed, then ran down the slight slope to First Platoon's position.

The platoon was already down a squad, and Esther couldn't allow it to fall. She turned off her display, needing no distraction and screaming like a banshee, she covered the ground at a dead run, firing at any target that presented himself. She was dimly aware of Avalon and his six Marines pulling up behind her.

The seven of them hit the line like a piledriver. Esther shot two Amals before they knew she was there. One went down, and the other spun around, his body armor stopping her darts. No matter. Esther delivered a butt stroke to the man's chin. Body armor or not, he dropped like a rock.

In front of her, an Amal soldier had a Marine on the ground as he tried to drive a vibroblade of some sort through the Marine's armor. Esther drew her Ruger, dropping her M90, and tackled the Amal hard. As the two crashed to the ground, she reached up and pulled on the Amal's face shield, stretching the monolayer over his neck. She put the muzzle of her Ruger against his throat and fired.

The little Ruger didn't have much range, but at point-blank, the round tore through the monolayer and destroyed the man's throat.

Esther jumped to her feet, but to her surprise, there were no more Amals. First Sergeant Watson, his right arm hanging limp, gave her a nod from where he stood.

"My mama's going to thank you, Skipper, for keeping her favorite son's scalp intact."

Adrenaline flowing, Esther had to take a few deep breaths to calm herself. She slowly turned around, taking in the scene. Staff Sergeant Avalon, or what was left of him, lay a few meters to her side. Almost idly, she wondered what weapon had done that to him. She turned her display back on. The company was down to 57 effectives, but the fighting was petering out. A few Amals were retreating.

Did we hold? Did we win? No time for that. I need to collapse the line.

"I'm reassuming command," she passed to the XO.

"Staff Sergeant Tor," she started until her AI informed her that the platoon sergeant was KIA.

Without a commander or platoon sergeant, she shifted to the first sergeant to take over the platoon.

"First Sergeant, we need to contract our company frontage. Take First and shift left until we have a defensible line."

"Aye-aye, ma'am."

"XO, what's your disposition?"

"We're consolidating now. We're spread out too thin to withstand another assault like that. Uh . . . do you think they will? I mean, attack again?"

As if on cue, a voice interjected itself on the universal net, the one all military units are required to keep open by the Accords.

"Captain Lysander or her successor, this is Step Commander Avery of the Amalgamation Sunset Security Forces. You've acquitted yourself well, but there's no more need for loss of life. I am formally requesting your surrender. You will be treated as per the Accords, and after this unfortunate disagreement is over, you will be able to return to your families."

Esther took a deep breath, gathering her thoughts before answering, "Step Commander Avery, this is Captain Esther Lysander, United Federation Marine Corps. From where I sit, I don't see a reason to surrender. We beat back your attack and destroyed your Karzai. I'm not sure you have the means to defeat us."

"Granted, taking out our Karzai was a surprise, and I tip my hat to the valor of your Marines. But if you look to your northwest, I think you might change your mind."

"What's he saying?" the XO asked on the P2P.

"I'm not sure, but let me look."

Esther walked back up the slope and onto a protruding rock. She knew she was making a target of herself, but she didn't think the enemy commander would break the standards of the universal net. She zoomed her display and swore to herself.

Up on a ridge, two klicks away, had to be 300 soldiers. Right in the middle of them was another Karzai.

Esther did a quick rundown of the company's remaining combat load. Besides having no mortar rounds left, her remaining small arms rounds were at low levels. Certainly not enough to withhold the Amals, even if those 300 were all that were left, something she highly doubted.

"Colonel Rzeminski, I've just been contacted by—"

"We've been monitoring it, Esther," the battalion commander said.

"So, you know. I'm down to 57 effectives, and I can see at least 300 of them, along with another Karzai."

She waited for him to say something, and when he didn't, she asked, "What do you want me to do?"

"For something like this, Esther, it's your call. You are the commander on the scene."

"Surrender" was a dirty word in the Corps. No one wanted to be the one to order it. Back in the old Federation, before the Evolution, a colonel, Derek Asherton, had been executed for surrendering despite facing overwhelming odds. The Federation didn't execute commanders anymore, but the rules had been changed. Only the commander on the ground could make that decision now, and it was illegal for an offsite commander to make that decision, one way or the other. Esther understood this, but still, she hoped the colonel would give her some guidance. She could tell he was aching to tell her what to do, but the law wouldn't allow that.

"Can I ask, sir, when I can get air?"

"I'm being told the Wasp can get airborne within 70 minutes. Then another seven minutes to your position."

So, if I can hold out for 78 minutes, I can get air to blast these suckers back to their component atoms.

"Roger that. I understand."

"Whatever you decide, Esther, I'm going to support you."

You mean if it comes to a court martial, she told herself bitterly.

"Thank you, sir."

She switched back to the universal net.

"Step Commander Avery, are you familiar with General Anthony McAuliffe?" she asked.

There was a pause, then a "That disappoints me, Captain Lysander. Yes, I am familiar with the general and what he said at Bastogne during World War II. I take it that you are going to give me the same reply?"

"That's right, Step Commander. 'Nuts.'"

"Well, I was hoping you were going to be reasonable, but given your past and your heritage, I'm not surprised. So be it. Avery, out."

"Nice call, Skipper. I couldn't live with being beat by a merc unit," the XO said.

"A highly professional merc unit," she replied. "And would all of the Marines say the same?"

"Probably. Yes, ma'am, I think they would."

"What you didn't hear was the CO telling us we had 78 minutes before we can expect air. So, if we can hold out that long, we can get ourselves out of this mess. If not, I can always call up the step commander again."

"Won't happen, Skipper. We'll hold out."

"If I go down, Ralph, the company is yours. Keep the lines of communications open with Avery."

"If you go down, Skipper, with all due respect, then the call will be mine. You can't order me now one way or the other what to do if you aren't around."

He's right. Well, if it gets close to that time, I'd better still be around to make the call.

Esther's AI screamed out a warning, causing her to instinctively duck. The alarm was only temporary, however, and her shielding only dropped by a few percentage points. Off in the distance, the Karzai had fired. Two klicks in this atmosphere was a long shot even for it. Esther knew that Step Commander Avery was only reminding the Marines of what was coming. The firing wouldn't begin in earnest until it stopped somewhere around 1200 meters out, 200 meters beyond the range of their Hatchets.

"Let's see if we can send out an ambush team," she told the XO. "Let me know what you think."

"Step Commander Avery, I'd like to propose a 30-minute truce to allow for the recovery of the dead and wounded," she passed, switching to the universal net.

"So, you have time to get that Wasp here? I don't think so. The dead and wounded can wait for another hour."

Hell, it didn't hurt to try.

She wasn't surprised that the Amal commander knew about their aircraft issues and knew when they get could the remaining Wasp on station.

Esther spent the next five minutes consolidating her lines. Each fighting position had to be able to support the adjoining positions, and with only 57 Marines left in the fight, the original positions were just too spread out.

The XO reported back to her that the areas forward of the FEBA still had Amal soldiers, so sending out an ambush team to take out the Karzai as it made its way forward wouldn't work.

She had the company gunny and Doc Deep Strength, assisted by a team of four Marines and the remaining three corpsmen, start triaging the dead and wounded, getting as many of those who had a chance at resurrection zip-locked and in stasis. That lasted for only ten minutes before incoming fire made that too dangerous, and she ordered everyone into their fighting holes. She took her place between Second and Third Platoons, sharing a hole with Sergeant Sripituksakul.

Fifteen minutes after her response to the step commander, the Karzai stopped 1300 meters from her lines and started firing. At this range, it was deadly to the Marines. Four more were lost within moments. Esther knew they needed to keep rounds going downrange, but she didn't want to expose her Marines to the Karzai's touch.

The company still had a large number of dunker grenades, and using one of her two remaining drones to spot targets, her gunners could loft the rounds out of their holes. This wasn't very effective, but it did slow down the infantry advance.

Not slow enough, Esther thought as she checked the time.

There was still 50 minutes before she could expect air. Esther knew that would probably be too late.

"Last chance, Captain. Think of your Marines," Step Commander Avery passed on the net. Esther ignored him, and a few moments later, he said, "It's on you."

The incoming fire increased. What had been an Amal advance to contact was now a coordinated assault with a large base of fire supporting the main assault force. There didn't look to be any subterfuge; they were planning to simply overwhelm the remaining Marines.

And it was working. With small arms and Karzai fire, Marine after Marine was dropping. There was a wet sound beside her. She turned to see Sri slumping to the bottom of their hole, his head a bloody mess. She shook her head as if that could erase the sight of her dronemaster. She had to remain in control if the company was to have any chance at getting through this.

The company was down to 41 effectives. Chambers was the only other officer still fighting, and she'd lost most of her SNCOs. Esther took a moment to take in the Dragonfly feed. More than a hundred Amal bodies littered the AO, cut down like sheaves of wheat, but still, they came. Again, Esther was reminded of Pickett's charge, but this time, she thought the attackers would prevail.

With one more look at the time, she knew she'd failed. They couldn't hold out. She started to call the step commander, but her throat caught. She couldn't bring herself to do it.

But does holding out any longer do us much good? Will it really affect future operations?

She wasn't sure. Future operations were all well and good, but this was the here and now, and these were her Marines dying around her.

There was the crack of a large gun in the distance, and Esther braced for the shock of incoming.

Great, what else have they brought to the table?

"Skipper, do you see this?" the first sergeant asked, his voice filled with excitement.

Esther had been focusing on the area right in front of the FEBA. She zoomed back out, and a wonderful sight greeted her.

Not the burning Karzai, although that was great. But four Marine M1 Davis main battle tanks rushing into the AO.

She cleared her display and stood out of the hole to get a real view. The tanks had come over a rise and were now deploying, guns blazing. She could see them tear up through the rear of the lines.

A round glanced off her helmet, and she ducked down, but still stayed high enough to watch. It took the Amals a moment to realize what was happening, but not before 20 or 30 of them had been killed. Esther could almost feel the panic set in.

Not all the Amals panicked, though. One of the tanks stopped dead as smoke began to rise from its rear.

"Golf Company, let them have it," she passed on the company net.

With a roar, the remaining Marines rose up and rained death among the Amals. With the tanks bearing down on them, Amal soldiers started to break off and flee. Those who stayed to fight were killed.

Another of the four tanks was hit and ground to halt, but it never stopped firing. Esther had ridden in a Davis before as part of her orientation, and she'd even fired a round at the range, but until this moment, she never really grasped how much firepower one of the big beasts had.

"Step Commander Avery," she passed on the universal net, "I will accept your surrender on the same terms you proposed to me."

There was no answer, not that Esther expected any. Esther didn't have enough troops to pursue what was still a much larger force, and tanks, while they could wreak havoc, were not made for chasing down infantry.

What had been a trickle of Amals fleeing became a torrent. Step Commander Avery had evidently ordered her soldiers to retreat.

Esther tried to call the tank platoon commander, but there was no answer. She was able to reach the CO, though.

"The attack has been broken," she passed.

"What's going on? We're getting conflicting reports," he demanded.

"The tank platoon arrived, and it kicked Amal ass, sir."

"The tanks? Where have they been?"

"I don't know, sir. I can't raise them on the comms."

With the Amals fleeing, the firing petered out. One of the two mobile tanks approached the lines. It stopped, and Esther could see one of her Marines pointing in her direction. The tank smoothly pivoted, then drove along the lines to her. Esther got out of her fighting hole and stood waiting.

The Davis stopped in front of her, and Esther could read the name painted on the main gun barrel: *Anvil II.*

Her mouth dropped as the hatch opened and a familiar head popped out.

"I heard you needed some support, Captain," Staff Sergeant Noah Lysander, UFMC, casually told his speechless sister.

TARAWA

Chapter 1
Noah

"Did you have a good time?" Noah asked Shiloh as he drove into the base housing complex.

"Yes, Daddy. I liked the penguins."

"The penguins? That's what you liked?" he asked shaking his head. "They were people in penguin costumes. What about the sharks? We're they rigid?"

"Uh, that's rabid, Dad, not 'rigid,'" Hannah said with all the gravitas a twelve-year-old could muster.

"Rigid, rabid . . . how about *riiiibetttt*?" Noah asked, making a frog croak.

Hannah rolled her eyes, but Shiloh laughed, which warmed his heart. He loved hearing his youngest laugh. He looked up in the rear-view mirror, but his oldest, Chance, hadn't looked up, his head buried in his PA, much as it had been all afternoon at the aquarium.

"How about you, Chance. Did you have a good time?"

Nothing.

Noah gave up. At fourteen, Chance was no longer the little boy he'd been even a year ago.

Where have the years gone by?

Except, he knew where the years had gone. Wayfarer Station, Alexander, a year on Hodgkin's Retreat, and more deployments that he could remember. He'd missed so much in his children's life. At least here on Tarawa in a shore billet, he could spend more time with them. Shiloh was still his little girl. How much longer, he didn't know, but he planned on enjoying every moment he could with her.

Noah almost grabbed the manual control as the Evo turned left instead of the right into Basilone Village, the married SNCO quarters and where the family had lived on Gallipoli Lane for a year. With a rueful grin, he sat back in his seat, letting the AI drive into Espinoza Village.

"So, what's next? What do we do next weekend?" he asked.

None of the kids said anything, and he said, "What am I, just a frog?" before letting out another deep ribet.

"No, Daddy, you just look like a frog!" Shiloh said, laughing uproariously.

He reached over to give her side a poke, and she screamed, squirming to get away from his finger.

"Dad, don't get her riled up," Hannah said. "Mom's going to be pissed at you."

"'Pissed?' Did you just say 'pissed?'"

"Oh, come on, Dad. It's not like you haven't heard that before."

"Maybe not, young lady, but I don't need to hear my daughter talking like that."

"Whatever, Dad," his middle child said, folding her hands across her chest.

Damn, she sure looks like her mother right now, he thought as a small pang hit his heart.

The hover pulled up in front of the house, a needless ding letting them know they'd arrived. The girls immediately piled out and ran to the front door.

"You coming, bud?" he asked.

"Yeah, just a sec," Chance said, punching madly on his PA in a flurry before slipping it in his pocket.

"You know, those things are voice activated. Modern technology, you know, brand new eight centuries ago."

"You don't live with two sisters who pry into everyone's business, Dad," he said, hopping out of the hover.

That one hurt, Noah thought as he walked up to the front door just as the girls opened it.

"Evening, Major," he said to the tall infantryman at the door.

"Evening, First Sergeant. Any problems?"

Noah hesitated, wondering if he should mention Hannah's "pissed."

Screw it. I'm not going to be the bad guy.

"No, not a thing. Everyone was on their best behavior.

"Noah?" a familiar voice called out, eliciting the usual heart thumping.

Miriam walked up to the door, wiping her hands on a hand towel. She looked great, as always. More than that, she looked happy.

"Next week, would you mind picking them up at 1400 instead of noon? Hannah Belle's got a dental appointment, and I wanted to be there to go over the procedure with Dr. Hsung."

"The palate adjustment?"

"Yeah. I know it's nothing, but I'd just feel better if I knew exactly what will happen, and I didn't want to take off work during the week."

"No, that's OK. Fourteen hundred's fine. Uh . . . unless you want me to be there, too?"

"No, it's OK. Don't bother yourself. I'll have her back, and you can pick them up then."

"Well, OK, then," Noah said, awkward as always when it was time to say goodbye.

The divorce had only been finalized for a year-and-a-half, and Miriam had been remarried for just six months. That should be enough time to adjust, but in many ways, they were still married in his mind.

"Oh, and say hello to Esther for me. Tell her I'm sorry I couldn't see her today, but we'll have her over for dinner before she leaves," Miriam said.

"OK, I'll tell her," he said, and when the three adults just stood there, saying nothing more, he added, "I'll just go, then. See you next week."

The major nodded at him, then slowly closed the door. Noah stared at the door for a moment before turning around and making his way back to the Evo.

"Tell Ess I'm on my way. I'll be there in 15 minutes," he told his PA, then told his Evo to head to the Globe and Laurel.

Fourteen minutes later, he parked in the tiny lot behind the venerable club and entered, eyes searching the darkness for his sister. He spotted her in the back, sharing a cider with two other Marines.

"Hey, Noah, thanks for coming," she said as she spotted him, standing up and meeting him for a hug.

"We don't see each other enough, Ess, and with you in town for your conference, of course, we've got to meet up."

"This is First Sergeant Noah Lysander," she said, turning to the other two Marines who both stood as well. "And this is Lieutenant Colonel Topaz Mendlebaum, 3/6's CO."

"Good to meet you, First Sergeant," the man, whose stocky, no-neck build and accent screamed Rio Tinto, the same homeworld of their old mentor, General Simone.

"You, too, sir."

"This baby-faced Marine is Lieutenant Colonel Archibald Reasoner, 1/17's CO."

Lieutenant Colonel Reasoner had quite a reputation, both as a military genius and as an old Corps stalwart. He'd earned four Silver Stars climbing the ranks to gunny before accepting a commission.

"It's an honor to meet you, sir," Noah said, meaning every word of it.

"The honor's mine, First Sergeant," the lieutenant colonel said, and he seemed just as sincere in his words as Noah had been.

Which was surprising to him. He'd had a successful career so far, all things told, and while he was his father's son, his career had had none of the flash as his sister's.

Introductions made, Noah stood awkwardly for a moment. He wasn't sure if he was supposed to join them or not, but Esther came to his rescue by saying, "Why don't you and I find a corner," then "I'll catch up with you guys in a bit."

"We'll be waiting. The next round's on you, and you can't skip out on that," Lieutenant Colonel Reasoner said.

Esther caught the eye of the young waiter and signaled him to bring another round to her friends, then looked around for a table. As usual, the weekend crowd had the place fairly full, but she spotted an empty spot, and they walked past hundreds of flats and holos of hundreds of years of notable Marines as they made their way to it. Their father had his own wall-holo, but it was along the back wall of the main room of the tavern, along with all the former commandants.

"How's Miriam? The kids?" she asked as they sat down.

"They're fine. I took them to the aquarium today."

"And Chance?" she asked, eyebrows raised.

"He was just along for the ride. He had his nose buried in his PA for the whole time. Shiloh liked the penguins, though."

"Miriam says to tell you she wants you to come for dinner before you leave."

She hesitated, and Noah could see her gears turning, before she said, "Maybe Wednesday. They've got us pretty well shepherded for the entire conference."

Every year, the commandant hosted a battalion commander's conference, and unless a battalion was in action, it would take an act of God for anyone to miss it. This was Esther's second conference, having taken over 1/8 15 months prior.

"So, what's up, Ess? Just a social call? I'd be happy if it was that, but you've got something on your mind."

Despite the time and separation, twins were connected in ways that other people just couldn't understand, and Noah knew that she was going to ask him something. He just couldn't figure out what it could be.

She smiled, leaned back, and said, "Well, yeah, now that you mention it. Do you know Sergeant Major Killington? Norm Killington?"

"Your sergeant major? No, not really. He's got a reputation for being somewhat of a hardass, but that's about it."

"My ex-sergeant major. I fired him just before leaving for the conference."

"No shit," Noah said, shocked.

A sergeant major was the highest rank an enlisted Marine could achieve, but there were still career paths forward within the rank. A battalion sergeant major was a boot sergeant major, if the term could even be used in conjunction with E9. A successful tour with a battalion, then it was upwards and onwards to bigger and more prestigious units, culminating in the very top as Sergeant Major of the Marine Corps. Any sergeant major who said he or she didn't aspire to that position was either lying or afraid of failure, and sergeants major generally weren't afraid of anything. By shit-canning Killington, Esther had essentially stopped his career.

Esther could be a hard-ass, too, but she wouldn't have taken such a drastic step without good reason and without weighing her options. Noah looked at her, waiting for her to elaborate.

"Let's just say we had differing opinions on how the battalion should be run, and he decided to try and bypass me to get things done his way.

Dumb move, Killington, Noah thought.

His sister had mellowed over the years and was no longer the self-centered, career-driven Marine she'd been. But she was still a force to be reckoned with, and Noah wouldn't want to cross her paths with her. If Killington was trying to work behind her back, simply getting shit-canned was probably the least Esther would have done to him.

"Well, it's your battalion, Ess. If you had to fire him, then that's your choice. Uh . . . how did the division sergeant major take it?"

"I told her right after I told the CG. She wasn't happy, to say the least," Esther said with a rueful sounding chuckle. "But like Colonel Falstaff and the CG said, it was my call. Sergeant Major Upo asked me who I wanted to take Killington's place, and I told her I'd let her know when I got back."

A division sergeant major, even one who was one of the names in the hat for the next Sergeant Major of the Marine Corps, did not assign sergeants major to the battalions, but she still had to be treated with respect as belies her rank. The CG listened to her, and he would be the one to assign a sergeant major from within division personnel. There might not be any unassigned sergeants major—if Esther commanded a regiment, one of the battalion sergeants major could jump up, but for a battalion, the CG might resort to a first sergeant who'd been selected for E9. Otherwise, he'd have to ask HQMC for a fresh body.

"So, who are you thinking of? Anyone I know?"

"Yeah, you could say that."

"And . . . ?" he asked when she didn't say anything else.

"I want you to be my sergeant major."

Noah looked at her in shock, then laughed out loud, breaking the quiet murmurs of the other patrons in the tavern.

"No, really, who?"

"I'm serious, Noah."

"First of all, Ess, if you haven't noticed, I'm a first sergeant, and a fairly boot one at that. I won't be eligible for E9 for three or even four years at a minimum. Second, have you forgotten that we're twins? We haven't served together since 3/14, and you weren't too happy about that, if memory serves me right."

"I was an idiot then."

That took Noah aback. He agreed with her assessment, but he never thought she'd have admitted it.

"Maybe then when we were both non-rate grunts, but this, I mean . . . this is something different. You and me at the head of a battalion? This isn't a good idea, Ess. Remember father and Uncle Joshua?"

"I've thought about that," she said. "I've thought about that a lot, to be honest. Giving those orders to his own brother-in-law, well, you know how that affected him all his life. But, hear me out. I'm not going to be ordering you to stay behind like that. We're getting a little long in the tooth to be kicking down doors and taking names. That's for the young Marines. You and I'll be in the CP, fighting the battles from there, not out with the lance corporals."

"Long in the tooth?" he wondered, looking at his twin.

She had kept in tremendous shape, and he knew she could give most lance corporals a run for their money at any physical challenge. For that matter, Noah himself could kick some butt on a company run.

"And it's not as if we're going to war," she added. "We're just gearing up for an Outer Reaches deployment. All showing the flag and exercises with our allies."

"I don't know, Ess. Think of the politics. I mean, if you . . ."

"You mean if I want to pick up colonel, what would this look like?"

"Well, yeah, as you put it so bluntly."

"I've thought about that, too. Look, I've probably alienated every sergeant major in the division, hell, maybe the Corps, by firing Killington. He was a pretty popular guy. And if I don't have someone who's got my back, do you think I'm going to do well enough with the battalion to even be considered for O6?"

"I don't think it's as bad as all that, Ess. There's a reason you shit-canned Killington, and the other E9's will know that."

"And still, they'll hold a grudge for not letting them take care of it in-house."

"Uh . . . now that you mention it, why didn't you? I mean, that would have solved your problem and kept your hands clean?"

"I couldn't. He challenged me in front of the troops. I had to take action right then and there."

Shit, Killington, you were even dumber than I thought.

"Hell, Colonel Falstaff heard about it before I marched down to regiment, and he already had the S1 drawing up the orders."

"So, it's not as bad as all of that. He gave you no choice."

"Look, Noah, whether I had to or not, I need someone who I know has my back. Someone who can relate to the Marines, who can nudge when I push. The only person I know for an absolute certainty who will have my back is you. I'd be honored if you'll take the position."

Noah sat back, then took a long swallow of juice, more to give himself a few moments than that he needed a drink. The idea was crazy. Him, a sergeant major? Serving with Esther? He had to admit the idea intrigued him. But he realized it was never going to happen. No matter what friends his twin had in high places, he was not a sergeant major and wasn't going to simply be appointed as one.

"Ess, I really appreciate your confidence in me. It touches me, to be honest. But this isn't how the Corps works, you know. I'm a first sergeant, and they're not going to have an E8 as the senior enlisted in the battalion. Heck, you probably have E8's senior to me."

"I have one, and he's due orders in three months."

"Still, it's not going to happen."

"It can. I spoke with the commandant about it last night. He's on board with the idea.

General Rzeminski had been Esther's battalion commander with 2/11, the same battalion when Noah, leading his two tanks, had broken the Amal assault. Noah wasn't surprised that they'd kept close contact. That was the way the Marine Corps ran and had probably run since the Roman Adiutrix. But even the commandant couldn't just snap his fingers and have it all fixed.

"On board with your brother, an E8, as one of his battalion sergeant majors?"

"Not an E8. Well, technically an E8. But you'll be frocked to E9. It will be temporary, of course, and you'll still get paid as an E8, but you'll wear the rockers of a sergeant major and hold the title."

"Frocked? We're not the Navy, Ess."

"But the authorization to frock is in our code as well. If a Marine is serving in a billet one rank above his or her permanent rank, that Marine can wear the rank and enjoy the privileges if authorized by the commandant."

"But we don't do that. The Navy does, but we don't."

"Yes, we do. Just not often."

Noah's mind was whirling. He knew this was a bad idea, very bad. Siblings just didn't serve together, going back to the 20th Century when five brothers, the Sullivans, all died on one ship during the WWII Battle of the Guadalcanal. His own father, as a platoon commander, had requested his brother-in-law to serve as his platoon sergeant. Fighting the capies on G.K. Nutrition Six, he had to order their uncle to stay behind and delay the capies enough for the civilians to be evacuated, knowing full well that it was a suicide mission. Noah thought their father never got over that. And now, here was his sister, asking him to serve with her.

"Ess, you've taken me by surprise. I really, really think this is a bad idea—"

"Noah," she said, raising a finger to his lips to stop him. "Don't say anything yet. I know, especially with dad and Uncle Joshua, that this is a hard decision. But I wouldn't ask you if I thought this would be bad for the battalion. I think you're the right person for the billet. So, I'm here for four more days. Let's meet back here at 1500 on Thursday, if you can make it, and let me know what you've decided."

When Noah didn't say anything, she asked, "Can you think about it?"

He nodded and said, "Sure, Ess. I can give you that. I'll meet you back here on Thursday."

"Thanks, Little Brother," she said with a smile, but one that didn't strike Noah as being much of a happy smile.

She stood up, leaned over the table, and gave him a hug. She didn't say anything but left to go back to her fellow commanders, who greeted her with raised glasses.

Noah watched her for a moment as she jumped back into whatever conversation she'd been having before. Esther was a good Marine, a good commander. He trusted her in that she'd had to fire Killington. But there were more than enough sergeants major who could fill the billet, E9's who wouldn't come with the baggage that he'd bring with him.

And then there was their relationship. They were still pretty casual, just brother and sister despite their differing ranks. If they served together, how would that work? His job—a battalion sergeant major's job—was to advise and commander in all manner of things, even when it was something the commander didn't want to hear.

Noah knew this was a bad idea, but he also knew that his sister disagreed with that. He had four days to make up his mind, and at the moment, he had no idea what he was going to do.

Chapter 2
Esther

Esther checked the time; it was 1507. Noah was late, and she didn't know what that might mean. She'd thought long and hard about asking Noah to be her sergeant major, and despite the fact that everyone—Noah included, seemingly—thought this was a bad idea, she was certain he'd make the best sergeant major for the battalion.

What she'd told Noah about how her firing of Killington had gone over with the rest of the E9 mafia had been true. It wasn't that there wasn't another sergeant major who'd take the position. It was a battalion, after all, much better than a school or other non-combat unit. By firing Killington, however, Esther had seemingly made a statement that she wanted a yes-man. Nothing could be further from the truth, but perceptions were what mattered. Esther needed someone to act as a counterpoint to her. Her XO, Major Mark Frazier, was smart and organized, and he wasn't afraid to offer suggestions, but she wasn't sure he'd oppose her if she were making a mistake.

Noah would.

Jim, who she trusted more than anyone else, had recommended that she just make due with whoever was assigned to her. General Rzeminski had told her he thought it was a bad move when she'd broached the subject with him, but she'd been adamant, and in the end, he'd gone along with her request. Now, it was up to Noah.

In a way, she was being selfish, she knew. If the pairing were a catastrophe, he'd go down the tubes the same as she. He'd probably never see E9 permanently. Even with an acceptable tour, there would always be the cloud hanging over him that he only got his battalion because of the Lysander name.

Still, she hoped he'd accept.

She took another sip of her Coke. A cider would fit the bill better, but she'd been fighting the battle of the booze for years, and in the middle of the afternoon, she wouldn't allow herself to already be going for the heavy stuff. She'd be on the shuttle by 1730, and another hour or so after that, she'd let herself have a drink or two at the ship's bar, one of the many advantages of traveling on commercial liners rather than Navy ships.

Four minutes later, Noah came into the Globe and Laurel, looking around as his eyes shifted from daylight to the murky tavern. Esther raised a hand, and he headed her way, sliding into the seat across from her.

"Coke?" he asked, eyebrows raised.

Noah had quit drinking after Miriam had filed for divorce, and with the evangelical enthusiasm of the converted, had lectured Esther on her affection for drinking. There was the slightest bit of validity to his arguments, but she'd never let drinking affect her performance. She was in control of it. The mere fact that he was on her case about it, however, was proof that he'd stand up to her, if need be, in the battalion.

"It's still in the afternoon, Noah."

"What about the old saying that it's seventeen hundred somewhere?"

"I'm not that bad, little brother. Besides, I've got a berth on a commercial liner out. I can wait until we leave the system.

"But forget about all of that. Have you thought it over?"

"Yeah, Ess. I have," he said, pausing for a moment. "You know, this is a bad idea."

"Some people have said that," she said.

"And, at the company, I've got regular hours. No deployments."

"Oh, come on, Noah. You mean to tell me that you like being in Headquarters Battalion? You like chasing down all the officers at HQMC to get them to update their next of kin rosters?"

"Not really, no. OK, it's not like it's a normal company, Ess, but every weekend, I see the kids. For the first time I'm there for them."

Why change now? she thought, but knowing to leave that unsaid.

Noah had always promised that he'd be different than their father, that he wouldn't be an absentee parent. But when the Corps sends you half-way across the galaxy, you went. Being a full-time parent and being a Marine just didn't coincide, and he'd chosen the Corps. She could understand why he wanted to take this opportunity to be with his kids, at least on the weekends. But if he'd wanted to be a full-time parent, he shouldn't have reenlisted. That ship had sailed back when he was a staff sergeant.

"So, you're turning me down?" she asked, trying to keep the bitterness out of her voice.

"It's not a matter of you, of turning you down, Ess."

"Then what is it?"

"I love you, Ess, more than you know. But this kind of decision, well, it's not made for love or family ties. I've got to think of what's best for the Corps. And yes, what's best for me."

Esther let out a sigh, and said, "OK, I understand."

"So that's why I'm accepting the position."

"It's OK, I know it was a lot to ask."

"I'm accepting, Ess."

"Yes, I heard you. You're . . . you're accepting? You're saying yes?"

"I'm saying yes. I already told Captain Gilfoyl, and they're cutting me orders within ten days."

"But . . . I mean the kids. What you just said."

"That was the main thing that held me back, Ess, to be honest. I like being with them. But, you know, father wasn't around much, and we turned out OK, right?"

"Uh, yeah, we did."

"And so can they. Miriam's a good mother, and Major Howard, he's a good man," he said, barely faltering over Miriam's husband's name.

Esther caught that and knew he was putting on a brave front.

"But one thing you said was right on. You need someone who's got your back. I don't mean a lapdog, but who's really got your back, even when that means telling you something you don't want to hear. You're good, Esther, but sometimes, you're your own worst enemy."

"Uh . . . thanks? I mean, thank you. I need that. Hell, the battalion needs that. We're good, but we need to get better. I'm counting on you to bring the—"

"You don't need to convince me, Ess. It's done. I'll evaluate the SNCOs and all the rest when I get there, then decide how I'm going to tackle things. But not right now. I've got a shitload of things to get done before I leave, and that starts now. I really can't stay and chat, so I've got to run. I'll be right behind you, and you can forward me anything you think I need to know before I report aboard."

"You can't stay for a bit?"

"No, really, I can't. This is all rather sudden, as you can imagine, and I've got a lot to do. First, I'm heading to see the kids right now, to give them the news," he told her while standing up.

"Oh. Yeah, I can understand that. Well, OK. I'm glad you're coming, and I'll send you some notes about the battalion and where we're at now. And, then, well, I guess, I'll see you on Last Stop."

She stood up, and not quite knowing what to do, reached out to hug her twin. She held him tighter and longer than normal, but the next time she saw him, she'd be his boss. They'd still be Ess and Noah, but the institution of command would be between them as well. For one more moment, Esther wanted simply to hug her brother, to feel his broad shoulders knowing that he always was there to protect her.

Finally, she let him go.

"OK, then, I'll see you soon," he said, wheeling and walking out of the tavern.

Esther watched him go, then sat back down, taking half a sip of Coke before pushing the glass away. Noah had just agreed to be her sergeant major, and that deserved a celebratory drink, mid-afternoon or not. She signaled the waiter, started to order a cider, then thought something a little stronger was in order and changed that to a Crissie on the Rocks.

Pulling out her PA, she connected to Tarawa's commercial comms hub. This was going to cost a pretty credit, but she didn't care. Within moments, her call was put through to Sahara, all the way out in the Fourth Quadrant.

"Did he accept?" Jim asked, knowing why she was calling.

"Yes, he did."

"Well, OK, then. Now it's up to you to make it work."

"I know, and it will. He'll be good for the battalion."

"And good for you?"

"I think so. I need someone to keep me on an even keel, and with you half-way across the galaxy, it has to be him."

"Just, well, remember, he's your brother, but he's a Marine, and he'll be taking his duties seriously."

The waiter returned with her drink and placed it in front of her.

"I know he will. Which is why I wanted him. OK, this is going to cost a fortune, but I wanted to let you know."

"Thanks, honey. You two will do well. I've got confidence in you."

"Love you," Esther said.

"Love you back," Jim answered before cutting the connection.

Esther took a long sip of her Crissie, savoring both the smoky nuances and the strong kick. She felt a little guilty for taking Noah away from his kids, but they were career Marines, and that was part of the price of admission. She and Jim were different. They weren't going to have kids until they finally got out. It was bad enough never being stationed together, just snatching periods of time together when they could, but adding kids to the equation would make it untenable.

She took another long swallow, letting the strong drink warm her belly to match the warmth she was feeling in her heart. She had a loving husband who supported her, and now her twin brother would be at her right hand in getting the battalion into shape. It couldn't get much better than that.

LAST STOP

Chapter 3
Noah

Noah looked at the plaque of the line of commanding officers of the First Battalion, Eighth Marines, "The Cutting Edge." There, the last name on the list, was "Lieutenant Colonel Esther Lysander."

Right next to that plaque was another with the line of battalion sergeants major. The last one in that list was Sergeant Major Norman H. Killington. The next spot would be his.

Noah still wasn't sure if this was a good move. The Marine Corps had never had siblings at the head of a battalion, and while the opportunity probably hadn't been too numerous, it just hadn't been done.

"Sergeant Major, welcome aboard!" a corporal said, his white duty belt all Noah needed to know that the corporal had the battalion duty, and more than that, that he was expecting him. "The XO told me to fetch you as soon as you arrived."

"Lead on, Corporal. What's your name?"

"Corporal Spain, Sergeant Major. I'm with Bravo Company."

Noah knew that first impressions were important, and almost at the speed of light, Corporal Spain would be letting the rest of the battalion know the new sergeant major had arrived—along with his impressions of him.

He and Esther had agreed not to advertise the fact that he was only a frocked sergeant major. The senior SNCO's would be able to figure it out simply by checking the Enlisted Blue Book, which had lineal numbers and dates of rank. Noah would still be with the first sergeants. The junior Marines, enlisted and officers alike, probably wouldn't bother to check that. If asked, Noah would tell the truth, but he wasn't about to proclaim to the world that he

---

was only frocked. He wore the star in the middle of his rank insignia, and he needed to act the part, not relying on his lack of time in grade as a first sergeant as any sort of excuse for his performance.

Corporal Spain rapped on the hatch outside the XO's office, then said, "Sir, the sergeant major's here."

"Send him in."

"Welcome aboard, Sergeant Major," Spain said as he turned to go back to the duty desk.

"Welcome aboard, Sergeant Major," the XO repeated, standing and coming around his desk to shake Noah's hand. "You checked in OK? I was expecting you a little earlier."

"At regiment, yes, sir. Not in battalion," Noah said, not mentioning that his meeting earlier in the morning with Sergeant Major Upo at division had taken a full two hours.

It had been painfully obvious that the division sergeant major was not a fan of Noah serving as his sister's sergeant major. Noah still wasn't sure if that was because of their relationship or if she was upset that he was only a frocked sergeant major and one pulled from outside of the battalion. If he were a betting man, he'd pick the latter. She hadn't been antagonistic, per se, but Noah was 100% certain that she'd have her eyes on him, and she'd call him on the carpet the first time he screwed up.

"OK, no problem. I was just a little surprised. Well, the *commanding officer—*"

OK, he sure stressed the "commanding officer," not "Colonel Lysander" or your sister. I kind of expected that.

" . . . is at division right now, but she'll be back before COB. After we're done here, you can finish your check-in, then be back here around 1600 to report in to her."

"Aye-aye, sir."

"And . . . well . . . before that, I just wanted to talk to you a bit. Please, sit down," Major Frazier said, pointing out the couch alongside the bulkhead.

He pulled his chair out from behind his desk and positioned it in front of Noah as he took his seat.

"I don't have to tell you that your position here is unique, to say the least. And, uh, well, a sergeant major is the commanding officer's link to the enlisted Marines, and there is a special bond between the two. You, of course, have an open door to the CO. You don't need anyone's permission to stick your head in her office for a chat."

I know that. So, what's your point?

"But, as the commanding officer's, well, brother, none of us want to see any accusations of favoritism here."

"Has there been any mention of that since I've received my orders?"

"No, not at all. The junior enlisted seem to think that it's pretty copacetic, to be sure. At least from what First Sergeant Khan—the first sergeant's been acting sergeant major since Sergeant Major Killington was transferred."

Fired, you mean.

"And the senior enlisted?"

"Well . . . ah . . . there's been a little pushback. Nothing you can't handle, I'm sure, but you can imagine . . ."

Yeah, I can.

"Well, anyway, back to what I was saying. You've got an open door, of course, with the CO. But for a while, at least, I'd like you to come to me first, with anything major."

I don't have to do that, Major. You know that.

"You don't have to, of course," he said as if reading his mind. "But First Sergeant Khan and I think it might be a good idea, you know, to keep us in the loop.

Not going to happen, Noah said to himself. *Damned right Khan would want to "keep in the loop," but he's not acting sergeant major anymore, and he's going to have to learn that quickly and focus on Alpha Company. As far as you, Major, well, I'll just have to see.*

"When appropriate, I sure will inform you, sir. You're the XO, after all," he said instead.

That seemed to mollify the major somewhat. Esther had been full of praise for the man, and Noah didn't want to come in as an adversary. Still, he wasn't going to change the way the Corps ran because the XO and Dylan Khan were worried. Either Noah was the sergeant major or he wasn't. From his perspective, he was in the billet, and he'd served as expected of a sergeant major.

The major then switched to small talk for five minutes, most of it going in one ear and out the other. Noah was relieved when the man stood up, shook his hand once more, and told him he could finish checking in.

As he walked back down the passage to the S1 and personnel, he mulled over what the XO, said, and perhaps more importantly, how the XO spoke. He didn't see any underlying resentment in the man's tone, but reading between the lines, he did reveal that there might be resentment with First Sergeant Khan. Noah was determined to come in strong, but he didn't want to alienate the battalion's SNCOs, particularly the Alpha Company first sergeant. Everything was a balancing act, and Noah had to navigate that without falling off.

Welcome to the battalion, Noah. Welcome to the battalion.

Chapter 4
Esther

"How's he doing, Mark?" Esther asked her XO.

She didn't have to specify to whom she was referring.

"Not bad, I guess, ma'am." Major Frazier said, sounding almost reluctant.

"Forget he's my brother for a moment. You can be straight with me."

The major hesitated as if couching his words, before finally saying, "He's a little headstrong. First Sergeant Khan has been offering his assistance, but your brother, I mean, the sergeant major, he doesn't seem too inclined to take it."

Not surprising, Esther thought as she tried to keep a smile off of her face.

She knew Noah, and he'd be trying to establish himself, particularly with his sister as the commanding officer. He'd been doing that his entire career what with their father's place in the Corps.

"You still think this was a mistake, don't you?"

"It was your call, ma'am. Not mine."

"But you think it was a mistake. What I did."

Major Frazier nodded his head, then said, "Yes, ma'am, I did. Not because I think the sergeant major can't handle the position, but only because of your relationship. I told you that before, and I still believe it."

"And I appreciate that. I value that you aren't a yes-man, like Major . . . uh, well, better left that unsaid."

She'd been about to call out Major Marcy Holdenstaff, Carol Depepe's XO over at 3/9. That smarmy major was the ultimate yes-man, and she was doing Carol no good at all. Esther thanked her lucky stars that she had Mark Frazier, who besides being damned competent, was brutally honest.

"I think you're wrong, though. I think my brother will do fine in the billet."

Am I really sure about that? Just because he's my brother?

Bringing Noah in had been a calculated gamble. Esther understood risk, but she'd fenced with the devil before and so far come out victorious each time. Was she tempting fate here, however? Was there even a payoff for bringing Noah in?

Noah had a way of relating to his junior Marines, and that was a valuable trait for a sergeant major. But there were other sergeants major with the same trait. No, what Esther valued was the firm knowledge that Noah would have her back, no matter what. That was what gave her the confidence that she'd made the right choice.

And he'd let her have it with both barrels if he thought she was wrong. With Major Frazier's blunt honesty and Noah's lack of hesitation in calling her out, she had two sounding boards.

If I'll listen, that is.

Esther had a habit of thinking she was always right. It would be a sea change for her, but it did her no good to have the major and her brother if she didn't make use of them. Right then and there, she swore that she'd heed their advice.

Chapter 5
Noah

"They're part of your force, Colonel," Noah said, keeping his voice steady when all he wanted to do was to yell at his sister. "Use them!"

Esther looked up from her display, a look of annoyance Noah recognized from their years together.

She looked at Major Kurtzman, her S3, for a moment as if couching her response, then said, "Sergeant Major, I think you've got armor on your brain. You even agreed that this is not armor territory."

"Not great armor territory, ma'am, but that doesn't mean armor can't function. We know they've got a tank platoon, and our Aardvarks' 20mms are our most effective anti-armor weapon we have at the moment."

Esther seemed to gather herself, then said, "Which they can't get to us, Sergeant Major. Bringing the Mamba's forward will make them vulnerable to infiltration, and we're going to need our tracs when we displace."

The words may not have been overly confrontational, but Noah could hear the steel in her voice. He might want to yell at her, but he also knew she was about to blow up at him. Around them, the rest of the CP kept at their stations, but he could almost see their ears perk up as they listened to see what happened.

In the two months since Noah had reported aboard, this was the battalion's first action, and for all the "Of course I'll listen to you, just as I do all my staff," Esther didn't seem to be hewing to that concept. He was about to erupt in frustration, but that wouldn't do anyone any good. The bottom line was that Esther was the battalion commander, and it was her battalion to command, not his.

"Aye, aye, ma'am. I understand. I'm going to check the perimeter," he said, wheeling about and stalking out of the CP.

Esther, like many officers in the Corps, was too focused on infantry. In her case, her small-unit predilection was even more pronounced with her time in recon and lack of service even with PICS. The infantry *was* the Corps in many of their minds, and it was certainly the way to climb the command hierarchy. To many of them, the supporting arms, and even more so with logistics, were there merely to serve at best, almost being distractions at worst.

Until you need that arty or tank support, or you need a resupply of munitions.

Noah slowed his breathing as he made his way to the fighting holes. As the sergeant major, Esther had tasked him to assist Captain Peaslee, the headquarters commandant, form the battalion staff into a defensive perimeter. When the Marines, officer and enlisted alike, were not actively fighting the war, they slept, ate, and shit in fighting holes that put them into a position to defend the CP from attack. Not all battalions did that, preferring to use a rifle squad or even a platoon, but Esther believed in putting her fighting strength forward, something to which Noah heartily agreed. She didn't want to waste manpower by holding part of it back.

Not that the CP was in the best position, in his opinion. The SOP was to have the headquarters commandant and a rep from comms physically select positions for the CP. However, with changing battle conditions, this procedure usually fell by the wayside, with the S3 picking a position simply based on a map study. The current position was good in as far as limiting enemy surveillance, but if attacked, it was not very defensible.

"You OK, sir?" he asked Captain Tranh, the S4, as he walked up on the man's fighting hole.

"Sure thing, Sergeant Major," the officer said as he squeezed more F-rats out of the tube.

From the expression on his face, Noah thought the man actually liked that crap. They were all eating F-rats on this mission, but they were merely fuel to be able to fight, not something that actually tasted good.

"I'm going to catch a few Z's here in a few moments so I'll be ready for the displacement this evening, but don't worry," he said, patting the stock of his M90, "I'll keep on eye open in case the bad guys come."

Noah knew that some of the officers thought it was a waste for them to spend time in fighting holes. While no one had challenged the CO on that, he could sense their disapproval. Captain Tranh, however, didn't seem to mind at all. As with all things, the Captain seemed to embrace life as a Marine, even if that meant sleeping curled up in the muddy bottom of a hole.

Noah left the captain to his mashed turkey ala king and made the rounds. With a third of the battalion staff with the XO and the Bravo Command, with most of the Alpha putting in long hours, and with most of those out in the perimeter sleeping, the effectiveness of the defense was shaky at best. But it was better than nothing, and it had the added benefit that if the CP were hit, not everyone would be taken out.

"Disbursement, disbursement, disbursement," he muttered as he walked the line.

Corporal Ikimura almost jumped out of her skin when he walked up on her, swearing that she wasn't asleep. Noah had to assure her it was OK. The corporal monitored the logistics net while on the job, and after 12 hours on duty, this was when she was supposed to sleep.

It didn't take long to make his rounds, and he started back up to the CP before he realized that wasn't a place he wanted to be at the moment. Looking back down the slope to where it dropped off into the dry river bed, he decided to head on down. The 90mm mortar section was an organic part of the battalion, after all, and the armor section was attached for the duration of the exercise. They were his responsibility just as much as the rifle companies were.

"I'm going down to the river bed," he told Ikimura. "Don't shoot me when I come back up."

"I wouldn't do that, Sergeant Major," she protested in earnest.

I'm not serious, Corporal, he thought as he raised one hand in acknowledgment as he started down the path.

He probably shouldn't be wandering alone between the positions, but he wasn't in the mood to pay attention to SOP at the moment. Esther was sure that their CP was secure, so if she were right, he'd be safe as well.

Ten minutes later, he reached the bluff over the river bed. The battalion's eight 90 tubes were arrayed in the near bed, out in the open to surveillance, but able to range the battalion's entire AOR. The armor section was along the near bank, getting as much cover as possible. Four Marines were visible—the rest of the crews were probably in their tracs.

"Who goes there?" a voice called out from some scrub in the best tradition of centuries of movies and flicks.

"The Sergeant Major. Ping me, uh, Lance Corporal Hiapez," he said after checking his own display.

"Uh, yes, Sergeant Major, I have you confirmed."

"Keep alert, Hiapez. It might not be me next time."

The bluff at the edge of the river bed was a good three meters high. Too far to jump, Noah half-slid down, using his ass as a brake. He hit the bed itself hard, but none the worse for wear. Brushing himself off, we wandered over to the first Aardvark. First Lieutenant Hep Constantine was on the ramp, leaning back, half asleep.

"Keeping busy, sir?" Noah asked.

"Right, Sergeant Major. Bus drivers always keep busy, right?" he said, not moving and only one eye opened a slit.

Noah knew what he meant. Sure, the Aardvark was a personnel carrier by designation, but it was also a fighting vehicle. All four of them were armed with the 20mm chain gun as their secondary armament: two were armed with the M717 plasma cannons in air defense modes and two had Weapons Pack 1, carrying the M905 70mm smoothbore cannon. Between the two M905's and the chain guns, they constituted the battalion's best anti-armor capability, and here they were, waiting in the riverbed for the next displacement of the CP.

Esther had been right in that the AOR was prime infantry country, not particularly conducive to armor, but the enemy had Mambas, the small lightweight tank that had greater maneuverability. Noah had plotted several avenues of approach to the CP that they could probably navigate, and even as a light tank, they could wreak havoc in the CP. The makeshift defensive perimeter wouldn't be much of an obstacle, but the Aardvarks would at least have a fighting chance against the tanks.

If they were positioned to be used against them, not simply parking in the riverbed.

"You know how it is, sir . . ."

"Yeah, after two months with the platoon, I'm beginning to see that," he said. "Sergeant Major, you're in armor. Is it always like this?"

The lieutenant had served his first tour as a grunt, like most officers, and had very little time in the fleet in armor.

"No, not really. It's just that this is primarily an infantry operation. You know, the terrain and such," Noah said, hating the fact that he was spouting the party line.

The lieutenant opened both eyes and stared up at Noah before saying, "I know you spend most of your time with Davises," referring to the Marine's heavy tank. "I may be with the 'Varks,' but I can see more than a few ways to cause hate and discontent with light armor."

"You're right, sir. There are ways. But armor would be very vulnerable trying to get within the battalion lines," he said, meaning it this time.

"He who will not risk, cannot win, Sergeant Major."

"John Paul Jones, the United States wet-water navy during its revolution. I recognize the quote."

"I figured you might. But it's true, nonetheless."

"Mind if I sit, sir?" Noah asked.

"Be my guest."

Noah took a seat on the ramp beside him, taking in the undeniable smell of Marine armor. That took him back. He might be the sergeant major of a Marine battalion at the cutting edge of the spear, but his best time in the Corps was as a tank commander of the *Anvil II*, and he missed those days.

He and the lieutenant started chatting about inconsequentials, but before long, they were talking about tactics. At one point, Lieutenant Constantine jumped up, and using a stick, started mapping out how he'd attack the battalion. Of course, that assumed a full tank and Aardvark platoon, but Noah had to give the young man credit. He'd come up with several ways that he, with far more experience, hadn't considered. It'd be awfully difficult for eight vehicles to take on a full rifle battalion, but he'd make it difficult for one. Noah was glad that the lieutenant was on their side. Esther was missing an opportunity here.

Finally, he checked the time, stretched, and stood up, saying, "Well, sir, it's been a pleasure. I mean that. But I need to get back to the CP. When this is all over, I'd like to pick your brains about it, if you don't mind."

"Sure thing, Sergeant Major. I'd be happy to."

Noah nodded to the Aardvark driver, who'd come out to take a piss, then stayed on to listen to the lieutenant lay out his concept of operations to Noah. As sergeant major, Noah was the senior enlisted advisor, and all the enlisted Marines and sailors were sort of under his wings, so-to-speak. But a SNCO was also a vital cog in the training of the officers, and his 40 minutes with Lieutenant Constantine had an effect on the young officer. For the better, Noah assumed. The lieutenant had gotten up as Noah stood, and as Noah stepped off, he was going to one of the other vehicles to check up on it.

Training officers didn't exclude the battalion commander, Noah knew, and with renewed determination, he started climbing back up to the CP. Now might not be the time, but he'd be shirking his duty if he didn't try and show his sister where she was wrong in this case.

Esther was a hot-shit Marine, he knew, and he readily gave her props for grunt and recon stuff. But no one was an expert in everything, and if he could get her to sit down with Lieutenant Constantine, for example, and pick his brain, then he'd be doing his job as her sergeant major.

Corporal Ikimura wasn't on the lines when he returned. Sergeant Halpin was in the fighting hole, fast asleep. Noah didn't say anything to wake him. He stopped as in front of the CP, ready to go in and do his job, when a faint whine caught his ears. It took a moment for that to sink in.

The Mamba was an electromag-drive vehicle, powered by an almost silent fusion generator. It made less noise than Noah's Avo hover back on Last Stop, but it wasn't silent. A crash of vegetation, then the shout of someone on the battalion perimeter confirmed what his instincts had told him would happen.

The Marines on the perimeter opened fire, but without much effect. They just didn't have the weaponry. Forcing down his smile, he strode into the CP where most of the staff were looking around at each other, waiting for the shoe to drop.

"Colonel, I think we've got a problem," Noah said in a gross understatement.

There was aloud crack of a smoothbore from outside, and Major Johansson, the head umpire assigned to the battalion, looked at his exercise display and announced, "I'm calling the CP out of action. Cease all comms immediately."

The war wasn't over. The XO, with the Bravo Command would take over, and with the line companies at full or almost full strength, the battalion still had a chance to beat 3/11, their opposing battalion. With the rifle companies on the alert now, the Mamba section didn't stand much of a chance, but they'd performed their mission. Lieutenant Colonel Depepe had taken out her opposing number.

That "opposing number" was fuming now, and Noah thought lightening was about to jump out of her eyes and strike everyone in the CP.

With what he knew to be a herculean effort, she calmly said, "You heard the major. Shut down everything."

She was pissed, no doubt about it, and inwardly, Noah reveled. Not that he was right and she was wrong, although there could be a hint of that inside of him. He knew, though, that Esther would never be caught like that again, and after all of this was over and he suggested that she sit down with Lieutenant Constantine for his input, she'd do it. Esther had a driving desire, no, a *requirement* to be right, and if she had to be schooled in that knowledge from others, she would.

Her pride was wounded, and she'd hate to face Colonel Depepe, who was her MCMAP sparring partner, and have this lorded over her. But better pride be wounded during peacetime than lives being lost in war.

The CP was shut down, and command shifted to Major Frazier. No one wanted to meet Esther's eyes, even if none of them had done anything wrong. Noah didn't want to look at her either, but for a different reason. She knew him too well, and she'd know he thought this was a good thing. Better that he waited until she cooled down before discussing it.

But he couldn't help be give her one last glance, and in that moment, she locked eyes with him, eyes that still burned with suppressed fury.

Your bed, Ess. You made it, he thought as he refused to break contact.

And to his surprise, her countenance softened, and with a wry half-smile, she nodded.

He'd expected her to come around, but not this quickly. His sister was maturing in the role, he realized. He smiled and nodded back.

"OK, listen up," she shouted. "We might be dead, but there's nothing saying we can't hash out what went wrong. I want all the principles over to the display in five. Be ready for a long session, Marines."

Noah had intended to gather the SNCO's, but he was principle staff as well. He told Gunny Vandervee to start packing up the CP, then walked over to where Esther was already staring at the display, going back in five-minute increments as she gathered her thoughts.

This was a good lesson for her and the battalion, but it was about to get hammered into their heads if he knew his sister. Suddenly, he wished he'd taken a piss break before coming back. This was probably going to be a long, long debrief.

Chapter 6
Esther

"Major Kutzman, Lieutenant Constantine, Captain Peaslee, Lieutenant Poul, and Sergeant Major, if you would stay behind?" Esther said as her staff and commanders filed out of the briefing room.

It had been a long, long day, first with the division wargame staff, then with her own staff. She'd gotten a pretty severe comeuppance in the battle with Carol and 3/9 when she'd lost the battalion CP. Luckily for the battalion, the line companies, led by Major Frazier, and persevered, giving the battalion an overall grade of 76—not great, but passing. They were still on track to be certified for deployment. Still, she'd been heartily embarrassed, and she vowed that wouldn't happen again.

"Thanks for staying back. To get right to the point, what happened with the CP was inexcusable, and I blame myself for that. But that's the past. What I want to make sure is that never happens again.

"Lieutenant Constantine, I've spoken with Colonel Williams, and he's cleared it for you to stay attached for another week. As for the rest of you, if you tap your PAs to the nub . . . "

The five Marines dutifully tapped the conference table feed nubs, then looked at what they'd just downloaded.

"That's FM1205, Command Posts. We, well, we sort of ignored most of that. If you look right there in the front, Paragraph 1.10.02, Captain Peaslee, as headquarters commandant, you are in charge of selecting CP sites after consulting with the communications officer. And while comms is vital, please note what it says on the second line: security is the prime factor."

Esther let that sink in for the moment.

She knew that in peacetime exercises, some things tended to slip. The ability to communicate became the major factor for a battalion CP. It had always been that way, and she was guilty as anyone. It took Carol Depepe and her Mamba attack to drive that mistake home. She had a squash date with Carol that evening, and the first thing she was going to do was to thank her. Carol was still going to lord it over her, and that was going to sting big time, but better in training than in a real situation.

"So, what I want now is for the CP SOP to be re-written. Captain Peaslee, this is going to be your baby. You've got Lieutenant Constantine for a week, so use his expertise well."

"Aye-aye, ma'am," the young captain said, his eyes alight. "I've got it."

Too often, the H&S Company commander was treated as a holding pattern while waiting for a line company. They seemed to be more staff than commander, and Esther could see Jeff rise to the challenge. This was his time to make an impact on the battalion.

She didn't know if the captain was up to it. Maybe he was. But she was going to make sure by having Major Kutzman supervise him. And then there was Noah.

"Sergeant Major, I'd like you to assist Captain Peaslee with the SOP."

Noah nodded.

You warned me, Noah, true that. Now prove that wasn't a fluke and you really know what you were doing.

"Between the two of you, I'd like this done within two weeks," she said.

She waited a moment to see if there was any reaction before saying, "Two weeks as in right before our ACD evals. Next time the battalion takes the field, I want the SOP to be in place.

"Any questions?"

There were none.

"OK, then. I look forward to seeing the end product. Let's get to work."

Esther watched them file out of the conference room. She'd been embarrassed by having her CP wiped out, and while she was tasking Peaslee and Noah to craft a new SOP, she knew it was still up to her. She was the commanding officer, and it all fell on her shoulders. Not Peaslee's. Not Noah's. Hers.

Chapter 7
Noah

"Where the hell is PFC Islington?" Noah shouted down the passage.

A head poked out of the chaplain's office, some 30 meters past the duty desk.

"I've got him here, Sergeant Major," Second Lieutenant Eikbush said tentatively.

"Shit, Lieutenant, are you going to keep the CO waiting? Think she has nothing better to do that sit around until you're good and ready?" Noah shouted back. "How about getting your ass and your PFC up here now!"

The day had gotten off to a bad start and gone downhill from there. With only six days before embarkation, the battalion was at 78% of its Class V load-out, but the PICS maintenance pack was at 42% with no word on when the rest would arrive. The CO had called a 0530 meeting with Captain Tranh and First Lieutenant Hortense (the supply officer) to discuss it, and as Noah was already onboard for the morning, he had joined them. After chewing out the Sup-O for letting it get this far, she called up Division and unloaded on the Division G-4 Maintenance Supply Officer, a fellow lieutenant colonel, just about burning up the line. Noah and the other two listened in, grateful that they weren't on the receiving end of that tirade.

Noah's relief had been short-lived, though. As soon as she got off her PA, the Duty Officer, Lieutenant Kaddioui, stuck his head in the office and told them that Corporal Jeh Frump from Charlie had just been in a hover accident coming in back to base.

"Sergeant Major! We're at six days, right?" his sister asked.

"Yes, ma'am," Noah said, his heart falling, knowing what would come next.

From seven days on in, all unmarried Marines and sailors were on Cinderella liberty.

"And if I'm not mistaken, Corporal Frump is not married."

Of course, you aren't mistaken, and you know it.

"That's right, ma'am."

"Then how in God's little green acre was Frump 'coming back to base?'"

"I'll find out, ma'am."

"Do that," she said with steel in her voice. "And find out if Frump is still deployable."

Noah beat a hasty retreat to his office, calling First Sergeant Quisenberry to get his ass down to the CP. Corporal Frump was in big trouble, but the First Sergeant had some explaining to do. How was Frump out in town and either no one knew about it or had simply ignored it?

A quick call to the Naval hospital gave him nothing. Frump had just arrived in the ER, but charge nurse promised to call back as soon as he found out anything.

A red-faced Cory Quisenberry knocked on his hatch.

The Charlie Company first sergeant held up his hand in surrender before Noah lit into him and said, "Before you begin, I'm looking into it now. And I have to tell you, I've probably got another 12 Marines in the same position.

"Not in the hospital," he quickly said when Noah started to stand up, mouth dropping open. "I mean, out in the ville. I . . . I just found out. I . . . "

"You what, First Sergeant?" Noah asked in an icy voice.

Noah had been treading somewhat lightly around Cory, who had the same date of rank as he did. He'd tried not to come down overly bearing, but he was pissed. Thirteen Marines were UA?[5] Because that was what it was. If they were not on the base, they were UA.

The Cinderella liberty for deploying units was chickenshit, Noah knew. It was an overreaction to a number of Marines doing stupid things over the past year or so and becoming non-deployable. Noah had begged Esther to take it up to the CG, which she'd done only to be shot down. And now Frump had justified the restriction.

---

[5] UA: Unauthorized Absence

Noah sent Cory off to make sure all his missing sheep were back in the fold—and to initiate charges. Then he called the other first sergeants and asked for a full accounting of all battalion personnel; not now, twenty minutes before morning formation, but as of 0001 that morning.

A half an hour later, Noah had to inform Esther that of the 33 Marines and two sailors who were subject to Cinderella Liberty and who were not in the battalion area at 0001, only six had been entered into the system as UA. Ten had arrived within 15 minutes of midnight, which normally could be taken care of by non-disciplinary action at the platoon or company level. The rest? Noah didn't have an answer for that yet, and Esther—his Commanding Officer—had blistered his hide, the first time that had happened since they were kids.

Noah didn't like getting his hide blistered, and he blamed his company first sergeants. He set up a meeting at 1500, and he expected answers. Nothing was going to take away the sting of his sister's rebuke, but he was going to make sure that she wasn't going to get the same opportunity again. This issue was going to be fixed if he had to get Esther to restrict the entire battalion to the barracks until they embarked.

At 0900, the first of five Battalion Commander NJP's was scheduled. The intent had been to clear the CO's outstanding cases before embarking. With all the new UA's, however, that wasn't going to happen.

The first four NJPs went smoothly. One was dismissed, one was referred to a summary court martial, and two Marines were busted a rank each, fined half a month's pay for three months, and restricted to the battalion for three months. They'd be staying on the ship for at least one liberty port, possibly more. And now, with his to-do list getting longer by the minute, Second Lieutenant Eikbush was playing hide-and-seek with his PFC.

"Sergeant Major, where's my next case?" Esther called out over the office intercoms.

"Just a moment, ma'am. I'll have her right in."

"Here's PFC Islington," Lieutenant Eikbush said at his open hatch.

"About time, Lieutenant," he said. "You go report in to the CO. She'll ask you for some background," he added before turning to the nervous-looking private first class.

"And you, get your ass in here," he said, grabbing the Marine by her upper arm and almost dragging her to his desk. "Read this."

PFC Islington picked up the docutab, then dropped it on the deck.

"Son-of-a-bitch, Islington, can't you hold onto it? You sure seemed pretty capable out at the Foxy Moxie."

"Sorry, Sergeant Major," the PFC said, her voice cracking, as she picked the docutab back up and started to read it.

"Any day, now, Islington, or do you intend on keeping the CO waiting?"

"Uh, no, Sergeant Major."

"Are you Private First Class Isadora Islington? Do you realize you are being charged with Article Nine-Oh-Two of the UCMJ, Disorderly Conduct?"

"Ye . . . yes, Sergeant Major."

"Then scan the damned thing and let's get going. You don't need to read every grubbing word."

The PFC raised the tablet, stared at the lens, and scanned her acknowledgement.

"About grubbing time. OK, let's get going."

He led the now shaking PFC out into the passage and to the CO's hatch.

Knocking loudly, he said, "Private First Class Isadora Islington, reporting for the battalion commander's non-judicial punishment."

"Send her in."

"Center yourself on her desk and report in," he told Islington.

He slipped in behind her while the PFC marched up to Esther's desk, and in a soft voice, reported in.

"Speak up, Islington," Noah told her.

At least this case was pretty cut-and-dried. Islington, out with three other Marines, got into a confrontation with a group of five civilians. There was an argument of some mundane matter, some back-and-forth, and one civilian either shoved or didn't shove Lance Corporal Quince Ianconto. No one knew exactly because the owner of the Foxy Moxie refused to provide tapes of the incident. What was sure was that Islington decided to take matters into her own hands and break a chair over the civilian's back.

Islington wasn't being charged with assault. The civilian wasn't pressing charges and refused to make a statement. She was being charged with destruction of property, to wit, one bar chair. The bar owner had her written admission that she had broken said chair.

The NJP proceeded quickly. Islington admitted to the charges, and Captain Kingery, the Charlie Company Commander, and the butter bar Eikbush, her platoon commander, both said that Islington was a good Marine, an asset to the battalion.

That was pure show, however, for Islington and maybe for the two officers. Noah knew Esther had made up her mind the moment they walked in. Islington was busted down a rank and given a forfeiture of half a month's pay for three months. Islington's knees almost buckled before she heard that both of these were being suspended for a period of six months.

Islington had pulled a bonehead move and had escalated a situation that might have been already over, but she'd tried to protect a fellow Marine. Noah understood her intent if not her execution, and he knew Esther felt the same way.

He brought Islington back to his office and explained what "suspended" meant to her. She read Esther's judgment, stated she accepted it (not accepting it would open her up to a special court martial where the punishment could be much greater), and scanned that in.

"You're lucky, Islington. I hope you know that. No restriction to the ship while we pull liberty, no loss of money, no loss of rank—if you keep your nose clean. Understand?"

"Yes, Sergeant Major. I understand."

"OK, go report back to your lieutenant."

He sat back down, the first moment he'd had to catch his breath since 0530. He leaned his head back when there was a rap on his hatch.

"May I come in, Sergeant Major?" Lieutenant Eikbush asked.

"Of course, Lieutenant, come on in."

Second Lieutenant Eikbush was one of the new "contract lieutenants." He came in with his lieutenant's bars guaranteed. He'd serve two years as an enlisted Marine before going to NOTC to be commissioned for four years as an officer. "Guaranteed" might be a strong word, too strong. If one of the CL's messed up as a junior enlisted, such as receiving NJP or failing NOTC, the officer term of the contract was null and void, and it was the full six years enlisted.

There had been quite a bit of pushback among the old salts, both retired and still in the service, but this had been a political decision meant to be more efficient and to bring the Corps in line with the Navy and FCDC. "CL" became a derogatory term, however, and each CL had to work harder to prove him or herself.

"What can I do for you, Lieutenant?"

"Sergeant Major, I know you've got much more experience than I do, and I realize that one of a SNCO's job is to train lieutenants."

"Yeah . . ." Noah said, wondering where this was going.

Is he nervous? Why?

"Well, if I didn't have PFC Islington in the right place at the right time, that's on me. And I'd expect you to tell me that."

Which I did. What's your point?

"But . . . I mean . . ." he started before visibly gathering himself. "I don't appreciate how you did that," he said in a rush. "I may be a boot lieutenant, but I'm still a commissioned officer in the Corps, and as such, I deserve the respect and courtesy of my rank. If you need to correct me, I will absolutely listen to you and take in what you have to say, but if you need to correct me, that should be done in private, not in front of one of my Marines. You've compromised me, Sergeant Major, and that isn't good for my platoon."

He stood up straighter and looked Noah in the eye as if waiting for an outburst.

What the grubbing hell? Who do you think you are, boot? You? You're calling me out?

Noah stood and leaned over his desk, ready to lecture the lieutenant on the facts of life when it hit him. Lieutenant Eikbush was right. Yes, he was a boot, and yes, he had a lot to learn. But he was an officer, and junior officer became mid-level officers, then high-ranking officers. Discipline was one of the bedrocks of the Corps. It was the foundation of what kept the entire structure standing.

Noah had been rude and disrespectful to the lieutenant. Not just him. To PCF Islington as well. He'd let this morning, he'd let his anger and frustration affect how he treated others. He'd let go of the respect all Marines should have for each other.

No one doubted that Noah, even as a frocked sergeant major, knew more about the Corps than the lieutenant could learn in 20 more years. And part of what he knew was military courtesy. It took this boot lieutenant with barely three years in the Corps to remind him of that.

"You're absolutely right, sir," he said, and he could see the relief rush over the young Marine.

It had taken a pretty large set of balls for the lieutenant to confront him, Noah knew. The fact that he did so to support his conviction was a good sign, a very good sign.

"I apologize for my actions. I can assure you it won't happen again, sir."

"Well . . . I . . . thank you, Sergeant Major. I . . . I'd better get back to the company, then. Lots to do."

"Stop in any time, sir, if you want to chat. As you said, it's our duty to help train up the junior officers."

"I sure will, Sergeant Major. And thanks."

He turned and started out of Noah's office.

"I'll still correct you when I deem fit, sir, but not in front of your Marines."

The lieutenant stopped, smiled, and said, "I'm sure you'll have more than a few opportunities to correct me, Sergeant Major. And I welcome that. The better commander I become, the better my platoon will be."

Noah followed the lieutenant to his hatch, then watched the young man walk down the passage.

"What was that all about?"

Noah turned to see Esther standing beside him.

"Oh, nothing much."

"OK, if you say so."

"He's going to be a good one, though," he said, more to himself than to her.

"Well, with those out of the way, what's the story on the Cinderella UAs?"

Back to reality, Noah.

"Not good, not good at all. We've got the 13 from Charlie, then eight from Bravo—" he started before she interrupted him.

"I want the names, Sergeant Major, on my desk, now. Then I want the company commanders. I've got to brief the chief of staff at 1100, and I want the answers to all of the questions he's going to ask me."

"Aye-aye, ma'am," he said. "I'll have them to you in ten."

"XO! In my office now!" she called out, stepping back across the passage and through her hatch.

Chief of staff? Better you than me, Ess.

He'd been concerned about telling his sister about the UAs, but that was nothing. Now that they were within a month of deployment, Esther no longer reported to the regimental commander. Her boss was the CG himself.

Heavy is the crown, he thought to himself.

His day had sucked big time so far, but he had a feeling that Ess' was soon going to be a lot worse.

FS MOUNT FUJI

Chapter 8
Esther

Esther dropped her assault pack on the deck, then flopped on the rack. She was exhausted, pure and simple. The last two or three weeks had been one crisis after the other competing with the normal frenzy of getting a battalion deployed.

It seemed that they had barely made it to the ship. If they'd been the Space Alert Battalion, they could have deployed within 12 hours. It would have been a frenzied evolution, but it would have been done. With six months to prepare, even given that much of that time was in the field with training and evaluation ops, a rational outsider would think that it would be easy to get the battalion on the ship and ready for duty.

A rational outsider would be wrong.

Nature abhors a vacuum, and the military abhors free time. Every moment was filled with one more requirement from division, one more emergency situation that needed Esther's personal attention. She'd been on stimsticks for the last week, surviving on fewer than three hours of sleep a night.

The idiotic Cinderella liberty issue had been typical of the crap that had been thrown at her. The CG had even questioned her leadership abilities and if she was capable of leading the battalion on deployment. She knew it had been too late for her to be replaced lacking an actionable transgression on her part, but she hadn't enjoyed being questioned, especially by General Lace-Reimer, who knew her well.

Luckily, Noah had grabbed the reins on that. He'd said he'd take care of it, and Esther didn't ask how. Fifteen Marines were scheduled for NJP during transit; the rest had been handled at the company level.

There's going to be a lot of sad faces when they miss out on Kukson, she thought, a smile creeping over her face.

Kukson, along with Vegas, Ramp it Up, and Pattaya, were considered the four premier liberty ports in Federation space, and that was where the turnover with 3/12 and the *FS Singh Harbor* was to take place. More than a few Marines would be stuck on the *Mount Fuji* with extra duty while the rest of the battalion enjoyed the pleasures of what Kukson had to offer.

Esther glanced up at the small clock above the hatch into her stateroom. She had two blessed hours before chow, two hours where she could catch some Z's. Stimsticks were all well and good, but they couldn't keep a person going forever, and extended use extracted a price on the body. Not bothering to get undressed, she brought her feet up to her rack and told the room to wake her ten minutes before first call for the wardroom.

Two minutes later, the ship's 1MC interface said, "Lieutenant Colonel Lysander, Commander Anderson welcomes you aboard, and he's requesting your presence in his stateroom for your joint deployment statement."

Esther groaned as she struggled to open her eyes. It was traditional at the start of a deployment for both commanders to issue a joint statement over the 1MC, stressing the teamwork required for a successful mission, that they were representatives for the Federation, blah, blah, blah.

Now? Can't this wait until after chow?

It was his ship and his call, however. They may be the same rank, but he was god aboard the *Mount Fuji*.

"Please tell the captain that I'll be there directly," she said.

She swung her legs off the rack, stepping up to the tiny sink and splashing water on her face. It didn't do much in to refresh her.

Leaving the stateroom, she gave one last longing look at her rack. At least she had first seating in the wardroom, and she'd be free after that.

"Three more hours," she told her rack. "Three hours and you and I have a date."

KUKSON

Chapter 9
Noah

"Eight Agathas, three house ciders, and a Manhattan," Cory told the tablewaiter. "I'm buying this round."

What am I? Noah wondered as the green light chimed the tablewaiter's acceptance.

He and Gunny Raison were not drinkers. The gunny was drinking water, and he had a soft cider, but as usual, they were left out when someone was buying a round. Noah never understood that. Non-alcoholic drinks were less expensive than the draft beer, cider, and the lone cocktail, and Noah had bought the first round to celebrate a liberty port without a single liberty incident. Yet the two of them were left out when it came to getting drinks from the others.

He shook his head slightly, but he remained quiet. Nothing was going to spoil his good mood. He checked the time. The last shuttle up to the ship left in a little over two hours. After that, assuming no one missed it, he'd be home free. An entire reinforced battalion, a Marine Expeditionary Unit of 868 Marines and sailors, had managed to spend three days on Kukson without a liberty incident. Esther had tasked him with that almost impossible result, and they'd just about managed it.

It had been surprisingly easy from a senior staff level point of view. Noah had called the entire battalion into the mess decks before the first liberty was called. Kukson was one of the premier liberty ports, and the troops' excitement had been palpable. Noah had given them the normal "have fun, but you are representing the Federation Marines" speech before he lowered the boom. Any liberty incident would result in the immediate and total curtailment of liberty—for all hands.

The look of shock on the Marines' faces as he said that almost made him laugh, and he had to keep control.

"By liberty incident, I mean as reported by the local police. If Lance Corporal Schmuckatelli gets plastered and falls down puking in the gutter and gets hauled away by the police, that is a liberty

Jonathan P. Brazee

incident. If Lance Corporal Schmuckatelli gets plastered and falls down puking in the gutter and some of his buddies, that means you out there, haul his ass back to the shuttle and pour him aboard, that is not a liberty incident, and then his buddies can go back out and enjoy themselves. And as far as Lance Corporal Schmuckatelli, if he's on the shuttle, no harm, no foul."

He paused for a second to let it sink in. It took a moment, but he could see it on their faces as they began to understand. It was really a pretty straightforward concept. A Marine took care of another Marine, pure and simple. If the Marines policed themselves, then they could party to their heart's content. If they could not police themselves, then liberty would be curtailed.

He told Command Master Chief Rajput his plans for the Marines, and the ship's senior enlisted sailor decided she was going to put the same plan in place for the ship's crew. Together, they'd discussed how strict they were going to be with the rules, and if an incident on day one would affect liberty on day three, but to both of their surprises, there had not been a single reportable incident.

If he did nothing else on this entire deployment, Noah was going to take that as a major win.

The bar they'd picked had a trolley system, like a miniature roller coaster, that led the drinks to the table. Twelve covered glasses, like cars in a train, trundled down to land on the table. As it was his round, Cory took over, spreading the beers, ciders, and the Manhattan to the other Marines.

"Another Sunhills Green and a water," Noah said quietly into the tablewaiter, waiting for the green light of acknowledgment.

Gunny Bill Keating was an avid golfer, and he was trying to describe some supposedly amazing shot he'd made that morning. No one else was paying much attention, and the gunny took to standing, grabbing Top Dwaine McCurry by the shoulder. First Sergeant Khan threw a wadded-up napkin at the gunny, who ignored it.

Noah sat back and just drank in the scene. They were a good crew, he knew. He couldn't have assembled a better bunch of senior SNCOs. He'd been worried about how he'd be accepted, both for his relationship with the CO and with him being merely frocked, but after some initial awkwardness with a couple of the E8's, things had settled down. He wasn't particularly close to any of them, but they seemed to accept him as the sergeant major.

His PA buzzed. He took it out of his pocket and saw that he had a message from Esther. He made his excuses, then stepped into the hall leading to the heads where the ambient noise was a little less.

"We've got a mission," Esther said.

"Ok," Noah acknowledged. "Um . . . should we recall the troops?"

He wondered what the mission was, but this was his personal PA, and she couldn't pass that over the commercial net. With a simple command, however, he could initiate a recall over that same commercial net.

"I don't think that'll be necessary, Noah. Let's just let the normal shuttle schedule run. But I want you and the two tops ready for a 0200 meeting aboard the *Fujiyama*."

Noah glanced back down the hallway to where he could see their table. Top Reston, the Operations Chief, was tottering in her seat.

"OK, I'll stop the spigot on those two," he told her. "Uh . . . how are you?"

Noah had quit drinking after Miriam filed for divorce, and he'd been pressuring Esther to cut back, at least, without much effect.

"A little tipsy, but I just took a Soberup."

Noah shuddered. During his downwards drinking spiral, he'd had to resort to the little pill more than once, and frankly, he'd rather suffer through the hangover.

"Thanks for the heads up. I'll see you at 0200."

Noah started back to the table. He had no idea what the mission was, but the enlisted leadership had to be ready.

"The drinking light is out, folks," he said as he reached the table.

"What? Why? We're just getting started," Cory said, lifting his beer.

"Duty calls."

Faces immediately sobered up even if bodies did not.

Noah held up his hand to forestall them, palm out, and said, "No recall. Liberty ends as usual. But make sure every swinging dick left is on that last shuttle. Missing movement is, well, I don't have to tell you. And you two," he said to the two master sergeants, "we've got a meeting at 0200 with the CO. I don't know how far into your cups you are, but they've got Soberups at the bar."

"Well, that's a fine how-do-you-do," Cory said without rancor as he took another long swallow of his beer.

"This is what we do, folks. So, enjoy your last two hours, because it's about time we earned our salaries."

VANITY

Chapter 10
Esther

"Mr. Ambassador, I'm Lieutenant Colonel Lysander. We're here to evacuate you. This is Sergeant Major Lysander, and if you follow him, he'll take you to the *Mount Fuji.*"

The harried looking white-haired gentleman looked up at her from his large, opulent desk as if he didn't understand. His eyes went from Esther to Noah to the four armed Marines who had accompanied her into his office.

"Sir, I told you about this. These are the Marines, and they'll take care of you," Kirk Fehrenkamp, the deputy chief of mission said.

"But, I thought the commander is the last to leave," the ambassador said, his voice wavering.

"This is a Federation embassy, sir, not an old wet-water Navy ship," Esther told him, glancing at the DCM.

He'd met her at the landing pad and explained that even in the best of times, the ambassador could be somewhat "scattered," was the phrase he'd used. The current situation only exacerbated that condition.

"It's time, sir," the DCM said. "You go, and I'll take care of the loose ends here."

An explosion from off in the near distance rocked the office windows, the sound muffled only somewhat by the embassy's sturdy construction. The ambassador didn't seem to notice.

"We've got at least 200 people at the gate now, begging to come in," Major Ralph Kurtzman, her S3, passed to her on the P2P. "The ones in the rear of the mob are taking sporadic fire."

With the ambassador looking right at her, she kept a slight smile on her face as she sub-vocalized, "Our orders remain in place. No one gets in until the embassy and the ambassador are secure."

"Understood."

"I can't leave now. Greta, she's . . ." he started before turning to the DCM and asking, "Kirk, where is Greta? Why isn't she here?"

"Sir, I've got Captain McLamb and Alpha Company at the residence. They have your wife and will be off the planet's surface momentarily," Esther answered for the DCM.

"It's time, sir," Fehrenkamp said softly, as someone might speak with a child. "You need to go."

Esther didn't have time to sweet talk a man who had so evidently lost it, if he even had "it" in the first place. She was about to order the four Marines to bodily lift him from his chair when the DCM stepped forward, and taking the ambassador's arm, helped him up. There was no doubt in her military mind that the DCM was running the show and probably had been for some time, but she could also see that he genuinely cared for the ambassador.

The old man let the DCM get him up and start him from around the desk.

The ambassador took three steps, then said, "Wait!" He moved back to his desk, then reached out to take the pen that was sticking in a wooden block. "My pen," he told the DCM as if it was a vital piece of embassy gear.

"Sir, if you will go with the sergeant major now, we'll have you up to the ship in no time.

"Sergeant Major, if you will take care of the ambassador now?" she said, raising her eyebrows and tilting her head at her brother, her sign that he needed to get the ambassador out as quickly as possible.

Two distinctive reports of a Marine Windmoeller and Holscher reached Esther, followed by panicked screams from outside the gate. One of her two snipers had engaged a target.

Hell, there goes the "no engagement" orders, Ether thought.

Admiral Jallaby, the sector commander, had briefed her while the battalion was in transit. It was imperative that the embassy remain secure and that the ambassador be removed from harm's way, but until the Federation knew who was going to come out on top, there would be no taking sides in the conflict. Part and parcel to that was that if possible, there would be no engagements.

Which was pretty ridiculous, in her opinion. They were going into a hot zone, and with warring sides, the Marines would more likely than not to have to use deadly force to protect Federation citizens or locals. As a captain, Esther had commanded a secret mission of snipers, and she held them in utmost respect. Sergeant Jack Hilborn, one of her two snipers, had taken the shots, and while he might not be Master Guns Medicine Crow, Esther trusted his judgement, Admiral Jallaby's directives be damned. Standing inside the embassy building, she wasn't about to second guess the sergeant.

The ambassador hadn't seemed to register the shots. He evidently didn't realize that this was now a shooting mission.

"If you'll come with me, sir?" Noah said, taking the DCM's place on his arm and signaling Corporal Prostov to take the other.

He came close to carrying the ambassador as the Marines escorted the man out of his office.

Esther asked for a sitrep on the gunshots, and her AI flashed that two armed men had fired upon the crowd at the gate. Four of the people were down, their condition yet to be determined. The two men had been taken down by Sergeant Hilborn, probably KIA.

"He wasn't always like this, you know," Fehrenkamp said, interrupting her train of thought. "It's just been over the last six months."

Then he should have been removed six months ago, Esther thought. *Would we be in this mess if someone competent had been in charge?*

That wasn't a very charitable thought, Esther knew. The Dorado Front had been around for years, and Esther wasn't sure that even a competent ambassador could have accomplished much once the DF began to sweep aside the government forces.

"So, what's the status of the evacuation? Where are we at with the classified?" Esther asked, which technically wasn't under her responsibility.

With the ambassador out of the picture, the removal and destruction of sensitive materials was the responsibility of the DCM, his Regional Security Officer, and the commander of the Marine Security Guard, Gunnery Sergeant Tika Tasuaalo. Although a Marine, Gunny Taluaalo did not answer to Esther despite the fact that she commanded the NEO, but rather to the DCM.

If Fehrenkamp thought Esther was overstepping her bounds, he didn't say anything, instead telling her, "Gunny T is destroying the classified as we speak. She should be done in 15 minutes."

"If you don't mind, I'd like to speak with her when she's done. I'd like her view on the situation."

Which the DCM could take as a rebuke, she knew. Some Second Ministry folks felt like second-hand citizens to the First Ministry and the military, and they could be prickly when they thought they were being disrespected. To ask to speak to the gunny could infer that she didn't trust the DCM and his staff.

Which was partially true. Not that she didn't trust them over all, but for military matters, such as defending the embassy, she'd prefer to speak with someone who understood Marines and Marine tactics. Esther and her staff had gone over the embassy's F101, the plan for the defense and evacuation that each embassy created, and it had seemed reasonable, but she still wanted to speak to the gunny face-to-face.

"No problem. I'll let her know," the DCM said.

"We've lifted off," Noah passed on the P2P. "I'll be back on the return trip."

"Your ambassador is off the ground. He'll be aboard the *Fujiyama* in thirty minutes."

"Thank you, Colonel. Now, if you don't mind, I'd like to go over the one-oh-one with you. I've already given your Captain Tranh the list of our key players and their locations. All other remaining non-essentials are at the staging areas A, B, and C. As you can see . . ."

Esther listened as the DCM went over the ground situation. She was impressed with the degree of thoroughness, and she couldn't think of much to ask. DCM Fehrenkamp evidently was at the top of his game. She forgot about asking for Gunny Tauaalo and instead dealt directly with him as they determined where would be the best placement of her Marines while they waited for the final decision on whether to implement a full evacuation.

"Let's take a look at the grounds," Esther said when the DCM was finished. "I'd like to get a visual in my mind of the layout."

The DCM led Esther out of the office, one of his security team jumping out in front of the two. With almost 240 Marines in the compound, she didn't know how much good a single bodyguard was going to do, but she held her tongue.

Fehrenkamp led her to the roof of the embassy. The ambassador had been lifted off the planet in a Marine Albatross, but the bulk of the evacuees were leaving on one of two ship's shuttles.

"What're the numbers now, Top," she asked Master Sergeant McCurry.

"Two-oh-three gone, ma'am. We've got eighty-six here," he said, pointing to the line of people filing in F-2.

"How many does that leave us with?"

"Sixty-nine. One last load. F-1's due to be back in 42 minutes."

"And that leaves how many left at the embassy?" she asked, turning to Fehrenkamp.

"Thirty-three, including the security guard detachment."

Esther did a quick calculation in her head. Captain McLamb and his two platoons from Alpha had already taken off from the residence without a hitch. Bravo and Charlie were in the compound along with nine from headquarters. With the embassy's 33, that left her with 263 bodies to get off the planet if the final order came. Each shuttle could carry 90 pax, and the two Albatrosses could carry 30 each in a pinch. Call it 240 if they packed it in tight, to include all 24 PICS Marines. Which meant they could not lift off with one flight unless she ordered the PICS Marines to molt and leave the combat suits behind, something she was loath to do.

"Do you need all of those thirty-three?" she asked the DCM as they started back down the ladderwell to the ground level.

"That's my requirement. No choice on those numbers."

Esther pulled up her disposition on her display. Bravo was holding the front gate and most of the perimeter. Charlie had one platoon completing the perimeter, one inside the embassy at the ground floor, and one helping Top handle the first wave of evacuees.

"Captain Kingery," she passed on the command net. "I want Third Platoon to return to the ship. Get who you can on F-2, then the rest on F-1 when it returns. Send a squad from Second to take Third's place loading pax."

"Aye-aye, ma'am. But if I may suggest, let me leave one squad from Third. They've bene working with Top McCurry and know what he wants. I'll take a squad from Second to make up the numbers."

Esther thought about it for a moment, then concurred. She simply needed to lower the number of bodies on the ground, and what he said about his Third Platoon already working with the Top made sense.

Her AI, which was continually scanning the nets, decided right then that she needed to hear what Captain Gill was saying to the Three.

" . . . no ID, but he says he's Federation."

"Show me visuals," Esther ordered her AI.

Her AI picked two, one from the front and one from the side. A middle-aged man, dressed in safari chic, had pushed himself to the front of the mob at the gate. Around him, people were shouting for attention, demanding to get into the embassy.

If the man's Federation, why is he out and about while the DF marched into the city?

"Get a retinal scan," Major Kurtzman told the captain. "I'll run it through the system."

People shoved closer to the gate, smashing the man flat against it. They seemed to sense something was changing, and they wanted to take advantage of it.

"You need to act now, Ralph," she passed on the P2P. "Send out a snatch team, get that guy, and isolate him away from the embassy until you can scan him for anything we don't want in here. Then you can identify him."

"Roger that, ma'am," the major responded before giving the orders to Captain Gill.

A snatch team was normally used to penetrate a violent crowd to snatch an instigator. Very few mobs could or would stand up to the bulrush of a well-trained team, and the battalion had drilled incessantly at this.

Two of the PICS Marines were standing sentinel at the gate, more for show than anything else. But not entirely. On Captain Gill's command, the two Marines moved forward to the gate and opened it about two meters, their shear bulk nicely filling the gap. When they stepped forward, the front of the mob recoiled. The moment the two PICS Marines stepped to the side, five more Marines, packed tightly, pushed out into the crowd parting them. With a coordinated pivot, they enveloped the man like some sort of giant, armed amoeba. Immediately back stepping, they returned to the opening of the gate and slipped back inside the compound as the two PICS Marines slammed the gate shut.

The entire movement took 14 seconds, too quick for the stunned crowd to react.

"Pretty impressive," the DCM said from where he'd watched on his handheld screen. "No one in the crowd was even hurt."

"That's what we train for," Esther said.

Not that we always get it right, even in training, she admitted to herself.

She was pretty pumped to see the snatch performed flawlessly.

The snatch team searched the man, and one pulled something out of his pocket. Esther immediately recognized a field holocorder, the same type carried by members of the press. A moment later, his identity was confirmed. De'Sander Yule was a credentialed reporter at large, meaning he was licensed by the Federation but worked as a free-lancer.

"Colonel? The guy's a reporter. Credentialed. Says his cards were taken by the DL when he was with them. What do we do with him?" Major Kurtzman asked.

"What do we do? We give him back his holocorder and ask him if he wants a lift off-planet, that's what we do," she told him.

"But, he's been with the DL all this time, ma'am."

"As it his right as a reporter, Ralph. You know that. Find out what he wants to do."

Esther knew what the major was driving at. This guy had been with the DL, so he had to have some good intel Captain Montoya, her S2 back up on the ship, would love to hear. But their hands were tied. As a Federation credentialed reporter, he had every right to pretty much go where he wanted, even to the enemy. And in this case, the DL wasn't an enemy of the Federation, just to the local government. He probably ran afoul of local laws, but that wasn't the Marines' concern. To them, he was simply another Federation citizen, but one who could choose to remain until the planet came crashing down around his ears, if he so desired.

"His choice, Ralph. Search him, then send him to Gunny Vandervee at the cafeteria. If we can get him off planet, we'll do it. If not . . ."

Which is bullshit, Lysander. I can imagine the CU going batshit if we left him.

Technically, Esther could leave him on the planet. He'd arrived during a conflict of his own free will. But the Correspondents' Union was a powerful force that transcended governmental boundaries, and they could make things tough for her if they so desired.

"Roger that, ma'am," Kurtzman passed back to her.

With Vandervee on her mind, she called him up, asking, "Gunny, how many non-Federation citizens do you have there?"

"Fifteen, ma'am. Seven Brotherhood, three Confeds, three Alliance, a San Marcan, and Cassovite."

"OK, not as bad as I thought. You've got a Federation reporter on his way. Keep him with the rest. Are they demanding lift off-planet?"

"Just the Cassovite."

The fifteen people had either been at the embassy on official business, or the ambassador—no, probably the DCM—had given them refuge when things went to shit. The Brotherhood and Confederation citizens probably didn't want to be seen as being "rescued" by the Federation, so they wouldn't ask for a lift.

If it gets hot, though, I bet you change your tune.

The Cassovite was a different story. A tax enclave of the wealthy, Casson had no navy nor much of anything else.

A rush of displaced air made Esther's ear's pop. She looked up, but she couldn't see the aircraft that rushed just out of view. She heard and felt the ordnance that the plane dropped, though.

"Did anyone get eyes on that aircraft?" she passed on the open net.

"I did," Sergeant Hilborn passed from his perch on the embassy roof. "It was DL. A Spyder. It dropped its load two blocks over."

A Spyder was a Gentry-made atmospheric craft, cheap, reliable, and effective for what it was designed. The Marines could knock it out of the sky with any number of weapons, and she had to assume that the Vanity military could, too. The fact that it was flying over the capital with seeming impunity was pretty telling that the situation was going south quickly.

"That was a DL Spyder," she told the DCM. "It dropped its bombs two blocks to the north. What's there?"

"The Ministry of Commerce and the Alliance of Free States embassy."

Damn, I wish I could get drones out there! she wished for the umpteenth time. She needed to see if the Spyder had targeted the ministry building or the Alliance embassy.

Her orders, however, were nothing Federation past the embassy walls, and that included her drones.

"Gunny," she asked Vandervee on the P2P, "get one of the Alliance folks to call their embassy. Let me know if it's still standing."

"The Spyder's coming around for another run," Hilborn said. "I can barely pick it up, but it's coming back, no doubt about it."

"I'm coming back up," Esther said.

With the DCM in tow, she ran up the ladderwell to the roof, six floors up, all the time scanning her various feeds, cursing the limitations placed on her Marines. A NEO wasn't considered a combat operation, but Marines could die all the same.

Top met her at the door that opened onto the roof, one arm out, pointing to where Hilborn had picked his firing position, the other one motioning back-and-forth like a traffic cop directing her where to go.

"I've got a shuttle inbound, ETA four minutes," he told her.

"Wave it off until we see what's going on."

A Marine Albatross could more than handle a Spyder, but things would be a little dicier for one of the *Mount Fuji's* shuttles.

She ran up to Hilborn, who pointed to the planetary west, over the city center. She accepted his feed, and a split second later, her AI had centered the Spyder in her face shield display. The plane was still ten klicks away, so maybe 45 seconds. Her AI kept calculating a probable target location, but there were still too many variables at play.

"Sector Ops," she said, and the *Mount Fuji's* comm center patched her through to Admiral Jallaby's operations center back on Port Florence. "I've got an incoming Spyder that has already dropped ordnance. Request weapons free."

There was a momentary pause, one in which the Spyder closed the distance, and then the comms operator came back with, "That's a negative. The DL aircraft targeted a government building, not our embassy. I repeat, negative. You are not granted weapons free."

Esther shook her head, her frustration mounting. "Weapons free" meant her Marines could engage as they deemed fit. Without it, they had to be fired upon first in order to return fire.

She turned to Sergeant Hilborn to ask him exactly where he thought the plane was heading, but he was glassing the area outside the gate with his rifle scope. As he should have been. He and Corporal Tendine, his spotter, had a job to do, and with Esther there, they could ignore the Spyder.

"Oh, I see it," Fehrenkamp said.

Without any optics, the Spyder was a little hard to spot, but if the DCM could see it, time was running out. Esther zoomed out her display, and sure enough, the Spyder was visible as it split several high rises and kept coming.

Her AI kept intoning the approach, but Esther tuned it out, relying on her own eyes. It looked like the plane was lining up for another run at its previous target, and she had just started to relax when the Spyder juked to its right, putting it directly on line with Dykstra Boulevard, the street out in front of the embassy.

"Incoming!" several voiced filled the net as the Spyder release two iron bombs, clearly visible to the naked eye, before pulling up and out of its approach.

The iron bombs (and old term that merely meant non-guided) were slowed by expanding tailfins, which gave the Spyder enough time to get out of the blast zone. It also made it easy for her AI to determine the point of impact. The bombs would not hit the embassy itself, but rather the street outside—right where the crowd was gathered.

The bombs hit towards the back of the crowd, the twin concussion blasts hitting Esther one-two. Screams erupted from the crowd.

"Captain Gill, I want a CASREP,"[6] Esther ordered her Bravo Company commander as smoke billowed into the air. "Use your PICS. No straight-leg infantry."

The crowd didn't seem to be turning against the Marines, but panic had a way of making people act irrationally, like the drowning person dragging down the lifeguard trying to save him. She didn't want any of her Marines dragged down that way.

She looked over the edge of the roof as two more PICS Marines joined the two at the gate, and together, the four Marines slipped out, carefully pushing their way through the crowd. Esther tied into Sergeant Pawelczak's feed, and the carnage was shocking. Burnt bodies struggled to pull themselves out of the impact area, and more burnt lumps of what had been people only moments before littered the street. Esther could almost smell the blackened flesh through the feed.

The bastards had used incendiaries. There would be no chance of resurrection for most of the victims, and the "lucky" ones who survived faced months, if not years, of painful regen.

Esther wasn't supposed to take sides, but this was beyond the pale. The Ministry of Commerce was bad enough, but this was a war crime, as far as she was concerned.

---

[6] CASREP: Casualty Report

"There is a second craft incoming," her AI intoned.

Esther looked up, and back towards the city center, her AI pinpointed a second Spyder, staring the same approach.

"I'm opening the gate," she told the DCM. "We've got another plane making a run."

Technically, Esther didn't have the authority to do that. But when Fehrenkamp said nothing, she ordered Captain Gill to open the main gate. Immediately, the gate began to open, and the crowd started to surge inside.

"Keep them isolated," she ordered her company commander, then to Major Kurtzman, "No one intermixes with our Marines or the remaining embassy staff. Get them on the ground; then I want every single one of them scanned. Biologicals, too. If they don't cooperate, I want Marines standing them down."

The embassy had only two scanners that could detect the new biological explosives that could be hidden on or inside a living human being. She needed each person scanned, and if it took Marines holding weapons on them to gain their compliance, so be it.

"Fifteen seconds to arrival," her AI said, snapping Esther back.

She glanced at the gate; fifty or more people had pushed their way in, but the opening was too small for the mass of people. More were out on the street, both trying to get inside the grounds and wounded and unable to move.

"Engage the Spyder," she ordered on the open net.

At the edge of the building, one of her two M249 crew served guns opened up. Down on the street, though, Lance Corporal Dennis Bird, with the Weapons Pack 4 on his PICS, targeted and fired his Mini-Joe, a small, but extremely powerful missile. Equally effective against armor or aircraft, the Spyder didn't have a chance. The missile struck true, tearing off a wing and sending the aircraft spinning off to its left and into a line of houses.

Esther may or may not have just disobeyed orders. The embassy hadn't been attacked yet, but she wasn't going to stand by and let civilians burn. She could argue that her four PICS Marines had been in danger. They hadn't been, of course, if the second Spyder was using incendiaries as well. A PICS was protection enough against mere flames. But she'd argue that she didn't know with what else that Spyder was armed.

Worry about that later, Lysander!

Below her, in the embassy courtyard, Bravo Company had its hands full trying to gain control of the panicked people.

"Ralph, no DL fighter comes near the embassy building. I'm declaring an exclusion zone," she said as she wheeled about to run to the door, then taking three stairs at a time, down to the ground floor and out into the courtyard.

"Lieutenant Phoenix, get those people down on the ground, face first," she shouted at one of the Bravo lieutenants as she ran up to Captain Gill.

"Jean, we've got dead and wounded out there on the street. Use First Platoon to bring them inside the embassy for Doc Lorton to start treatment."

First Platoon was the company's PICS platoon, and Doc Lorton was Bravo's senior corpsman. The wounded civilians had to be treated, but not by abandoning security.

"Colonel, can I have a word with you?" someone shouted out.

Esther turned to see the reporter, holocorder out, running up to her.

"Not now!" she shouted back.

"Let Sector Ops know what happened," she belatedly told Major Kurtzman.

Probably not necessary, she told herself. *I'm sure they already know.*

At least Sector Ops wasn't getting in her hair. She may or may not have crossed the line, but they were letting her deal with the situation for the time being. If she messed up, that would be address that later.

"We've got EC's approaching," Major Kurtzman passed to her.

Esther switched her display. Some thirty or forty red avatars appeared, all moving forward and converging on the embassy.

Now, they could be friendlies, she knew, and not "ECs," for "enemy combatants." But something told her the good major was right. More avatars kept popping up on her display as people they represented were acquired by her limited scanners.

"Ralph, I want this broadcasted.

"This is Lieutenant Colonel Esther Lysander, United Federation Marine Corps. To all personnel, the area around the Federation Embassy is now a no-go zone. All personnel are warned to stay at least 200 meters from the embassy. Anyone entering this exclusion zone will be subject to lethal force. I repeat, if you come into the area, you will be fired upon."

A moment later, Esther heard her voice going out over the embassy loudspeakers.

"Again," she ordered her Ops O.

"Can you do that?" Fehrenkamp asked as he stepped up beside her.

"Probably not. Hell, half of those homes and buildings there are within 200 meters, and I'm sure there are people inside of them. But those are DL fighters coming, and I don't want them to get any closer."

"We're not at war with the DL," the DCM reminded her.

"No, but we have a humanitarian duty to protect civilians. I'm not going to let them get slaughtered. And with most of those civilians now inside—"

She held up her hand as Major Kurtzman told her the advancing DL fighters were continuing forward, and the first of them were visible.

"Sergeant Pawelczak, bring your team back in," she ordered, bypassing the company commander.

"We've still got wounded out here, ma'am, that gotta get inside if we're going to save 'em. We can handle any piss-ant fighters."

Almost on cue, the sound of firing reached her. Instinctively, Esther drew her Ruger, spinning around to face the gate. The last of the civilians were pushing inside, trying to reach safety.

Except one.

A middle-aged woman stopped and looked back to where the firing was building. She reached for her belly, and just as Esther shouted out, disappeared in a blinding flash of light.

The blast knocked Esther on her back, and in a daze, she struggled to sit up. She put her hand on something that gave, and looking down, she saw that "something" was a human leg.

Captain Gill was rushing forward, but to the gate, not to her. A moment later, ten PICS Marines rushed forward. Esther switched to the company net where Captain Gill was forming an assault team with her PICS platoon.

With Gill having things in hand, Esther slowly stood up, checking herself. To her surprise, she wasn't really hurt. Her bone inserts had protected her as they'd been designed to do. Several other Marines were in the process of getting up, and Esther finally had the presence of mind to check her personnel display. Every member of the battalion was represented by a steady blue avatar. Some of them might be dazed as she was, but no one was hurt bad enough to have their avatar switch to a light blue of a WIA.

The civilians were not so lucky. Those standing next to the suicide bomber had been torn apart by the blast.

"You OK, Colonel?" Major Kurtzman asked, his voice stressed.

"Yeah, I'm fine," she responded, and she realized she really was fine. She'd been only momentarily dazed. She'd had worse back in pugil stick fights in bootcamp.

"We're engaging," Captain Gill passed.

"Kick some ass," Esther replied on the P2P.

The scans didn't show the fighters to have any heavy weapons, and small arms would be ineffective against PICS Marines.

Idiots, she thought. *Don't they know we have PICS?*

Unless they do know and have a surprise up their collective sleeves, she second-guessed herself.

"All hands, engage the ECs if you have clear fields of fire," she ordered on the open net.

If the DLs had a surprise, Esther wanted to keep them from springing it. And a concerted, aggressive assault could do just that.

"Stop, Jean," she passed as she saw Captain Gill about to leave the embassy grounds. "Let Lieutenant Gaspar take it."

The captain looked back to Esther, then gave a rueful grin and a half salute. The captain was not in a PICS. Lieutenant Gaspar, as the platoon commander, was. Esther understood the desire to run to the sound of guns, but the captain couldn't needlessly risk herself.

"Get the rest of the people scanned. Just because one suicided doesn't mean there isn't another planted in here."

"Aye-aye, ma'am. I'm on it."

Outside the walls, the heavy reports of the PICS' HGLs and lighter drone of their M114 rifles drowned out the firing of the DL soldiers. On her display, Esther could see red avatar after avatar fade out as the fighters were literally torn apart.

"Looks like they're on the run," she said, turning to the DCM.

Her voice caught as she saw him, one leg bloody and almost severed. Unlike Esther, he didn't have body armor. Beyond him, the reporter lay, his torso torn in half.

"Fred, I want all your corpsmen here," she passed to the Charlie Company commander.

She knelt beside the DCM who looked up at her and simply said, "Damn!"

"Looks like some heavy regen for you, Kirk. But you'll be fine," then "Doc Harris, come take a look at the Deputy Chief of Mission.

"I'll leave you in Doc Harris' good hands. Take care of yourself."

Esther had a fight to command, and she couldn't let herself be constrained by concern over individuals.

But the battle, such as it was, was over. The PICS Marines' assault had broken the back of the DL fighters. At least 20 had been killed before the rest broke and ran.

Esther had Captain Gill order her Marines to bring in the rest of the civilian wounded from the street, then had Top McCurry take over the screening of those now inside the embassy grounds. Only after that was done did she report in to Sector Ops.

The Navy rear admiral who'd been monitoring the battle took the report, then passed it on to the Sector Commander. Three minutes later, the order came down to abandon the embassy.

It took two full lifts, not the one lift Esther had originally envisioned. All of the wounded were taken to the *Mount Fuji* first, where even the ship's first-class hospital was taxed. Other nationals, both those who'd already been at the embassy as well as some from the Alliance embassy two streets away, were also given rides off-planet. But finally, with all the classified destroyed, it was time for the Marines.

"Are you coming, ma'am?" Major Kurtzman asked from the ramp of the Marine Albatross.

Esther took a last look around. She'd chastised the ambassador when the man said he wanted to be the last one to leave, but here she was, the last Federation Marine at the embassy.

"Yeah, Ralph, I am," she said, stepping up on the ramp and letting the crew chief lead her to her seat. "Let's get out of here."

FS MOUNT FUJI

Chapter 11
Noah

"Do you have anything to add?" Commander Steve Anderson asked Esther.

"Just this. I want all of you to get the word back to the Marines and sailors that I'm proud of each and every one of them. NEOs can be tricky with all the rules of engagement, but despite that, we accomplished the mission. We evacuated the ambassador, the embassy staff, and 163 non-combatants, all without a single Marine casualty."

Not quite, thought Noah. *We've got a few burns being treated and a busted eardrum, but close enough for government work.*

"All things considering, the Cutting Edge showed once more why we are the best battalion in the Corps."

"Well, if that's it, I guess we'll close off for now. Division heads, I want your after action reports in by COB tomorrow," the ship's CO said.

"Companies and senior staff, same here. COB tomorrow," Major Kurtzman shouted out as the commanders and senior staff got up from their seats.

"Command Master Chief, can I see you for a moment?" Noah shouted out to his Navy counterpart as she started to exit through the hatch.

"What duya got, Noah?" Sisa asked as Noah reached him.

Command Master Chief Sisa Rajput was a short, stocky sailor with as keen a mind as anyone Noah had ever met. If it had anything to do with the navy, then she was the duty expert.

"We've still got problems with the berthing spaces. Two-twenty-four-G, two-twenty-four L, and two-ten-two-A, don't have air conditioning, and with all the bodies in them, it's getting pretty hot. Pretty rank, too."

"I know, Noah," Sisa answered. "And we're trying the best we can. The *Fujiyama* was supposed to go into the yards a year ago, but with the ops temp, well, you know how that is."

"Yeah, I do, but we've got to get this fixed."

"We've got a request for repairs for when we pull into Hang Sen 1."

"That's five weeks from now," Noah protested.

"That's the best we can do, Noah. The station's got full retrofit capabilities."

"I know that. But what are we going to do in the meantime?"

"Look, we don't have a qualified tech onboard. And it's not just you Marines. Five of the ship's crew's berthing spaces are in the same boat."

"No air maintenance techs? How do we keep breathing?"

Maintaining breathable air on a ship was one of the main functions of the crew.

"We're breathing fine. We've got that covered. But this is an old ship, and the cooling and circulation are outdated. We don't have anyone who can fix that."

"But can't they, you know, jury rig something?"

"Not without risk of shutting down the O2 generation, Noah. Believe me, we've tried. And we'll still try, but I think we're going to have to wait for Hang Sen."

It seemed unbelievable that with all the Navy's reliance on engineering, they couldn't figure out a way to shunt cool air to the affected spaces. Normally, the system was foolproof, all part of the same set-up. But even if the cooling was separate on this ship, there had to be sailors who knew how to fix it.

"Hell, I bet Coffman could fix it," he muttered.

"Who's Coffman?" the command master chief asked.

"Coffman. Lance Corporal Jim Coffman. He's one of the armor mechanics, and among other things, he keeps the overpressure system on the tanks functioning."

"Tanks? You don't have any tanks onboard."

"Well no, but our T/O says we have to have him, and if we fall on prepositioned equipment somewhere, we'll wish we had him."

Sisa had a point, though. Most of the maintenance on the Marines' many systems was performed by civilian techs. However, the Corps tried to minimize the numbers of civilian techs for forward deployed units, so Marines were given secondary training to take over tasks normally done by the techs. Coffman was technically still a rifleman with the Headquarters security element, but he was also trained in armor maintenance. The battalion had no rolling armor, so he was helping out with PICS maintenance despite having had no training with the combat suits.

"So, you say he understands overpressure systems?" Sisa asked, her voice laden with unspoken meaning.

"Well, yeah. But a Davis overpressure system isn't like a Navy ship of the line."

"Air is air, Noah."

"What, you're suggesting that I hand Coffman over to you to try and fix the ship's air?"

"If you want air in berthing before we hit Hang Sen. I mean, what can it hurt? If he can fix it, fine. If not, what's to lose?"

Noah started automatically to object. One one hand, Marines didn't work on Navy ships. Other than cleaning their spaces, if they started performing the ship's crew's work, then that was a slippery slope. Before he knew it, Marine doing Navy tasks will have become the status quo.

On the other hand, cooperation between the Marines and Navy was vital for a successful deployment, and his Marines were the ones suffering at the moment. If there were the slightest possibility that Coffman could fix the system, then it would benefit them all.

He started to tell Sisa that he'd bring it up with Esther, but at the last second, he pulled back. Why did she have to know? She was the commanding officer, and she couldn't get stuck down in the weeds.

Plus, she'd probably say no, he knew. She was much, much more by-the-book than he was. He made up his mind.

"OK, I'll send you Coffman. If he says he can work on it, fine. But if he can't, you send him back."

"Sure thing."

"Oh, and one more thing. Let's, uh, let's keep this between us. I don't want this broadcast over the 1MC."

The command master chief mimed locking her lips, then putting the key in her breast pocket.

"Mum's the word, Sergeant Major. This is an E9 need to know only. No officers involved."

Noah suddenly realized that she wasn't keen on making this widely-known, either. Noah didn't really know Commander Anderson, but the Navy higher-ups might not want people to know that they had to reach out to a Marine lance corporal for an engineering fix.

That's one big difference between officers and SNCOs. They worry about the big picture and how things look while the command master chief and I only care about getting things done.

"I'll send him down after chow. I hope he can fix this tub."

"It will take a lot more than that to bring the *Fujiyama* up to 100%, but it'll be a start, Noah."

"OK. Well, take care of him."

"Don't worry, we will."

Noah left the command master chief to find First Sergeant Pistorious. Josev could be by-the-book as well, and Noah would have to smooth over his ruffled feathers over this. But he'd come around. The SNCO mafia stuck together, after all, doing what had to be done.

And that was how the Marine Corps had kept functioning for over 400 years and counting.

Chapter 12
Esther

Esther ducked through the door, then stopped as someone crossed her path in the passage intersection.

"Uh . . . Noah, was that Lance Corporal Coffman I just saw up there?"

"Could be. He's on the ship, after all."

"But why was he in blue Navy overalls?"

"Don't worry about it none, Ess. If he's in overalls, there's a reason, and that's way below your paygrade."

"But not below yours, Noah, from the tone of your voice. And you are telling me to ignore it."

"I'm not telling you anything. You're the commanding officer, after all. I just think you don't have to worry yourself about every little detail."

Esther wanted to ask more. She didn't understand why one of her Marines was in a Navy uniform, but she could also tell that Noah didn't want to explain anything.

"Just tell me there's nothing illegal, or immoral, for that matter."

"Nothing like that."

"OK, then. Let's see what the captain has for us."

The two passed the wardroom and knocked on Commander Anderson's hatch.

"Come on in," the commander shouted from inside.

"What's up, Steve?" Esther asked as the two entered the surprisingly spacious stateroom.

"I think you might want to see this," the commander said before instructing his PA to display something.

"Holy shit," Noah said as an image appeared on the holoscreen.

"That's me," Esther said stupidly.

The image had been taken down on Vanity at the embassy. She had her Ruger drawn and was looking damned fierce. Behind her, an explosion filled the rest of the image, the bright white and yellow highlighting her image.

"De'Sander Yule," she said as she realized who'd taken the holo.

"Right. An instant before he died. His family found the image in his personal effects, and it's gone viral since."

"I didn't . . . I wouldn't . . . " Esther started before being interrupted by the commander.

"Doesn't matter. It's out now, and creating quite a buzz."

"Can we quash it?"

"Quash it, Ess? Are you kidding? You look grubbing amazing!"

"Your brother has the right of it, Esther. Admiral Jallaby has already authorized the payment to the family for the rights to it—approved by General Rzeminski, of course. We're going to use it," Anderson said, excitement in his voice.

"But—"

"But nothing. That's a great shot, and there's the fact that the reporter lost his life taking it. The public will eat it up."

Esther stepped closer to the projector field. She did look great, she had to admit. She looked, well, heroic, like she was ready to defend the Federation to her dying breath. But she hadn't been doing anything heroic at the moment, just reacting to the sounds of firing.

Esther understood the need to let the public know what they did to keep them safe. But this wasn't it. The image was not a true reflection of reality.

And a man died to take it, she reminded herself.

"I'm not sure this is appropriate."

"Whether you think so or not, Esther, I'd say it's out of your hands. Be prepared to see a lot of it for the next however long."

When she was younger, Esther had been willing to use her father's name to get ahead. She'd drifted away from that over the years. Niggling at the back of her brain was the thought that if she weren't her father's daughter, this image would not have taken off.

Noah and Steve evidently weren't concerned about that. Both were oohing and aahing over the image.

It is what it is, she told herself.

Esther wanted to be known for what she did, not for looking like a warrior queen going into battle. She'd have to do a lot more with the battalion to overshadow a fierce-looking holo.

NOVYY DONETSK

Chapter 12
Noah

"Are all of you ready?" Noah asked the Major Frazier,

"We're pumped and ready to perform, Sergeant Major," the XO answered.

"I'll give you the heads up when it's time, sir."

Noah left the performers and went to the door leading into the vast ballroom. Sandra Kolls, the planetary governor, was still into her welcome speech. He checked the time—she'd been talking for over 20 minutes and didn't show any signs of slowing down. Sitting beside her was Esther, who was doing a credible job of looking interested. For the first time, Noah was glad that she'd made him the point man for the Patron Day celebration. Otherwise, he'd be up there on the dais as well.

It wasn't that Noah disliked patron day celebrations. He'd always loved them. As a child, the pageantry had almost overwhelmed him, and the historical perspective was something that had tied him to his father. Now, as a deployed unit, there was just too much on his plate to worry about everything that went into a patron day, especially 1/8's patron day of Nov 16, less than a week after the Marine Corps Birthday celebration.

The governor was droning on and on, from how Novyy Donetsk was settled by Ukrainian dissidents, but over the centuries, welcomed people from all backgrounds without prejudice, blah, blah, blah. Noah knew that the patron day celebrations had a purpose beyond reminding Marines of tradition. There was the political aspect of it. The entire concept of each line battalion having a patron Marine Corps or naval infantry from the extant Earth and planetary units when the modern Federation Marine Corps was formed help tie the Corps to the people. When his father was the CO of 2/3, the "Fuzos," he'd been an honored guest back in Lisbon each year for the Military Outlook and Beyond Conference. The Portuguese took great pride in their relationship with the battalion.

First Battalion, Eighth Marines might not have quite the same degree of a relationship with the Ukraine, but Novvy Donetsk, one of the two Ukrainian-settled worlds in the Federation, was more than happy to assume the role of host, and with the battalion deployed aboard the *Mount Fuji*, it had only taken Navy scheduling to make sure the battalion was on the planet for the celebration, the first time 1/8 had been on Novyy Donetsk in almost ten years. And the planet had certainly rolled out the welcome mat.

As a junior Marine, Noah would be enjoying the three-day interlude. As the sergeant major, he was up to his ass in alligators. Already, the battalion had three liberty incidents, but this time, he couldn't restrict liberty. The federal government wanted the Marines to be out and about, to remind the citizens of the planet what their tax credits bought for them. Novyy Donetsk bled Federation blue, but it never hurt to consolidate support.

At last, the governor reached the end of her speech, introduced Esther, and gave her the podium.

"Governor, Administrator Gilsap, citizens of Novyy Donetsk, I'd like to thank you for the warm welcome you've given your First Battalion, Eighth Marines, the Cutting Edge."

She had to stop while the crowd erupted into applause. She looked calm, but Noah knew she was nervous. Fearless in battle, Esther didn't like public speaking. Noah had listened to her speech five times over the last two days as she fretted over her time in the spotlight.

Which was pretty ridiculous, Noah thought. Whatever she said, it was pretty evident that the people would love it. Politics went both ways. The Marines were getting good PR, but so was the local government, and the people were grateful that they had an entire Marine battalion and the *Mount Fuji* on an official visit.

"On September 4, 232, during the War of the Far Reaches, a Marine platoon was pinned down outside a small, nameless settlement on Sahra'. The lieutenant and platoon sergeant were killed, and the remaining twelve Marines, most of them wounded, faced upwards of fifty enemy soldiers, enemy determined to wipe them out."

There was an appreciative murmur from the crowd. Some of them knew what was coming, and Noah gave a satisfied smile. He'd been right when he suggested Esther focus on this story.

"One Marine, though, was not deterred. Private First Class Anton Dovzhenko—." She had to stop again for applause before continuing with ". . . had been a Marine for less than a year, but he understood, at the deepest level, what it meant to be a Marine. It means serving the Federation—not just the government, but the citizens. And it means serving your fellow Marines.

"With ammunition dwindling, and the enemy massing for one last push to wipe out the rest of the platoon, PFC Dovshenko started to crawl out of the depression where the Marines were holed up.

"'Where do you think you're going?' his sergeant, the senior surviving Marine asked."

There was a rustling among the crowd. They knew the story, but as Noah looked over them from his vantage, that wasn't taking anything away from their enjoyment of hearing it again.

"'Well, Sergeant, I'm going to kick some ass,' he told him."

There were whoops from the crowd.

Whether Dovzhenko had actually said that was open to debate among historians, but in the Hollybolly flick made shortly after the war, that's what he said, and that became the accepted lore.

"'Get back here, Dovzhenko, that's an order,' the sergeant told him. And you know what he said back, don't you? He said, 'You know Sergeant Pillsbury, my comms are out, so I can't hear a word you're saying.'"

Interrupted again by an enthusiastic audience, Esther was visibly relaxing. She looked up, caught Noah's eye, and winked.

"I can tell by your reaction that you know exactly what happened next, but you know what? I'm going to tell you anyway. Private First Class Anton Dovzhenko low-crawled down the hill to where the enemy was getting their final brief. And Dovzhenko decided to make his introduction as only a Marine knows how. With one burst of his rifle, he killed the commander and those standing next to him. Hurling grenades, he became a one-man tornado, dropping the enemy right and left. And what did they do? They ran, that's what they did. They ran from one Marine.

"When the relief arrived later that evening, they found twenty-two dead enemy at that spot. PFC Dovzhenko was found two hundred meters away, with ten more dead enemy he'd killed as he chased them. *Chased* them! Thirty trained soldiers, running from one Marine."

She looked up again and caught Noah's eye, then took a deep breath and said, "Well, you can't blame them for that. Thirty-to-one are pretty steep odds . . . against them!"

She and Noah had discussed that line. It was corny, and Noah had leaned against it, but she wanted to say it. And from the laughter in the audience, she'd been right. Noah gave her a little salute.

"PFC Anton Dovzhenko was posthumously awarded the Federation Nova for his actions on Saha'. Camp Dovzhenko, on Tasis II was named in his honor. So why am I telling you this story? I know you already know it. Because Anton Dovzhenko was one of you. He was born and raised on Novyy Donetsk. Yesterday, your governor graciously escorted me to the statue you have of him in Izyum, his hometown.

"Many, many of your best and brightest have served in the Marines, the Navy, or the FCDC, cementing the bonds with the rest of the Federation. You've produced sports stars, masters of commerce, and three Federation ministers, but as far as I'm concerned, not one has shined more than Anton Dovzhenko.

"And so, it is with great pride that I bring the First Battalion, Eighth Marines, here to your planet for our Patron Day celebration. I can't think of a greater honor."

And that was it, short and sweet. Neither Noah nor Esther knew that the governor would drone on for so long, but that probably made the impact of Esther's speech all the more powerful. It was a succinct and moving reminder of the connection between the citizens of the planet, and not just the Federation at large, but with the Marines in specific.

Telling the story hadn't been without trepidation. On the dais was also the Sahra' commercial attaché. He didn't seem to be upset, but then again, he was a politician, and he had to be skilled at hiding his feelings. Enemy then, a trusted friend now, still, he and Esther had discussed this, and in the end, they went ahead, but by just saying "enemy" instead of anything more specific.

He turned back to the holding area and shouted out, "Marines, head's up. The CO's done, so we've got a few performances by the locals, then you're up. Get yourselves ready."

The Marines stirred as they slowly gathered together. The drummers went over their rhythms, sticks silently beating the air. All of them were volunteers, putting in long hours for one, maybe two performances a year. Despite the work load, there was always a long waiting list to be accepted.

Back out in the ballroom, several local groups put on performances. Noah listened with half-an-ear, just waiting until it was the Marines' turn. Finally, after some sort of folk dance performed by pre-teens, he got the OK.

"This is it, Marines. Go to it."

A Marine Corps beating was one of the highlights of tradition. When the Federation Marine Corps was formed from the 48 extant Marine Corps at the time, there had been a competition to see who would form the basis of the new Marine band. Not surprisingly, the US Marine Corps band, made up of who were essentially professional musicians, won the competition—as judged by senior Marine and Navy officers—and became the bulk of the new band. The members would no longer be professional musicians and would come from the ranks, but they would serve alternate tours with the band. "The Chairman's Own" couldn't be complete amateurs, was probably the thinking.

However, the Royal Marine Band, especially the Corps of Drums, caught the attention—and hearts—of the rank and file. Almost immediately, separate Corps of Drums sprang up in almost every unit. They followed Royal Marine traditions, including the faux leopard skin worn by the members. All corps members were Marines first, drummers second. They were infantry, armor, artillery, support, or whatever and practiced when they could. Rank had no bearing, and they kept up a degree of mystery about themselves. Practices were almost always hidden from public view, and their performance plans might as well have been Corps-wide operation orders stamped TOP SECRET. Noah had been tasked with putting the show together, but as he wasn't a member of the Corps of Drums, not even he knew what they were going to do.

The lights went off in the ballroom, and the drum corps silently marched past Noah to take their position.

"Now," he passed to the light operator, and a moment later, a spotlight snapped on Corporal Lee Spain, the battalion drum major, who was standing perfectly still, one raised hand holding a drumstick. He waited another 20 seconds before he started slowly bringing the arm down, like a mechanical man in a giant Swiss cuckoo clock. At the last second, he flicked his wrist, sending out a single drumbeat reverberating through the hall. After a moment, Lieutenant Eikbush, shrouded in darkness at the back of the ballroom, responded with a single beat.

Corporal Spain raised his hand, a little quicker this time, and brought it down for another beat. The lieutenant answered almost immediately. Spain repeated, and this became a 30-second case of dueling drums. With a shift that was hard to catch, suddenly, the two drums were pounding out an intricate beat together. More spotlights snapped on, illuminating 18 Marines standing in a line at the back of the hall.

The beating had begun.

The 18 Marines in the back started a slow, almost straight-legged march to close the distance with Corporal Spain. As they beat their drums, each man paused in turn for two beats, drumsticks raised and frozen, before joining back in.

The second-to-last man in the line was XO. He was the second most senior Marine in the battalion, but in the Corps of Drums, he was just another drummer, commanded by Corporal Spain.

The Marines married up, and Corporal Spain slipped into his position within the group. For the next ten minutes, the 19 Marines moved through a series of intricate maneuvers, never stopping their drums. When the two bass drummers came to the front and somehow performed a duet that would put a snare drummer to shame, the crowd erupted into cheers.

Noah could feel his blood pounding. He'd probably attended fifty beatings during his lifetime, both as a dependent and as a Marine, and they still never failed to move him.

Too soon, the Corps of Drums went into their finale, the crescendo rising as they moved like Dervishes, sure to crash into each other, but never quite doing so. The crowd was calling out and cheering, but the drums' pounding beat drowned the crowd out.

Just when Noah thought their drumsticks surely had to burst apart, they stopped dead, one stick raised, the other on their drums. They stood like statues, not moving. Noah could feel the anticipation.

The huge crash made him jump despite him expecting it. Eight PICS Marines had entered the hall. Around each one was an enormous leopard skin, and under the left arms of four of them hung huge kettle drums.

The 19 original drummers Marines broke their position to beat out a "Forward, march!"

As far as Noah knew, his father's old battalion, 2/3, had initiated the use of PICS Marines in a beating. Other battalions claimed credit, but Noah was going to stick with his father's claim. Now, they were part and parcel to almost all beatings, and they were a crowd favorite.

With the four kettle drummers pounding out a cadence, the other four marched forward, spinning around in a one-legged 360 as they took their place in front of the guests. They each slowly raised their right hands up high, almost in a Roman salute, then brought them down with a resounding crash to their chest carapaces, then beat a quick tattoo.

Grubbing cool!

The four kettle drummers, with the rest of the corps, turned to face the drumless four, answering the chest tattoo as they formed a half-circle around them. With the massed drums providing a back-beat, the focus was on the drumless four as they started an intricate dance, all the time beating on their own bodies. The sharp clangs were a contrast to the booming drums. Several times, the four turned to pairs with each one pounding on his or her partner's body.

The crowd was enthusiastically cheering, but they were easily drowned out by the combined booms of 23 drums and four drumless PICS. At another point, the four turned to the kettle drum PICS and used their hands to pound on the drums while those drummers rapped on them with their drumsticks.

When the entire group broke out of their formation and started weaving about each other, Noah's heart jumped to this throat. There was a reason why PICS and non-PICS Marines didn't mix. A slight mistake, a slight stumble, and there would be one Marine pancake. Yet they managed to march and cross paths with each other with precision.

The finale was amazing—Noah had no other word for it. The combined pounding of 27 Marines, simply blew the huge hall away. Noah wasn't sure what he was hearing through his ears and what was being pounded into his chest, and he didn't care. Corporal Spain had made the battalion proud.

Noah took a moment to look up at the dais. Commander Anderson was pounding on Esther's back. She was applauding, a huge smile on her face. A beating was for the rank and file, it was for the civilians who observed it. It was not simply to please the CO. Still, Noah was happy to see that she'd enjoyed it.

He turned back to the Drum Corps. They had frozen in place. Finally, Corporal Spain stepped up raising one drum stick before bringing it back down with a soft tap. Immediately, the Marines of the Drum Corps performed right and left faces, and with Spain giving them a beat, marched out of the ballroom. The applause was deafening. Noah hurried after them.

Noah and his father had often discussed what was important about a beating. It wasn't combat after all, and that was a Marine's job, not to entertain civilians. But there was an almost visceral connection with being a Marine that the beating uncovered. A beating, something taken from Marines long past, transcended the "job" of a Marine and touched on the *soul* of a Marine. Just as ancient homo erectus sat pounding on hollowed logs around a campfire, this set off a sympathetic beating in his very DNA. At this very moment, Noah was not a man who was a Marine; he *was* the Marine Corps. A small cell in the bigger organism, to be sure, but still, he was the Corps.

Noah reached them just as the last Marine entered the holding room and the solemn formation broke into individuals, cheering and backslapping each other. Sergeant Olsen from the armory was there to help the PICS Marines shuck their huge combat suits, and as each Marine emerged, he or she was hugged and high-fived. Noah, still feeling pumped, had intended on joining the celebration, but as he saw Major Frazier pick up the much smaller Staff Sergeant Souder in a hug, he held back.

This was their show, their moment. He wasn't part of it.

With a smile, he closed the door into the holding room and made his way back to the ballroom. With the official ceremony over, he knew he had to show his face and press the flesh. The Drum Corps entertained, a sergeant major shook hands. Everyone had a place in the Corps.

FS MOUNT FUJI

Chapter 13
Esther

"How in the hell did they manage that?" Esther asked, her temper rising.

"On Novyy Donetsk, ma'am, where we did our Patron Day celebration."

"I know where we did our celebration, Doc. I was there, remember?" she said, eyes rolling. "I mean how the hell did this happen?"

Navy Lieutenant Siren was an earnest battalion surgeon, but the woman had a habit of stating the obvious and sometimes missing the key point.

"The two visited a civilian free birther clinic and had their implants removed, ma'am."

Free birthers. What the hell?

On most new planets, governments wanted people to go forth and multiply. Planets had to be populated, whether by birth or immigration. However, on many of the older planets, the teaming masses created a huge burden simply to give each citizen their UAM-approved minimum standard of life. The UAM BPA, the Basic Propagation Agreement, made it a crime against humanity for a government to use forced sterilization or any other method of involuntary birth control, but it did not forbid governments to offer incentives for reversible birth control.

The "free birthers" were a loosely organized group that felt any form of birth control still fell within the category of crimes against humanity, and aside from fighting legal battles, they offered services to people who wanted birth control methods to be removed or reversed.

"We hit Novyy Donetsk 40 days ago, Doc. I thought it took at least three months for the effects of an implant to fade away. How can O'Shannon be pregnant already?"

"Three months is the normal rebound period, ma'am. Obviously, Sergeant O'Shannon is particularly fecund."

"Fecund, Doc?" Esther asked, trying not to roll her eyes.

"Fertile, ma'am. It means easily able to become pregnant."

Hell, Doc, I know what "fecund" means. I was just wondering why you didn't say "fertile" in the first place.

"Yes, I know. But how are you sure they had their implants removed on Novyy Donetsk?"

"I saw the medical report, ma'am."

"If I may interrupt, Colonel?" Lieutenant Commander Hans Julian, the *Mount Fuji's* XO and acting legal officer asked. "It doesn't really matter when they had it done."

Esther stopped and reset herself. He was right. Whether Sergeant O'Shannon and Corporal Rhee removed their implants on Novyy Donetsk or before, the fact was that they had done it, and that was what mattered.

"So, we now have a pregnant squad leader in Bravo Company. According to you, Doc, Sergeant O'Shannon is determined to carry the child to term."

"That's correct, ma'am."

Esther hadn't needed a response from the battalion surgeon; she was merely thinking out loud.

"Well, whether she is or she isn't, I want both of them brought up on charges."

"Both of them?" the XO asked.

"It takes two to tango. They both were willing participants in this."

"Roger that."

"Uh, Colonel, there's going to be a problem with that. The BPA," Commander Julian said.

"Why? I'm not getting in the way of Sergeant O'Shannon and Corporal Rhee's fundamental right to procreate. I am merely charging them with removing their implants."

"Which you can't do."

"Sure, I can. Having the implants is a requirement for a Marine or sailor to be deployed," she said.

She imagined she could almost feel her own implant, a centimeter or so into the muscle of her left arm, just under her armpit.

"Yes, it is a regulation, one upheld by the courts. But the BPA specifically allows for anyone to remove birth control methods at any time."

"What?" Esther blurted out. "You mean, we can require Marines to get implants to be deployed, but they can take them out at any time?"

"That's about it."

Esther looked over to Noah who gave her a slight shrug. She could tell this little tidbit took him by surprise, too.

"What about if they lied to Doc Siren here, I mean, if they really had them taken out, say, before we actually embarked? The free birthers would fake a medical report if asked. The two had, what, four days back on Last Stop where they could have done that, and the free birthers would fake a medical report to say they had it done on Novyy Donetsk," Major Frazier asked.

"I'd have to check, but I don't think they would be required to inform anyone that they had the implants removed," LCDR Julian said.

"That's not my point. O'Shannon is pregnant now, but normally, it takes three months for that to be possible. So, if she and Rhee lied to Doc Siren, that in and of itself is a violation of the UCMJ."

That could work, Esther thought.

She stole a glance to Noah who subtly shook his head.

He's right. I'd be opening a can of worms, and I'm not going to get drawn into that kind of a mess. Better just end it now.

"I'm not going to have a pregnant sergeant within the battalion. For all I know, she goes out and loses the baby, and the free birthers say I'm a criminal against humanity. So, Captain Gill, from this moment, Sergeant O'Shannon is assigned to H&S. Same with Rhee," she told Captain McLamb. "At the first opportunity, both Marines are to be put on any available transport back to Last Stop where I'll request that they be transferred out of the battalion.

"Would that be allowed, Commander?" she asked the ship's XO.

He seemed to contemplate that for a moment before he nodded and said, "I'd say so. You have the full authority to transfer anyone within your battalion, and you can send anyone back as well. It would be up to your command whether they actually transfer the two out of the battalion, of course, but even if you didn't, you could have them as part of your rear party."

"Then let's do it. XO, keep me informed. OK, let's move on. Captain Montoya, you're up."

"Thank you, ma'am. As you now, we're now in Condition Charlie for piracy in the Delvier Sector. There has been an increase in chatter . . ."

It was looking more and more that the Dark Tide was planning a bold action of some sort in the Delvier Sector, and the *Mount Fuji* was standing by. Civilian vessels were being told to avoid the region. Condition Charlie was a heightened, but not extreme, condition of alert. Esther had been in Charlie half-a-dozen times in her career where nothing developed. But HQMC had canceled the battalion's joint exercise with the Confederation army, and that was not done lightly. Noah thought, however, that maybe the Confederation had done the canceling as the battalion was only in Charlie. Either way, there was a feeling of excitement beginning to build throughout the ship. With only three months left for deployment, they might be seeing some action.

With that in mind, she should be paying more attention to her S2. But her thoughts were drifting to Sergeant O'Shannon and Corporal Rhee. Both were good Marines without any disciplinary problems. Yet they had decided to remove their implants, something they knew could have career-threatening consequences. All to have a baby.

Esther felt her own implant begin to burn.

It's your imagination, Lysander. You can't feel it.

She and Jim had discussed children, of course, but always as part of some far future plans. They were both too dedicated to the Corps, and both had careers that they hoped were still only beginning.

Still, in a small way that she could quite understand, she envied O'Shannon.

"Ma'am? Do you want to see that?" Captain Montoya asked.

Esther looked around, confused for a second. She had no idea what the S2 wanted to show her.

"Yes, go ahead," she said, leaning forward and trying to look engaged.

Come on, Lysander. Command now and worry about a family in 20 years.

Chapter 14
Noah

Two months later, Noah was going stir crazy. The battalion was still in Condition Charlie while the *Mount Fuji* cut square circles in space. The excitement over the possibility of action that had gripped the ship had slowly atrophied into utter boredom punctuated by outbursts of frustration and fistfights. As the sergeant major, Noah knew it was up to him to keep the battalion from falling apart, but at the moment, he was more interested in simply sitting in the chief's mess, out of the reach of the bulk of his Marines.

He idly spooned his Leicestershire Stew, pushing the mass of glop from one side of his plate to the other and back again, never actually lifting any more of the mess to his mouth. He wasn't being reasonable, he knew. The stew was fine, one of the more popular recipes in the ship's fabricators. But as the *Mount Fuji* had not pulled into any port for going on ten weeks now, and as she hadn't had an underway replenishment, the ship was out of the fresh vegetables and fruits he liked. The officers still had a few supplies in their stasis pack, but the chiefs had consumed the last of theirs two weeks ago.

"Sergeant Major?" First Sergeant Quisenberry asked, sliding into the seat beside him.

"What do you need, Cory?" he asked, trying to put a hint of interest in his voice, interest of which he was totally devoid at the moment.

"It's Lieutenant RP again," he said. "He's driving Gillespie crazy. Now he's got the platoon using toothbrushes to clean berthing because they failed his inspection."

Noah tried not to roll his eyes. First Lieutenant Moses Radiant Purpose was a royal pain in the ass. He knew everything and held almost everyone else in disdain. The problem was that he was almost as good as he thought he was, at least as far as tactically. As far as being a leader, he left a lot to be desired.

"And what does Captain Kingery say?"

"He said he's going to talk to the lieutenant, but, you know..."

Yeah, I know. Just because RP is a Torritite, you think Esther or I needs to get involved.

"Look, Cory, you're from Pannington, right?"

"Yeah, you know that."

"So, if the chaplain starts acting up—"

"The chaplain? He's not going to act up."

"Let me finish. Let's just say he apostates, becomes the minion of the devil and starts demanding newborn children for sacrifices, since he's from Pannington, too, is it now your job to rein him in?"

"That's different, Sergeant Major," the first sergeant protested.

"The hell it is. You want me, or really, you want me to get the CO to take care of RP because we're half Torritite."

"No, that's not what I mean."

"Yes, it is. And just like last time you came to me, Lieutenant Radiant Purpose is your headache, yours and Captain Kingery's. You take care of him."

He turned back to his stew, this time actually taking a bite, which pained him to admit wasn't half bad. He hoped Cory would take the hint and leave.

But no, he was like a terrier on a rat. "We've tried, but the captain can't fire his ass—"

Whatever feeble excuse the first sergeant was going to say was interrupted by the 1MC.

"All Navy and Marine Corps principle staff are to make way to the wardroom at once. I say again, all Navy and Marine Corps principle staff are to make way to the wardroom at once."

Noah and the first sergeant looked at each other for a moment, First Lieutenant Radiant Purpose forgotten. Nothing specific as to why they had an immediate meeting had been said in the announcement, but between the two of them, they had almost 40 years of service. They knew it in their bones.

They jumped up from their seats and ran out of the chiefs' mess and down the long passage to the wardroom. It was go time.

Chapter 15
Esther

"F1 is leaving the hangar bay," the yeoman said, his voice the model of efficiency.

Esther didn't feel so calm as she stood by the projection stage, a 60 cm-long hologram of the *SS Calypso Queen* hovering a meter high over the base. A grand dame in her day as a cruise liner, she'd fallen victim to the ever more extravagant ships that pulled in vacationers and was now relegated to hauling contract workers from world to world. On board now was a crew of only nine—and 2,677 workers headed to Fortuna.

Why the ship's captain had decided to cut through the Delvier Sector would be something for the investigators to determine, but right now, those 2,686 souls were the responsibility of the *FS Mount Fuji* and First Battalion, Eighth Marines. And on the near side of the stage, next to a hologram of the *Mount Fuji*, Esther could see the ship's shuttle, with Wes McLamb and one of his platoons on board, leaving for the crossing to the *Calypso Queen*.

With only the two ship's shuttles, the two Marine Albatrosses, and nine rekis, the battalion was not really organized for ship-to-ship warfare. The shuttles had minimal firepower, and the two Marine craft, which were now standing off the seized ship, were not much better. While armed, they were the airborne equivalent of an armored personnel carrier instead of a heavy tank. If the opposing ship were an enemy ship-of-the-line, the Marines' only possible mission would be to inspect the dead vessel if the *Mount Fuji* managed to defeat it.

But the *SS Calypso Queen* was a civilian liner with no offensive weaponry. The *Mount Fuji* had disabled her engines with one surgically aimed cannon shot, and now it was unable to maneuver. Together with the *Mount Fuji* two kilometers off, both vessels were still hurtling through space, but the *Calypso Queen* could not alter course nor speed, hence the not technically accurate term "dead in space."

The liner might not have offensive weapons, but the 20-30 Dark Tide pirates would be armed, and the ship could be rigged to blow. Esther could be sending two Marine companies to a booby-trapped ship.

"Any signs of an explosive chain?" she asked the sailor on the D-Scan for the fourth time in the last half-hour.

"No, ma'am," OS2 Halle responded, never taking his eyes off his screens.

Esther knew he'd pass the word if he picked anything up, but she couldn't help being anxious. There were many ways to scuttle a ship that didn't require typical explosives, and she wasn't confident that the *Mount Fuji's* sensors could pick some of those methods up before it was too late.

She looked around the CIC, the heart of a ship's operations. The sailors and most of the Marines were in vac suits, ready for a breach. Esther and Ralph Kutzman were in their EVAs, only lacking the propulsion units before they'd be able to transit to the liner.

Esther didn't have to actually make the crossing—in fact, she probably shouldn't. But once the ship was secured, she'd have a better idea of what had to be done if she was on the scene rather than sitting in CIC.

That's my story, and I'm sticking to it, she told herself.

In reality, Esther couldn't bear standing in the middle of the *Mount Fuji* safe and sound while her Marines went into harm's way. She'd hold back from the breach, but as soon as she felt she could justify it, she was going to cross over.

"F2 is leaving the hangar bay," the yeoman intoned as if this was just one more training mission.

The breaching party could have simply ridden a reki or EVA'd to the liner, but the shuttles did provide slightly more protection. With breaching tubes aboard, Alpha's two platoons would emerge from the shuttles on either side of the *Calypso Queen*, force their breach, and secure them for the waves of EVA

Marines from Bravo and Charlie who would actually seize the ship.

"Cheetah One, Two, and Three debarking," the yeoman said.

Esther looked back to the ship's monitors. With the shuttles out of the way, the ship's crew had been positioning the rekis. The first rank of three rekis, had already been ported to the hangar curtain and was now in open space while other Marines boarded their space sleds. The hangar deck, run by Lieutenant Smythe, was working like clockwork. Esther wasn't worried about that. She was worried about what would happen when the rekis reached the *Calypso Queen*.

The reki was nothing more than an open sled with a propulsion system. Marines in their vacsuits stood like sardines in old-fashioned cans while the sleds transported them up to 50,000 klicks through open space. There was no life-support and no armor. Until McLamb and his security element secured the breaches, the Marines in the rekis were vulnerable to most weapons, even small arms. The ship's scanners hadn't picked out anyone waiting in ambush, but a pirate could be hiding cloaked on the liner's hull, ready to take a potshot at the Marines in the open sleds.

Still, the rekis were faster than simple EVA-suited Marines, and once McLamb's Marines breached the ship, Esther wanted the assault element to sweep into the ship with overwhelming aggression.

All three lifts of rekis took off, and the remainder of the force formed up to make the crossing in their EVA suits. Esther watched on the screen as the Charlie Company Marines marched up to the curtain in squad ranks of 13, then gracefully launched themselves into space. In the hangar bay, there had been an up and down; as soon as they reached open space, they started orienting on each other as they moved into formation for the crossing. Each squad maximized their dispersion to preclude the infamous one shot that could take them all out.

Esther was proud at the precision with which the battalion was moving. Still, she felt like she had to get involved. She looked over to Major Kurtzman, but he was on the net talking with someone. She could have listened in, and she was sorely tempted to, but she had to let her Marines do their job without her continually looking over their shoulders. Instead, she kept the battalion command net open.

The two shuttles slowed to a stop some 200 meters from the ship. Within moments, Captain McLamb and his two platoons had debarked and were crossing the remaining distance, each breaching team heading to their position on the *Calypso Queen's* hull.

"Order the shuttles to their stand-off station," Commander Anderson ordered.

A moment later, the shuttles' avatars started to pull away. Esther didn't like the fact that the shuttles were pulling back. If things went south, she wanted them to be able to recover the McLamb's security element. The possibility of things going south, however, was exactly why Steve was pulling his shuttles back. He couldn't afford to lose them.

And that was why Fred Kingery's assault element had halted about 500 meters from the ship. If the *Calypso Queen* were rigged to blow, the debris would act as shrapnel, traveling hundreds or thousands of kilometers outwards. Five hundred meters of vacuum would not diminish the force of any shrapnel, but it would lessen the chance that anyone would be hit. Every 100 meters away decreased the chance of shrapnel hitting someone by better than 99%. McLamb and his security element would be wiped out, but most of the assault element and support elements would have a good chance to survive.

Esther looked over to the schematic of the *Calypso Queen* displayed on a 3D screen on the bulkhead. The scans couldn't differentiate between passengers and pirates, but it wasn't difficult to surmise that the three larger masses were where the passengers were huddled, and the several smaller groupings represented the pirates. At the moment, none of them were near the two selected breach points.

"Ready to breach," Wes McLamb passed on the command net.

Major Kurtzman looked over to Esther expectantly.

There were two primary methods to force entry into a ship: breach tubes or the airlocks. Marines tended to avoid doors on the ground and airlocks in space. They were too easy to booby trap, and the enemy tended to defend them. McLamb had two of the *Mount Fuji's* engineers with him to break through the locks, and the ship's owners would undoubtedly prefer that course of action. Esther didn't give a rat's ass about the cost of repairs, should it come to that. Her main concern was for the security of her Marines.

There really wasn't a choice, in her mind.

"Breach," she told the major.

She shifted her combat PA to a split screen and pulled up the feeds of Sergeants Visquez and Ben-David, the two team commanders. She watched the duel feeds as the four Marines of each breaching team began to move forward, like pallbearers carrying a coffin. The breaching tube was a very primitive, but effective method of getting into a ship. It was essentially an airlock with a plasma gate on one end, a cutting blade on the other. The tube was placed against the skin of a ship and locked into place. An ion vibration blade would then begin to cut into the skin. Only the most hardened ships could withstand the blade for more than a few moments. For most ships, and the *Calypso Queen* would fit in this class, the breach could be cut in less than ten seconds. For sturdier warships, the blade could be exchanged for a molecular dissolution projector or even shaped charges.

The back end was initially closed off, but once the air pressure between the tube and the breached ship stabilized, the cover would be removed so the plasma gate would allow passage while keeping atmospheric integrity.

Ben David's team made contact with the *Calypso Queen* first, and breaching tube locked into place. Esther pulled up the tube's readouts as the ion generator blade began to rev up the blade. A moment later, Visquez' team reached their position on the other side of the ship.

"We've got movement inside the target ship," one of the CIC sailors shouted out.

Esther looked up from her PA to the ship's schematic. She could see that the pirates were rushing to the two breach sites. She'd hoped that the Marines could breach and be inside before the pirates could react, but that evidently wasn't going to happen.

Marines could and have conducted ship breaching in the face of heavy fire, but the cost in Marine casualties could be quite high. The SOP was to breach where the enemy wasn't, then secure the breach until there were enough Marines inside the ship to prosecute the assault.

For a ship like the *Calypso Queen*, the breach itself could take as few as ten or fifteen seconds. But with the rest of the security team standing off out of concern for boobytraps, a more realistic time to get Marines inside was closer to 45 seconds, and it was obvious that the Dark Tide pirates would get to the sites before the Marines could seize them.

Intel gave a probability that the pirates would blow the ship at 46%. For all their propaganda about seeking independence and religious freedom, in reality, they were little more than a criminal gang seeking financial rewards. A destroyed ship might set the stage for negotiations during future ship hijackings, but it would give them nothing for this seizure.

Still, 46% was too much to ignore.

Make a decision, Lysander!

With the blades already cutting into the *Calypso Queen's* skin, and the fact that the pirates were rushing to defend those two sites, Esther didn't think they were going to blow the ship, at least not at the moment.

"Dozer-One and Dozer-Two, slow down your breach. Do not enter the ship. Dozer-Three and Dozer-Four, advance and conduct breaching operations at the alternate positions. Security element, abandon your stand-off positions. I want you on Dozer-Three and Four's asses. You've got 30 seconds to get in that ship."

Thirty seconds wasn't doable. It would take Dozer-Three and Four that long to get to the ship's skin, even longer to get their tubes into position and begin cutting. The key timeline, however, was from the moment each back-up breaching tube touched the ship until Marines were inside the ship.

No military plan survives contact with the enemy, and this was no different. Dozer-Three and Four were just the back-ups in case either One or Two had mechanical issues. The alternate positions had been selected simply because it was SOP. With the full schematics of the *Calypso Queen*, the two breach sites selected were the two best sites from both a technical and military point of view. With Esther's conviction that the pirates were going to try and defend the ship and not blow it, at least yet, and their quick reaction, Esther had changed the plan on the fly. The point of main effort shifted to Sergeants Trotter and Julian and their back-up breaching teams, and along with the rest of the security element, they immediately closed in on the ship.

Esther had been nervous during combat before—well, not so much during as before it commenced. At the moment, however, she was almost beside herself. It was extremely difficult for her to stand back and let her Marines go into harm's way. She'd have given almost anything to be out there, to be with the teams as they cut their way into the ship.

She performed a quick check with Visquez and Ben-David. Dozer-One was 21% through the hull, while Dozer-Two was at 30%. According to the schematic, twelve pirates were waiting just on the other side of Dozer-Two and another ten were just now arriving opposite Dozer-One.

You just keep waiting there, boys.

Sergeant Trotter's Dozer-Three reached the hull of the *Calypso Queen* and within five seconds was cutting through. A few moments later, Dozer-Four reached the ship.

Esther keyed in the S3 and brought Captain Kingery, the assault element commander, up on the P2P. "Fred, break off Eikbush and RP. I'm going to stop Dozer-One and Two the moment Three and Four have breached. Hopefully, the pirates will react to the breach and abandon One and Two. If they do, send those two in."

Esther knew she should just give her intent to Kingery and not tell him who to send in, but she was not as confident about Lieutenant Torten and Staff Sergeant Francisco, the Second Platoon commander and platoon sergeant. Kingery was rightly so putting them into positions where they had to work together and develop, but this wasn't the time for that.

"We've got more movement inside the ship. They're reacting to the new breach," the petty officer on the schematic shouted out.

Sure enough, two more groups had split off from the mass of what had to be the passengers. The two groups opposite One and Two were remaining in place.

"Breach clear!" Trotter passed on the net as he led his four Marines through the tube and into the ship.

"Dozer-Three, you've got eight pirates inbound, looks like about ten seconds," Captain Cynthia Strong, Esther's S-3A, passed to Trotter.

"Move it," Esther passed to Lieutenant Weisskopf, who was leading his Marines to Dozer-Three's breach. "I want you in that ship now. Trotter's about to be in contact."

She pulled up Sergeant Trotter's feed just as the first two pirates entered the passage at a dead run, only to be immediately dropped. Another pirate appeared momentarily before diving back out of sight before the Marine's could target him.

Esther barely registered Major Kutzman telling Dozers One and Two to stop cutting and remain quiet. Whether that ruse would work or not was overshadowed by the fight currently going on.

"Grenade!" one of the Marines shouted, his voice picked up by Sergeant Trotter's feed, which despite the motion compensators, became a mishmash of motion as the sergeant took cover.

He hit the deck, and immediately, his feed stabilized the view of the barrel of his weapon pointed upwards and down the passage. The blast barely shook the feed, and a moment later, two more pirates, clad in their signature multi-colored uniforms, burst around the corner, firing kinetics at waist level. Trotter barely had to shift his point of aim as he cut down the lead man, dropping him face-first on the deck. The second pirate fell a split second later.

"Coming in center!" a voice cried out.

Trotter didn't look back, and in a few moments, the first of Eikbush's Marines rushed past, ready to consolidate the breach.

"Dozer-One, Dozer-Two, commence breach," Major Kutzman passed on the command net.

Esther shifted her attention to see that the pirates who had been facing the two original breach teams had, in fact, abandoned their positions, probably sure that the two had been feints. She let a tiny feeling of satisfaction surface before pushing it back down to monitor the action. With Marines onboard, she was confident about taking the ship back. What still concerned her was the chance that the pirates had booby trapped the ship in case they realized the battle was lost.

Thirty seconds later, Captain McLamb's Marines were pouring through the Dozer-One and Two-s breaches. Lieutenant Eikbush's Third Platoon was in heavy contact with the pirates, but the young lieutenant was pushing the pirates back. Two Marines were WIA, but the platoon's discipline was simply too much for the pirates to withstand.

Esther intersected herself in the battle once more, ordering "Stone-One, do not pursue the enemy. I want you to move to this position and form a blocking force. No one is to get to the passengers."

"Roger that, "Lieutenant Radiant Purpose said, his confidence evident even over the comms.

Esther didn't know how many, if any, of the pirates were still with the passengers, but she didn't want any of the others rejoining them. The passengers and crew represented a huge bargaining chip, one Esther wanted to deny them. As more and more of the assault element entered the ship, she had an overwhelming force to root out any remaining enemy, so she felt confident that she could afford to use RP's platoon as a blocking force.

And the enemy numbers were dropping. As the running firefights continued, at least eight were KIA with three wounded and in custody. Captain Montoya, who was technically part of the support element but who was already onboard the ship, had just arrived on the scene to question one of the pirates.

Pirates were not protected by the Accords, so with Doc Stevenson injecting the pirate with Mylanozene, Captain Montoya would be ferreting out if the ship was in fact boobytrapped, Esther's primary remaining concern. Mylanozene had some serious side-effects, but it was fast-acting, and within 60 seconds, the S-2 would be able to start questioning. Esther just hoped the two-day interrogation course the Two had taken back on Tarawa before reporting in had sunk in.

And suddenly, it was over. The remaining pirates were surrendering. These were not the terrorists Esther had fought in the past. These were men and woman fighting for material wealth despite their claims to the contrary, and while their bosses might want them to make the retaking of the *Calypso Queen* as expensive as possible, the fighters evidently had other ideas.

"I'm transiting," she announced to the CIC.

"Are you sure that's wise?" Commander Anderson asked.

"I can't get a feel for what's going on from here."

"What about—"

"Captain Montoya is questioning the prisoners, and we're starting to sweep the ship. I won't go aboard until the sweep is completed."

The commander was right. Esther could perform her duties aboard the *Mount Fuji*. She didn't have to go to the *Calypso Queen*, and she certainly didn't have to go now. But she was too hyped to simply sit in the CIC. She had to get out there to her Marines.

"Mark, you've got it," she told her XO.

She wasn't passing over her command to him, but he'd be the one to monitor the situation while she was making the crossing. And if anything did happen to her . . .

Two minutes later, Esther stepped off the elevator and into the hangar bay. Noah was waiting for her, flanked by Sergeant Hilborn and Corporal Tenine. Esther accepted her security team—she'd actually expected Noah would have demanded more. She snapped her helmet into place and let one of the Navy deck hands attach her propulsion pack. After a quick integrity check, the deck hand gave her the green light, and along with Noah and her two bodyguards, stepped up to the curtain and pushed through it, her stomach giving its customary lurch as she went from normal gravity to zero G.

At only a klick away, the *Calypso Queen* looked huge. The two Albatrosses stood off either end, waiting to take action should they need to. EVA-suited figures moved around the ship, several clustered around the ship's aft where the *Mount Fuji* had disabled the drives.

With Noah behind her, Hilborn and Tenine took positions on either side of her as she goosed her jets to make the crossing. At max acceleration, then flip and max deceleration, Esther could reach the ship within a minute. That wasn't a good idea, though. More than a few Marines or sailors had come in too hot and suffered the consequences. Slow and steady was the more conservative course.

"CO, we've got a situation here," Fred Kingery passed on the P2P. "With the crew."

"What is it?"

"The Dark Tiders, well, they . . . "

"Meet me at Dozer-Three's breach. I'll be there in 90 seconds."

No one should be able to monitor a Marine P2P circuit, but Captain Kingery had been flustered, and she wanted to give him a few moments to compose himself.

"Noah, Kingery just called me. There's an issue with the crew."

"What is it?"

"He didn't tell me. Didn't sound good, though."

She switched to Captain Montoya's P2P, and asked, "Destiny, have you found out anything, yet? About booby-trapping?"

"I questioned two so far. Their commander had wanted to rig the ship, but it looks like they overruled her. The two I've interrogated both believe the ship is clean."

They "believe" is the relevant term here. Their commander could have done it anyway without their knowledge.

"Have you questioned the commander yet?"

"That's a negative. Seems like her crew killed her when she refused to surrender."

Well, shit. Not a good command structure. Sucks to be her, I guess.

"Understood. I'll be aboard in 30 seconds."

Esther had her EVA suit on auto, and it fired off a series of small jets, bringing her gently to the gate of Dozer-Three. Sergeant Hilborn slid in before her, which seemed overkill as she could see on her helmet display that only Marines were on the other side, but she let it slide. Better her Marines were more conservative when the situation allowed than be too rash.

She slid headfirst into the tube and right on Hilborn's ass, pulled herself to the breach where two Marines pulled her out and to her feet. Captain Kingery ran up just as she stood. He started his report, but she wanted Noah to hear it as well, so she held up a hand to stop him for the moment until her brother was standing beside her.

In a rush, he reported that the ship was secure, and all known pirates were accounted for.

"The commander is dead, right?" she asked.

"Killed by her own troops," he said. "That's what they say, at least. We're pulling the recordings. Not just for that, though, for the crew, too."

"I take it from your demeanor that the crew suffered at the hands of the pirates?"

"Yes, ma'am. What's left of them are in their bridge."

"Show me."

She started to follow when Hilborn and Tenine pushed their way forward past the two Charlie Company Marines who were there with Kingery. In other circumstances, their marking of their territory might have been humorous. At the moment, it wasn't.

The bridge was only 30 meters from the breach point. Esther steeled herself as she entered, ready to ask the remaining crew what had happened to their peers.

Only, there were no remaining crew. When Captain Kingery had said "what's left of them," he hadn't meant survivors. He meant what was physically left of their bodies.

The bridge was an abattoir. The bodies of nine crew members lay on the deck behind the line of controls. Each body was missing a head. The heads were propped up on the control shelves, lifeless eyes watching over the rest of their bodies. Blood had pooled up to three centimeters in places.

Esther had seen Marines blown apart, but she didn't think she'd ever seen so much blood in her life. The coppery smell was gagging, and she had to swallow several times to keep her stomach from rebelling.

"When did this happen?" she asked, her voice calm even if she wanted to shout.

"When we appeared off her beam," Captain Kingery said.

Which explains why the blood is still liquid.

Esther looked up to a brightly-clad body sitting in the captain's chair, her turquoise and yellow fatigues stained by a single wound of some sort to her chest.

"The pirate commander?" she asked, pointing with her chin.

"Yes, ma'am."

"And let me guess. Her crew says she did all of this?"

Captain Kingery nodded.

Esther didn't buy that one bit. Even with a vibroblade, it wasn't easy to cut off a person's head. And there was no way Esther thought nine merchantmen would simply lay there and wait for the commander to get to them. No, the pirate crew was involved up to their eyeballs.

But that wasn't Esther's concern. They would get interrogated by the best the FCDC had to offer. Montoya might not be an expert in extracting information, but the FCDC ITT teams were, and the pirates wouldn't be able to hide anything from them.

"Steve, we've got a big problem here," she passed back to the *Mount Fuji's* CO.

"Not that big, Esther. Chief Bullstaff and the CHENG think they can repair propulsion in four or five hours. The *Calypso Queen* can get underway by herself and transit to Reece Station."

"How are they going to do that without a crew? The Dark Tide commander killed them all."

There was dead silence for a moment, then a mystified, "What?"

"Cut off their heads. All nine of them."

"You're sure?" he asked in what was almost a pleading tone.

"Yeah, pretty sure. I'm standing in this slaughterhouse right now," she said before sending him her feed.

"Oh, my God! I . . . what do, I mean, I've got to report this."

"Yeah, I think that's a good idea."

"Can you get back here? We need to figure out what we're going to do."

"Are the passengers secure?" she asked Captain Kingery.

"Yes, ma'am. We're matching the manifest now with them."

"I'm on my way," she told Anderson, then to Noah, "I'm going back. Watch out for things over here, OK?"

"Roger that."

She turned to Hilborn and said, "Well, Sergeant, let's get back to the *Fujiyama*."

****

Four hours later, Esther leaned back in her chair, hands clasped behind her head while she listened to Commander Anderson go over once again why he couldn't leave an officer in charge of the *Calypso Queen*.

"I've got the XO and two more in sickbay, and now with this second contingency, I just can't afford the manpower."

Esther lowered her arms and swung back forward, saying, "But we can't just leave the ship floating in space."

"She won't be. The propulsion will be up and running in another twenty minutes."

"At 20%."

"Still, she can get underway."

Esther and the *Mount Fuji's* CO were in his stateroom, hashing out alone what had become a bone of contention during the meeting in the wardroom. She completely understood his position. He was shorthanded, and he'd just received orders to transit to the Boclyn System for a possible interdiction—ironically as result of intel received by their prisoners. Esther didn't give much weight to the intel, but she knew the Admiral had to act on it, and that meant taking the *Mount Fuji* away from the *Calypso Queen* long before a qualified crew could be formed and arrive to take the ship to Reece Station and the quadrant naval headquarters.

And of course, this had to coincide when the XO and two other officers were quarantined with one of the ultra-viruses which were making the rounds through human space. The ship's surgeon said this was a particularly nasty virus, and there was a good chance he'd have to put the three sailors into stasis until they could get a higher-level treatment.

Esther had one out, one way for the *Mount Fuji* to leave on her new mission while still allowing the *Calypso Queen* to get underway, but it was a long shot, one she didn't think would get accepted by the Navy brass. She wasn't sure she wanted it, either. The new mission would probably be a blockade, but there was always the possibility of boots on the ground.

Screw it. We can't just leave the passengers to fend for themselves.

"I have a possible solution," she said hesitantly.

"Unless you have a way to get a crew here via instantaneous transport, I don't see how."

"What if we had a crew already here?"

"I told you, Esther, Navy regs require a commissioned officer to take over an abandoned vessel. I can't spare one, and the Admiral agrees. And he was reluctant to give CHENG and the chief the time to even repair the ship."

"Do the regs say that the commissioned officer be Navy?"

"What? Navy? Well, no, not exactly. But he or she needs to be underway qualed. That's why I can't leave Ensign Evers, Wolter, Liang, or Lieutenant (JG) Ahaad."

"How about a ship's master rating?"

"A ship's master? That's a civilian rating, but probably . . . yeah, that would work for a non-combatant. That's probably what they'll send over if they can't get a naval officer, come to think of it."

"I've got one."

"Got one what?"

"A ship's master. Captain Peaslee. Before he became a Marine, he'd earned his ship's master license. Kept his rating up all these years, too. From what he told me, he signs on with commercial liners while on leave to earn extra credits."

"Peaslee? Your H&S Company Commander?"

"The very same."

"Hmm," Steve said before sinking into silence.

Esther could almost read the thoughts cross his face. The Navy, like any governmental organization, fiercely guarded its turf, and no matter how close the two services were, she didn't think they would want a Marine to take over a ship, even a commercial liner. The alternative, though, was to leave the ship abandoned in space until a civilian crew was ferried out to it. Would Anderson see it that way, however?

"Is his license registered? I mean, is it current?"

"Yes, it is."

Peaslee, you better not be shitting me.

It was the captain who had approached Esther with the idea. She hadn't checked up on his claim, so she was taking his word that all his paperwork was up to date.

It took a few more moments, but Anderson made up his mind, telling Esther, "OK, let's do it. I'll leave an engineering and bridge team on board, but if Peaslee is a master, then he's in command."

"You don't want to ask the admiral, first?" Esther asked, surprised that a Navy commander would take that kind of decision upon his shoulders.

"Yeah, I want to, but he might say no, and then where are we? Like you said, we owe it to the passengers.

"I'll order F1 ready to ferry over Peaslee, departing in . . . can he make 15 minutes?"

"He'll make it. I'll be sending two Marines with him, and I'm leaving the sergeant major on board, too. He's still on the ship."

"OK, sounds good. Let's just hope this doesn't blow up in our faces, Esther."

I'm with you on that, Esther thought to herself as she rushed to tell Peaslee, who was waiting in the wardroom, to gather his shit and get going. *Believe you me, I'm with you on that.*

SS CALYPSO QUEEN

Chapter 16
Noah

"What do they want now?" Captain Peaslee asked BM3 Sturdevant.

"Same thing. They want you to take the ship back to Solznetya 3."

"And I'm saying the same thing back to them. We can't take them back home. Our orders are firm; we're heading to Reece Station."

"They're saying you don't have the authority to make that decision, sir."

The captain rolled his eyes and looked over to Noah, who was sitting in the cargo officer's chair.

"You know and I know the regs, sir," Noah said. "But maybe they need to hear it from you."

Sturdevant looked up at Noah with obvious relief in his eyes. They'd been putting a lot on the shoulder of the young sailor, and Noah knew it was time to push the problem up the ladder.

"Maybe you're right. I'm not going to the galley, though. I'm staying right here on the bridge. Why don't you get two or three of the ringleaders and escort them back up here," the captain said.

"Make one of them Tennyson," Noah told the sailor.

"You'd think they'd be a little grateful," he said to Noah after Sturdevant left. "We did save them from the pirates, after all."

"Never underestimate the fleeting strength of gratitude, sir."

"Yeah, I know. I just want to get this voyage over and done with, and with as little stress as possible."

"I don't know, sir. What with you commanding a ship now, maybe you can put this on your resume and get a transfer to the Navy," Noah said.

The captain didn't bother to say anything but merely raised his middle finger.

He'd had it right, though. Noah was anxious to deliver the ship, then get back to the *Mount Fuji*, particularly if the battalion was going to be engaged again. He understood why Esther had put him on the *Queen*—he didn't really have a tactical billet should it come to combat, and the experience he'd been gaining as a sergeant major was exactly what the current situation called for. Captain Peaslee was responsible for the ship, but he was to make sure all the working parts meshed together to enable the captain to get the *Queen* back to quadrant headquarters.

It shouldn't be that difficult, even with the engines at 20%. There was more than enough food manufacturing, and the entertainment system was operational. He had the three-man team in engineering, monitoring the system and keeping it running. With two helmsmen, that gave him five sailors, which was light when compared with normal staffing, but still doable considering the high degree of automation on the ship. With Captain Peaslee, Sergeant Hilborn, Corporal Tenine, and the jack-of-all-trades Sturdevant, there were more than enough people to get the ship from Point A to Point B.

But now, it seemed as if the natives were getting restless—all 2,677 of them.

Noah had met with their corporate handler, a particularly poorly-qualified woman named Naomi Harris-Mink. It had quickly become obvious that she was in over her head, so Noah had been forced to deal with L'Troy Tennyson and Guang Morris, two men who'd taken over as passenger representatives. Morris seemed to have ulterior motives that Noah couldn't quite fathom, and that bothered him. Tennyson, on the other hand, seemed like a decent enough guy. Still, it should be an uneventful passage—*should* be.

A few minutes later, Sturdevant returned with four passengers: Tennyson, Morris, and two others Noah didn't recognize.

"I thought he was in charge," Morris said, nodding at Noah. "But Sturdevant said you are?"

Hilborn, who'd been sitting in the comms suite chair, stood up at the underlying belligerence in the man's tone. He subtly shifted his weight on the balls of his feet, and Noah knew he was ready to react. Noah caught his eye and gave a tiny shake of his head to call the sergeant off. No one needed a confrontation on the bridge.

"I'm the captain of the ship, yes, so I am in charge. I'm Captain Jeff Peaslee, United Federation Marines," he said in a calm, but firm, voice.

If Morris thought it odd that a Marine was in command, he didn't show it. He might not even know the difference between a Navy and a Marine captain.

"Well, if you're in charge, you need to take us back to Solznetya."

"And Rubble," one of the other men said.

"As I'm sure BM3 Sturdevant told you, I am required to take you to the quadrant headquarters. Once there, all of you will be taken to your final destination."

"We're not going to Fortuna," Morris said with conviction.

Captain Peaslee looked nonplussed as he said, "Where you go from there is up to you and the authorities. I'm only charged with getting the *Calypso Queen* to headquarters."

"I don't think you understand, Captain," the fourth person, a 60-something woman with short, gray hair. "I'm Geste Madigar, and I'm a lawyer."

A lawyer? Going out as contract labor? Did she get disbarred? Noah wondered.

"What we have here is a clear breech of contract. Sunshine Ahead, LLC, promised us safe passage to Fortuna. Obviously, that didn't happen, so the contract is null and void. As such, you are required to return us to our embarkation point, Solzentya 3."

"And Rubble," the third person interjected once more.

Noah had never heard of Rubble. He wanted to pull out his PA and query it but didn't want to be a distraction.

"If you are a lawyer, Ms. Madigar," Captain Peaslee said, "then you are aware of maritime law. The *Calypso Queen* was seized by pirates and was recovered by a governmental force, in this case, the Federation military. The ship was damaged during the process.

"At your hands," the lawyer said.

He ignored the statement, continuing, "The UAM Charter of Passage is clear on what happens next. We are to proceed to the nearest designated governmental facility where claims and counterclaims can be filed, and in this case, where repairs can be conducted."

"The Federation quadrant headquarters in the nearest facility? You know that's not true, Captain," she persisted.

"The quadrant headquarters is the nearest 'designated' facility, yes. And it's certainly much closer than the Solzentya system. With our limited drive capabilities, I'd be willing to bet that should you be returning to the system, getting new transport from Reece Station will be quicker in the long run than would be taking the *Calypso Queen*."

"So, you won't take us?" Morris asked.

"It's not a matter of my choosing one way or the other. My hands are tied. I would suggest that you simply relax after your ordeal. Even under limited drive, we'll be at Reece Station soon, and you'll be treated well there while things get sorted out."

Noah was impressed with the captain's demeanor. He was normally a little high-strung, particularly on the Battle Ball pitch, where he was a madman. Here, he sounded reasonable and understanding.

"That's your final word?"

"Yes, I'm afraid it is."

"This isn't the last you're going to hear from us," Morris said before wheeling about and stalking out.

Noah grabbed Tennyson by the arm before the man could follow the other three out and said, "Getting excited won't do anyone any good. We don't have a choice here, so if you can, just keep things calm, and you'll all get taken care of at Reece Station."

The man started to say something, hesitated as if changing his mind, then said, "It's not up to me. Things are getting . . . um . . . stressful."

He pulled out of Noah's grasp and followed the other three out of the bridge.

"Sergeant Hilborn, wake Tenine and get him here to the bridge. Full battle rattle. Then you get to engineering," Noah said.

"You think that's necessary?" Captain Peaslee asked.

"I don't know. But something is brewing. I feel it in my bones."

Captain Peaslee stood silent for a moment, chewing on his lower lip. Finally, he looked up at Sturdevant and said, "Follow Sergeant Hilborn to berthing and wake up Pristeen and Jackson. I want everyone either here on the bridge or in engineering. We can sleep at our stations.

"After you wake up the other two, I want you, Hilborn, and Tenine to pick up two portable fabricators and some Base A. I want one here and one in engineering."

Noah grimaced despite himself. Even a portable fabricator could gin up some adequate food, but with only Base A, that meant sustenance bars, as nasty a source of calories as had ever been invented.

"I think I should get to engineering," Noah told the captain.

It made sense. They could run the ship as long as they controlled the bridge and engineering, and with the captain on the bridge, Noah thought he'd be better placed with the engineers.

"Wait until Hilborn gets back. I don't want you wandering around alone."

Noah didn't think anything would happen for the time being. If something bad were going to take place, it would be after Morris and the lawyer reported the results of their meeting. If he moved right now, he could get down to engineering without a problem. But the captain was in charge, so he nodded. He walked over to the purser's suite where displays pulled up the ship's spaces. As a full-fledged, working cruise liner, the purser held the ship's number 3 position, and the suite was extensive. When the ship was downgraded, most of the suite had been pulled out. Still, Noah could pull up the main galley. It was crowded with what had to be the bulk of the passengers, and within a minute or two, the crowd parted to let Morris and the other three through and up to what had been the captain's dais in better days.

"I spoke with the captain of this ship," Morris yelled out before shouts of "We can't hear you" drowned him out.

It took a few moments, but someone handed him a PA with loudspeaker capability.

"As I was saying, I just spoke with the captain of the ship. He flatly refuses to take us back home."

There were shouts of anger among the crowd.

"Sir, you might want to watch this," Noah said to Captain Peaslee who came over to join him.

Together, they watched as Morris and Madigar address the crowd, which seemed to get more and more agitated. No one had made a call for violence yet, but Noah had a feeling it was only a matter of time.

Hilborn, Tenine, Sturdevant and the two off-watch sailors entered the bridge carrying the two fabricators. Noah took one more look at the screen before taking Hilborn and Jackson to head to engineering.

"Keep your head down, Sergeant Major. And keep the comms lines open," the captain said.

With Jackson carrying the fabricator, Hilborn led with Noah in the rear. Both Marines had their M90's at the casual ready, trying not to look too aggressive, but still able to bring the weapon to bear if needed. The bridge was towards the bow of the ship; engineering was aft. The main passage aft passed the galley. The three could have changed decks, to avoid the galley, but that would have had them following a rat's maze up and down, and that would have taken time. Noah thought a quick passage would serve them best.

"Pick up the pace, Hilborn," Noah said as the rumble of the crowd reached them.

They passed the fore starboard entrance without incident. Noah glanced through the open hatch, from where Morris' voice reached them. The passengers he spotted were all looking back to the dais, and no one saw the three as they passed.

The middle hatch was closed, which left only the aft starboard hatch. Once past the main galley, it was almost a direct shot, 70 meters aft, to engineering. Noah held his breath as they walked past the hatch, and they were in the clear. He just started to let down his guard when three men exited one of the heads, right in front of Sergeant Hilborn.

"Hey, it's them!" one of the men shouted.

The lead man didn't say a word but charged the three. Hilborn barely moved his feet, but just as the man reached him, he brought the butt of his M90 in a textbook butt-stroke. The man crumbled bonelessly to the deck, out cold. Instantly, Hilborn had his weapon raise, aimed right at the other two men.

"You two, freeze where you are," Noah said. "Sergeant Hilborn, proceed aft."

The muzzle of Hilborn's weapon never wavered from its aiming point smack dab on the next man's forehead. He swiveled as he passed the man, keeping him covered. EM2 Jackson gingerly stepped past the two men, looking like he was ready to toss the fabricator at them if they so much as flinched. And then it was just Noah.

"Don't even think it," Noah said as one of the men glanced up the passage to the galley entrance.

He passed the two, the muzzle of his M90 20 centimeters from them. This was bad, bad form. He had a weapon—they did not. He should be standing off, not getting close to them, but they had to get past, and the passage was only so wide.

He kept the two covered, switching to back-stepping as he followed Jackson and Hilborn. The two men looked at each other, then at Noah several times before they broke in unison and ran for the galley. Noah could have dropped them. Maybe he should have. But they weren't the enemy. They were contract workers caught up in a situation beyond their control.

"Run!" he told the other two as he swung around and bolted forward.

It didn't take them long to cover the distance to the engineering spaces, but he heard shouts from behind while Jackson scanned his eye to open the space. Noah took a glance back and saw 20 or 30 people pouring from the galley and start running toward them. The three slipped into the admin space and closed the hatch before the crowd had covered half of the distance.

Jackson was breathing hard, but it was the breathing of excitement, not fear.

He doesn't know any better. If they had reached us . . .

The admin space was small, barely 2 X 2, and held shelves with printed back-up copies of manuals. The hatch leading into the space was locked, but it was not designed to withstand a concerted effort to get inside, an effort that had just commenced judging from the pounding on it.

"Let's take it in," Noah said.

The inner sanctum was much more secure. The ship's designers didn't want curious passengers poking around vital spaces. Jackson scanned the hatch open, and the three entered to where the chief and EM3 Juarez were anxiously waiting.

"What's going on out there?" Chief Bostick asked.

"The natives are restless, so it looks like we're staying here for the duration."

"Well, fuck me royal," the chief said, sinking down into a stool.

That about says it, Noah thought as he took a seat of his own.

****

"It looks pretty bad, Sergeant Major," Captain Peaslee told him. "I see at least ten bodies."

Noah had hoped that with the bridge and engineering secured, things would quiet down for the duration. Fat chance.

Three hours ago, the passengers in the galley had broken out into fighting. Noah didn't have eyes on the galley within engineering, but Captain Peaslee told him there had been disagreements on where they wanted to go and what they would do to effect that. Now, a good portion of the passengers were roaming the ship in gangs while the rest tried to find places to hide.

"Not much we can do about it now, sir. We've got . . . hey, Chief. How much longer until we drop out of bubble space?"

"Six hours, fourteen minutes."

"We've got just over six hours. Do you have the message ready to send out?"

"Ready and waiting, Sergeant Major."

The *Calypso Queen* had seen better days, and much of her equipment had been stripped since then, and that included her meson comms. As per space regulations, she had a message torpedo, but that had been used to report the piracy, and she didn't have another. So, for them, while the were in bubble space, there wasn't a way to let anyone know what was happening.

Chief was going to drop them out of bubble space within the red zone, and the second they emerged, Captain Peaslee would send out the message. If they were lucky and the station security on the ball, they could expect help within another two hours. That left something over eight hours for the passengers to kill off more of themselves.

"We've got another fire," Jackson said as he watched his displays.

"Where's it at?" Chief asked as he stood and moved to the displays.

"E-2-23."

Four fires had already been started by the passengers. None had threatened the integrity of the ship, but smoke put a strain on the air systems, so Jackson, with firefighting on manual control, had methodically put each one out.

"Hit it," the chief told him.

With a flip of the switch, Jackson flooded the space with Borophylioxide, an artificial gas that smothered the fire. BPL was an effective firefighting substance, but it was also toxic in strong enough doses, which was why Jackson was on manual and the chief approved each release. Noah didn't know why space E-2-23 was important enough that the threat to life and limb was acceptable, and he didn't ask. As far as he was concerned, they set the fire, and if fighting it was going to result in a long recovery for any of them, so be it. After the first fire, Noah had gotten on the 1MC to pass that BPL would be used to put out fires and what the consequences were to exposure to it, but that hadn't seemed to make a difference. They still started fires.

A pounding on the outer hatch caught Noah's attention for a moment, and he dismissed it until Sergeant Hilborn called out, "Sergeant Major, you might want to hear this."

There'd been pounding several times, and twice what sounded like some sort of tool trying to penetrate the hatch, so Noah wasn't sure what was different about this time. He walked up to join the sergeant, and outside her could barely hear shouting. With a shrug, he turned on the speaker.

"... kill us, please, let us in for God's sake," a man's voice said.

Noah looked up and Hilborn, who had a conflicted look on his face as he asked, "Is that for real?"

"Please, we've got women and children. You've got to help us."

Noah leaned forward and pressed the speaker button, saying, "Who's trying to kill you?"

"Oh my God, you're there. The Solzentians, the ones who want to go back, that's who. They're taking over the ship!"

"And who are you?"

"We've got two men, three women, and two kids. Please, you need to help us. We can hear more of them outside, but they're trying to find something to break in, so they'll be back. Please, sir, let us in!"

Noah looked over to Chief and Jackson. Both had come closer, and both looked worried.

"What do you think? He sounded real to me," Noah asked.

He knew the man could be part of a trap. They hadn't been able to break in, and they could be trying to trick them into opening up. If it was, all four of them were at risk.

"I don't know," the chief said. "I . . . just . . . " he said, his words trailing off.

"Oh, God! Please! I think they're coming back now!"

"Grubbing hell," Noah said, unslinging his M90. "Hilborn, take the right. Jackson, on my command, open the hatch." He positioned himself on the left and told the sergeant, "If there aren't three women and two kids out there, cut every single one of them down."

He took a deep breath, took his M90 off safe, and said, "Open it."

A man was standing right up to the speaker—and behind him were the women and children.

"Get in, get in!" Noah shouted as they made a mad scramble inside. "You said two men! Where is he?"

"Jeorg went back out to try and delay them. You have to wait for him."

Noah hesitated a second, then said, "Sorry, I can't. Close it!"

Immediately he spun around and covered the man. "Hands up. You, too, ladies. I mean it."

Sergeant Hilborn stepped up beside him to add emphasis to his order.

"Jackson, I want you to carefully check each one of them, children, too."

The little girl was probably four years old, and she looked up at Noah in wonderment. The little boy, who had to be her brother, was quietly snuffling tears.

Jackson stepped up and patted the man down.

"His junk, too, Jackson. Check everywhere on him."

"He's clean, I think," the sailor said when he was done.

"Step over to your right," Noah told the man. "Jackson, now check the women. And same thing, check everywhere on them."

If the women were uncomfortable about the big sailor groping them, they only showed relief. That alone helped convince Noah that they were the real deal. Not enough to forego checking the two children, however.

Once he was convinced, he slung his weapon and asked, "What is going on out there?"

"Is Jeorg going to be OK?" one of the women asked.

"Hush, Lyza. You know Jeorg and his gift of gab. He'll be fine. He'll want to know you and the kids are safe," an older woman said, taking her hand.

"Sergeant Hilborn, go back to the hatch and listen. If this Jeorg comes back, let me know."

"Oh, thank you, sir," the woman named Lyza said as she pulled the little boy into her grasp.

"So, once again, what's going on?"

The older woman, with a confidence that surprised him, said, "Some of the passengers . . . well, maybe most of them, got cold feet after the damned pirates came. They said that the Sunshine Ahead people couldn't even protect us in space, so how were they gonna do it on Fortuna. We'd end up indentured."

"There are no more indentured citizens," Noah said.

"Indentured, contract workers, same thing. They've got you by the balls. Then the lawyer, Geste, she said we can sue for damages. We can get money and not have to work away from home. Lots of folks liked that.

"So, there's us—we're Solzentians—and the Rubbles, and some want to go home, and some want to honor our contracts. And then that Rubble hit Hank Agnew over the head with a chair, and things sorta came apart at the seams, if you can imagine that. We became animals.

"It was the Rubbles' fault, them and the ones who wanted the money," the man said, his first word spoken since he'd been searched.

"Some of us Solzentians wanted the money, Terrance. You saw that. It weren't all Rubbles causing the problems."

"So why did you think they wanted to kill you, and who exactly is 'they.'"

"Cause they killed Lacy and Kris, that's why. They woulda killed us if Kris hadn't slowed them down. As to who's 'they,' it's everyone else. No one knows who's on what side. If you aren't with them, you're the enemy."

Noah looked at the six people, wondering how society could break down so quickly. And all because of the pirates? That didn't make any sense.

"Well, you'll be safe in another eight hours, so why don't you relax the best you can. We should be safe until then."

****

Four hours later, Noah wasn't sure about that. There'd been some muffled sounds outside the hatch, which didn't alarm Noah too much, but had caused Lyza to run up, asking if it was Jeorg. Dylan, the older woman, had to come up and take her away to her two kids. After fifteen minutes, however, the sound changed to heavy pounding—not the pounding of fists, but of tools. Chief came up and put his hands on the hatch for a minute or so, then shook his head and assured Noah it would hold.

After another ten minutes, the pounding ceased, and Noah thought they were home free until Jackson reported a fire in the admin room, but extremely localized. He and the chief looked at the readouts, trying to figure out what was happening when an alarm sounded.

The chief put his hand on the door, then said, "Sons of bitches are trying to burn through the hatch!"

"Can they do it?" Noah asked.

"If they had the right tools, yeah. This is a cruise liner, not a Navy ship."

Noah had to feel the hatch for himself, reaching out before snatching his hand back in pain.

"Told you so, Sergeant Major."

"Jackson, what would happen if you flood the space with BLP?" he asked, sucking on his fingers.

"Won't work if they've got a torch. The O2 for combustion is inside the fuel lines, not in the air," the chief said.

"He doesn't mean that, Chief. He wants to lay them out!" Jackson told him.

The chief looked confused for a moment before it dawned on him what his engineer had said, and a smile crept over his face. "I like the way you think, Sergeant Major," he said, then, "Do it," to EN2 Jackson.

With a wicked-looking smile on his face, Jackson flipped his lever. The alarm went quiet almost immediately.

"I wish we had a visual on what's going on out there. I bet they're shitting bricks," the chief said.

"Not the ones who are out cold," Jackson said with a laugh.

"Are the bad men coming to get us?" a soft voice asked from behind them.

Noah turned to see that the passengers had stood up and were watching their every move. Tara, the little girl, was standing in front of Lyza, who had her arms protectively around her.

The little girl was younger than his own Shiloh, and she looked nothing like his daughter, but Noah was hit by a wave of almost fatherly concern.

"No, Tara, you're safe in here. Don't you worry."

She nodded, accepting what he said, but from the look on her face, Tara's mother was not so accepting.

Noah hoped to God that he hadn't lied to the child.

****

"I wonder how how Captain P is doing on the bridge," Sergeant Hilborn said. "Do you think he got his message out?"

"He should have. The bridge comms are self-contained," Chief Bostick said.

An hour after the abortive attempt to burn through the hatch, all comms and power to the engineering spaces had been cut off. The passengers had cried out in a panic until the back-up power came on four seconds later, but the comms with the bridge and the rest of the ship were not restored.

Engineering still functioned. Life support was not affected, and the ship still traveled through bubble space—it would be a poor design if a crazy passenger bent on suicide, for example, could take down a ship. But inter-shipboard comms passed through micro optics, and they'd been obviously located and cut.

Without alternative orders, Noah had carried on with the original plan. Chief brought the ship out of bubble space as scheduled and confirmed their position. The shift had been barely noticeable; in this one aspect, the old cruise liner was superior to a Navy ship-of-the-line. Noah wondered if the passengers even knew they had reached normal space and within spitting distance of Reece Station.

Now, for the ten people in engineering, it was merely a matter of waiting. Noah wished he knew what was happening outside their little enclave, but he had to accept that things were now out of his hands.

He idly watched Tara and Norton, her brother, play on the deck. Jackson had poked around and found two small Nympho dolls that one of the *Queen's* crew had squirreled away to titillate himself or herself during the long hours underway. After disconnecting their active functions, and with permission from their mother, he'd given the two porn dolls to the children, which for them were just another two toys, nothing "adult" about them. Tara was berating Norton at the moment, chiding him for breaking book and trying to make his doll fly. He had to smile at that. The more he watched the little girl, the more he thought she was like Shiloh, and the more he missed his kids.

"I think we have company again," EN2 Jackson announced.

Their connections with the rest of the ship might be cut, but the admin office was still part of engineering, and they could monitor the readings from it. They'd switched the rest of the ship to automatic, which meant, among other things, that the BLP would be deployed in case of every fire, but they'd kept their office space on manual.

"Watch the temps," the chief said as he walked up to the hatch, followed by Noah and Hilborn. He put his right palm on the hatch and after a moment said, "Yeah, they're at it again."

"Should I hit them?" Jackson asked.

The chief looked at Noah who nodded, then said, "Yep. Do it."

Jackson flipped his switch, then waited eagerly for readings that would indicate he'd knocked them out. He waited for a few moments, then frowned.

"I'm still getting readings. The temps are rising."

Chief put both hands on the hatch, and Noah had to follow suit, testing the surface first to make sure he wasn't going to get burned. The hatch was warm, and he could feel a very slight vibration.

"They're still coming," Chief said.

"But, what about the BLP?" Noah asked.

"They picked up some breathing apparatus somewhere, that or vacsuits. I'm only surprised it took them this long to figure it out.

"Do you think they'll be able to break in?"

The chief shrugged, then said, "Depends on what they're cutting with. I'm guessing we'll know soon enough."

"What's happening, Sergeant Major?" Dylan asked as she joined them.

"Your friends out there are trying to get in."

"Will they make it?"

"Don't know, ma'am. We're watching now."

"I hope you can do more than just watching. If they get in, well, I don't think they'll take kindly to me and mine, you know, seeing as how we ran away from them in the first place."

"I know, I know."

He looked around the space. About 15 X 20, it was mostly filled with controls and the CAH projector where the engineers could pull up a real time 3D rendering of any system on the ship. At the far end was an access tube where the engineers could make the most common adjustments and replace parts to the drives. There was no place where six civilians could hide.

"Where's that hatch lead to," he asked the chief, pointing to a one-by-one-meter hatch set low on the aft bulkhead.

"That's the cold room, you know, for the bubble initiator."

Noah only had a layman's knowledge of bubble generators. He knew they needed an "initiator" to spark off the generator, and that initiator worked at ultra-cold temperatures. After that, it was all black magic as far as he was concerned.

"Can they survive in there?" he asked, tilting his head at the civilians.

"For a bit, sure. But the room is kept pretty cold, you know. Every degree colder helps in keeping the initiator tubes cold."

"How long could they last in there?" Noah said, feeling the heat begin to emanate from the near side of the hatch.

"I'm not a doctor, Sergeant Major. I don't know. With the kids? Ten minutes maybe?"

That's not going to work.

Noah looked back at the hatch, his mind racing. He'd feel a lot better if they were out of any possible line of fire.

"Wait, can't we just turn off the cooling? I mean, we won't be needing bubble space again, right?"

"Sure, we could, I guess. That will fry the tubes, and that'll cost a lot to repair."

"I'm not too concerned about that at the moment, to be blunt, Chief."

"I guess you're right at that," the chief said with a laugh. "Jackson, kill the cooling for the cold room, and open up the hatch to it."

"But—"

"I know, just do it. See if you can force some warmer air from out here inside."

"Roger that."

Noah turned to Dylan and told her, "I don't know if we're going to be able to keep them out, so I want you and the rest inside the cold room. And it's cold, really cold. We're turning off the cooling, and we'll try to get some warmer air in there, but better let the others know. I can keep the door open, but if they break through, we've got to close it. If that happens, keep quiet and stay inside until someone comes and gets you."

It looked like she was going to argue, but then she nodded, and asked, "And if you don't come and get us?"

"Give it a few hours, if you can hold out. By that time, station security should be aboard."

"I hope it's you, Sergeant Major, who comes to get us." She pulled his head down and gave him a kiss on the cheek before she turned back to the others and started then to the hatch.

A short moment later, a cascade of sparks shot into the space from the outer hatch. There were shouts from the civilians as Noah yelled, "Go, go!"

"Hilborn, take the right again," Noah said as he took his own position on the left side of the hatch. "Chief, you'd better get back."

A flame pushed through the hatch as the sparks kept falling. An acrid scent burned Noah's nose, and his eyes watered. The flame pushed lower, leaving a three-centimeter gap above it. Standing to the side of the flame, Noah lifted his M90, put the muzzle up at the gap, and fired off a 20-round burst of hypervelocity darts. Immediately, the flame stopped, and Noah could hear shouting from the other side.

He took a moment to look back. The kids and two women were already inside the cold room with only Dylan and Auburn still outside. Dylan looked back, gave Noah a wink, and let Auburn help her in. A moment later, he followed her.

"Jackson, the moment anyone makes it in here, you close that hatch."

"Do you think they will, Sergeant Major? I mean, make it in?"

"I don't know, son, but Sergeant Hilborn and I are going to have something to say about that."

He wished he had weapons for Jackson and the chief. Hell, he wished he had a squad of Marines. Instead, he had two M90s with a couple of thousand darts each. Their advantage was that the only entry into the space was the single door. Their disadvantage was that there was only the single door—they had no way out. Like it or not, if there was going to be a fight, it was going to be right there.

The flames started again, and the cut slowly started to lengthen. This time, though, the flame was more focused, the gap narrower. Hilborn stepped forward and tried to fire out back at the top, but his darts ricocheted, some bouncing back into their space. Noah took a quick look and saw that the passengers had put something up to block the opening.

Smart boys.

He knew that whatever they had up against the gap was only temporary, probably being held up by manpower. Hilborn's and his darts were deadly, but they didn't have the mass to punch through whatever they were using.

"Are there any cleaning supplies in here?" Noah asked to no one in particular.

"I saw some back in that little closet," Sergeant Hilborn said, pointing to a door not a meter from the main hatch, right in front of Noah's face.

"I guess I could have opened my eyes," he muttered as he opened the door.

Inside were a variety of cleaning supplies, and as he hoped, an electrostatic broom. He grabbed it, then detached the broom head. He only wanted the handle. He positioned himself just to the side of the spark cascade, then told Hilborn to get ready. Carefully, he placed the end of the handle just inside the wider part of the cut, the section where they were blocking.

"Now!" he shouted as he put all his weight behind the handle.

He'd been correct. The plate was being held up by one or more people, and with Noah's sudden surge, he knocked it out of their hands. He pulled back, and immediately, Sergeant Hilborn fired off a string of darts into the hole while shouts sounded from the other side and the sparks ceased. Hilborn fired off another string of darts, possibly 100 in total.

"Fucking A, yeah!" Hilborn said as the plate or whatever was put back into place. "That'll give the bastards something to think about."

It was only temporary, Noah knew. But they were fighting time, and any delay was worthwhile. The burning started again, and Noah tried to push the plate out of the way again, but they were prepared now.

Noah, Hilbron, and the chief were almost mesmerized by the cut in the door as it sunk lower and lower. Noah had to shake his head and get back to trying to figure out a solution. He didn't have anything in the space with which he could try to block the hatch, so it looked more and more like he and Hilborn were going to have to play the Horatius at the Bridge role, keeping the bad guys out as they tried to enter through the limited space opened by their cutting.

"It's changing direction," chief noted from five meters back.

He was right. The cut started moving off the vertical line and curved to their left. Within a minute, it started curving back. If they continued the shape, they'd have cut a circle, perhaps eight or ten centimeters in diameter.

For a moment, Noah thought it was a mistake. A hole that size would allow Hilborn and him to fire out. But then it struck him. They weren't totally stupid. They had to know that. They were cutting the hole so they could get something in the space.

"Grubbing hell! Chief, what can they fire through that hole? Do they have grenades?"

"Grenades? I doubt it. This is a civilian cruise liner, not a Navy ship."

"What about some kind of gas?"

"I . . . I really don't know. I imagine there's something they could gin up with what's on the ship. Then they'd have to figure out some way to get it in here. Uh, let me think . . ."

"No time for that, Chief. They'll be through in another minute. All of you, emergency hoods on."

Noah grabbed two hoods and threw one at Hilbron while the chief grabbed two more for Jackson and him.

"I see four more in here. Give them to the passengers, and Jackson, if anything comes in, you slam that hatch shut, got it?"

"Roger that!"

"So, that's it? No weapons aboard?"

"Well, there's probably a weapons locker. You know, side arms, a couple of Pirate Hammers."

"A what, Chief?"

"You know, a Pirate Hammer. An anti-boarding weapon. Like a shotgun, but either a plasma or meson beam."

"Well shit, let's hope they don't have one of those," Noah said, then to Hilborn, "Get ready."

With a final flurry of sparks, the torch completed the circle, and a chunk of the door fell into engineering. Noah just started to move forward to fire when a blast of energy came through the hole, hitting the muzzle of his M90 and causing him to drop it.

Noah jumped back, his heart racing. He ducked and reached for his M90, giving it a quick one-over. The muzzle, for about 15 centimeters, was blackened, but otherwise looked fine. He didn't know the recycling rate of whatever was being used, so standing to the side, he held out his M90 and fired off a barrage of darts through the hole before darting back.

"Chief . . . " he started, then stopped as he looked back.

The chief was on his back, his arms bent at the elbow, forearms and curled hands pointed up. Jackson had just slid to his knees beside the chief and was lifting up on the man's head.

Noah recognized the signs of a disrupter beam. The chief's nervous system had been fried beyond hope of resurrection.

The slight whine of a recharging powerpack reached him, and he shouted, "Jackson, get out of the way, now!"

"But the chief!" Jackson said, a woeful expression on his face.

"I said get the fuck out of the way before they fire again!" he ordered as he swung around to pump more darts through the hole in an attempt to keep the gunman on the other side from firing.

Just as he pulled the trigger, another blast came through, and Noah's right hand went numb. Not numb as in his arm was asleep, but numb as if it just wasn't there. He dropped the M90 again and jumped back, landing on his butt as he scrambled to get out of the way.

He looked back to Jackson, afraid of what he'd see, but evidently, the sailor had listened to him, and he was prone and to the side. His face was twisted in fear.

"Get back to your station, Jackson. Be ready to close that hatch," he said, and when Jackson didn't move but kept staring at the chief's body, he added, "That's an order, sailor. Do it now!"

His voice must have cut through the young man's mind. He looked with a confused expression at Noah, then scrambled back to his feet and ran to where he could close the shack to the cold room.

"Shit, Sergeant Major! Are you OK?" Sergeant Hilborn asked from the other side of the hatch.

Noah looked down at his right hand, and he almost threw up. It didn't look too bad, but it had the signatory curled fingers of totally nervous destruction. His hand was lost. Noah felt light-headed, and he knew shock was setting in. With an extreme force of will, he looked away and picked up his M90 with his left hand.

"Nothing's changed, Sergeant."

Another blast came through the hole in the door, and Noah immediately fired a burst back through in response.

"Switch sides," he told Hilborn.

On the left side of the hatch, he'd fired his M90 with only his right hand, the hand that was now useless. Firing with his left hand was awkward from that side, so he needed to switch with the sergeant.

The two Marines kept up a steady stream of harassing fire as the torch started cutting again. Whatever the bad guys had used to block the upper cut evidently wasn't large enough for the hole itself, and Noah was going to take advantage of it.

As one point, someone stuck the barrel of what had to be the energy gun through the hole to try and angle enough to hit them, but Hilborn grabbed the barrel and got into a tug-of-war with it. The weapon discharged harmlessly while the sergeant struggled with it, and finally, the gunman was able to jerk it back.

Noah checked his ammo: he had 312 darts left. The number sounded like a lot, but darts were designed to be expended in large numbers. He could cycle through those in twenty seconds of sustained fire.

"How's your ammo?" he asked Hilborn.

"Four-forty-six," the sergeant said.

"Let's be a little more judicious with our rate of fire," Noah told him.

The cut was at the bottom of the door and was slowly working its way across. Noah figured they had twenty minutes max before the door was breached. They'd made a big mistake, though. If they had only cut the hinges, then the lock, they could have simply kicked in the door 15 or 20 minutes ago.

Noah had been ignoring his hand, but he couldn't help glancing at it for a moment. The weirdest thing to him was that there was no pain at all. It was just a useless lump of flesh at the and of his arm.

"Wish we had a couple of grenades," Hilborn said.

"If wishes were gold, we'd all be sitting . . ." Noah started before an idea hit him.

He leaned forward so that his mouth was close to the hole and shouted out, "Sergeant, get ready with the grenades."

Within a few seconds, the torch cut out, and Noah could hear shouts and scrambling on the other side.

Hilborn smothered a laugh.

Their reprieve was short, however. Within two minutes, Noah could hear movement, and he fired a ten-round burst through the hole.

"Very funny in there. Enjoy it while you can, assholes, 'cause we're gonna cut your guts out while you watch—"

The voice cut off with a shriek after Hilborn fired a burst through the hole.

"I guess he shouldn't have gotten so cocky," Noah said.

The torch started cutting again, turning the corner and starting up. Noah knew the end game was coming. In a few minutes, there would be a good-sized hole in the door, big enough for a man to get through. If he and Hilborn could defend the hole, they might live. If they lost their position, they would die.

"Short bursts, Hilborn. Don't waste darts."

"I'm ready."

With only ten centimeters or so for the cut to be complete, the torch went out.

"Oh, just get it over with," Noah said. "Let's get it on."

There was some shouting on the other side, but nothing that Noah could make out. He couldn't imagine what they'd be discussing. Surely, they already had a plan on what to do once the breach was completed. If they hadn't figured it out yet, all the better for the two Marines. Better yet would be if they had no plan at all, and just wanted a brawl. He didn't know how many men were out there, but if they were a mob, he and Hilborn had a much better chance of pulling it off.

Finally, the commotion on the other side seemed to die off, and the torch started up again. Just before the cut was completed, Noah, his nerves on edge, fired a five-round burst through the hole.

The torch immediately cut off and a voice shouted, "Cease fire! Cease fire!"

Noah looked up and Hilborn, confused.

Why would I cease fire?

In a much clearer voice, as if someone had their mouth close to the round hole cut earlier, a woman's voice said, "Cease fire in there. Who are you?"

Noah looked at Hilborn again and shrugged before saying, "I'm Sergeant Major Noah Lysander, United Federation Marine Corps. And who the grubbing hell are you?"

"I'm Security Specialist Six Anneka Larsen, Fortuna Station. We're here to help you, so if you don't mind, can you not fire on us?"

"Oh, thank God," Jackson said from behind them, but Noah wanted more proof than someone simply making claims."

"How about some proof of that?" he asked.

There was a pause, then something was pushed through the hole to fall on the deck. Noah resisted the initial urge to dive out of the way and instead picked up the object. It was a badge for the Fortuna Station Security Force, #4117. He tossed the badge to Hilborn, who looked at it, shrugged, and tossed it back to him.

It looked real, but even if it was, that didn't prove that those outside the hatch were security. Still, it made sense.

"Cover the hatch," he told Hilborn. "If this is a trap, you waste them and get this hatch closed."

Noah reached up, and with only the slightest hesitation, hit the hatch release. With barely a whisper, the door opened to six people in blue uniforms. Three bodies in civilian clothes (whether alive or dead, Noah didn't know) were on the deck. Another three people were sitting alongside the bulkhead, looking morose, hands zip-tied behind them.

"Sergeant Major, we're glad to find you alive," a short-haired woman in uniform said.

"Not half as glad as we are," Noah replied. "And if you don't mind, we'd really like to get off this garbage scow."

FS MOUNT FUJI

Chapter 17
Esther

"So, what have you decided about your hand?" Esther asked her twin.

Noah held up his arm, then rotated it, looking at his fingers. The hand had not been as badly injured as they'd first thought. The ship's surgeon told them that the disrupter blast had hit the knuckles of his right hand as he'd held his M90 out to the side to fire. Those three fingers were lost, and his forefinger damaged. He should be fine to go through regen, but that would take anywhere from six months to a year, depending on how well his body took to it. And that would mean Noah would have to be detached from the battalion.

"I'm thinking prosthetics. Doc says he can get externals shipped here, and I can use them to get around until after we get off the deployment."

Esther felt a rush of relief. She knew she should be concerned with her brother and his health, but she also wanted—no, needed—him with her. External prostheses were not the long-term solution, but he should be able to perform his duties without much of a problem.

"Thank you," she said, feeling that she should say something more, but not quite knowing what. This was just one more time where Noah had her back.

"I've gone over the reports and watched the recordings," she said, changing the subject. "You performed well, not that I expected anything less. I'm putting Hilborn up for a Bronze Star and Tenine for a BC1. Captain Peaslee's being nominated for a Legion of Merit."

She waited for the next question, but instead of what she expected, Noah asked, "What about the chief?"

"Not my call. Not General Lace-Reimer's call. Commander Anderson told me he thinks Chief Bostick's being put in for a Bronze Star."

Noah nodded, then said, "He was a good man. Just got caught in the wrong place."

Esther waited a few more moments, and when Noah didn't say anything else, she said, "I can't put you in for anything, you know. I mean, you'll get your Purple Heart, but I can't put you in for a medal."

"Article 4004.2b," Noah said.

Of course, he would look that up. Why am I not surprised?

Article 4004.2b for the UCMJ prohibited award recommendations made by relatives. It was an old change to the regs, from back 200 years when nepotism reigned within the Navy and, to an extent, the Corps. But the reg was still on the books.

"I thought Commander Anderson could put you up for something, but as your deployed commanding officer, it has to be me. I'm sorry about that."

If he was bothered by the slight, he didn't show it. "No big deal, Ess. I just did my job."

"You deserve something, though. You really did well. There's no doubt in my mind that you saved your group."

"Except for the chief."

"Yes, except for him. But you saved the rest. It was a very, very close thing, you know."

And it had been close. Another six minutes, and the violent passengers would have broken in, and Esther had no doubt as to what they would have done. Noah had delayed them just long enough for the security team to reach them.

On the bridge, it had never gotten that close. It was much more secure, and Captain Peaslee had been able to seal it off. But even with the bridge secure, if engineering had fallen, the ship could have been rerouted to wherever the rioting passengers wanted to take it. Without question, Noah had saved the ship and countless lives. As it was, over 300 people had been killed in the violence.

"I just, well, I wish I could put you up for something."

"Ess, don't worry about it. I don't care."

Esther wondered if that was true. A long-ago general, Napoleon Bonaparte, had once said of awards, "A soldier will fight long and hard for a bit of colored ribbon." But if anyone didn't care about awards, it would be her brother.

"Well, I just wanted you to know how I felt, Noah. And now, we need to start thinking about the advance party. I'm sending Captain Tranh to lead it. When we pull into Friesland, he'll return with his party by commercial liner. Do you want to be on it? I mean, you can get a head start on your permanent prosthetics."

"What, and miss Friesland?" Noah said with a laugh. "No, I'll stick around, I think, and return with the main body. You can't get rid of me that easily, Ess."

"Kind of a waste, though, isn't it? All the fine Friesland beer, and you don't even drink?" Esther said, glad they'd moved beyond awards and into their sibling give-and-take, just like when they were kids.

"There's lots more to Friesland than beer, sister dear. And I've never been there. We've got six days there, right? And I intend on enjoying all six of them."

"OK, you win. You'll come back with the main body. But who're we going to send to assist Tranh?" she asked, getting back to the business of commanding the battalion.

"I'm thinking Top Reston. He's got a new daughter who he's anxious to meet, and he'd be up to the task."

"Reston? OK, I can accept that," Esther said. "But I want the rest identified, too. We've got two more weeks before Friesland, and a lot to get done. I'd like your recommendations by COB so I can run them by the XO and Three."

And just like that, Noah was all business as the two of them planned the battalion's return.

LAST STOP

Chapter 18
Noah

"I still don't know why you don't go to Tarawa," Esther said as he pulled to a stop outside of the terminal. "It's free leave, Noah."

He had thought about going to Tarawa during the post-deployment leave, but in the end, with Major Howard getting promoted and his wetting down, he didn't want to interfere as the family celebrated that.

"I told you, Ess, I need to get used to Three Musketeers," he said, the excuse he'd decided to use.

He tapped the fingers on the hover dash, making a hollow sound. The "Three Musketeers," as he'd started calling the fingers and half a hand, had been ready by the time they'd returned. It had taken just two hours to amputate the dead fingers and replace them with state-of-the-art prosthetics. Within another four hours, they were part of him. He was still learning some of the finer feedback impulses, and that would take time, but as far as using them, it was as if he'd had them all his life. He'd planned on going through regen after his tour with the battalion was over, but now he was considering skipping regen and just sticking with the robo-fingers.

Their father had gone through regen, and he'd been one of the unlucky ones to contract the Brick, the Boosted Regeneration Cancer. The research leaned to the fact that genetics didn't have much to do with contracting the Brick, but Noah wasn't sure about that. If he didn't need regeneration at all, all the better.

"OK, but I feel bad that you're going to be all alone with a ghost battalion."

"Don't worry about me. There'll be plenty to do. We've got Valiant Tension coming up, and I can start the planning."

"That's in five months, Noah. There'll be time to get ready for that."

"Never too early, Ess. But look, you need to catch your shuttle. You and Jim, you have a good time, even if I don't have a clue as to why you're doing this. I mean, you're going to dive with them by choice? Isn't being a Marine dangerous enough?"

"They said they only lose one diver per dive, so all I have to do is swim faster than the next slowest diver."

Noah shook his head, refusing to laugh. It was an old line, probably going back to Babylonian times, but it was so Esther. He got out of the hover and walked back to the trunk, taking out Esther's bag.

"Look, you have a good time, clear your head, and get back here ready to work. I'll mind the fort while you're gone."

She turned on the bag's Follow Me and looked up as if to say something. Instead, she reached out and pulled him into a hug, much to his surprise. He hesitated only a moment before he put his arms around her and squeezed.

"Try and have some fun during the break, little bro," she whispered into his ear.

"I will, and you, too, sis," he replied.

They hugged for a few more moments before Esther pushed him away, quickly brushing what looked to be a tear from her eye.

"Take care of yourself," she said.

"I'm not the one who's paying to flirt with danger, Ess. You take care of yourself."

He watched her walk off to ticketing, her bag trundling behind her.

"Sir, this is a loading and unloading zone only. Please move your vehicle," a spaceport auto concierge said as it rolled up beside him.

"I'm on my way," he said, looking back to catch another glimpse of Esther, but she was already lost in the crowd.

The concierge waited until Noah was in his hover and pulled it out before it went off to search for other transgressors.

Now, what the heck am I going to do for the next two weeks? he wondered as he drove out of the spaceport.

EARTH

Chapter 19
Esther

Esther hovered at the edge of the Monad Shoal as the water began to lighten. She peered into the darker water of the deep ocean, straining to pick up signs of motion. A few fish swam by, oblivious to her, but she ignored them.

And then suddenly, as if beamed by a Hollybolly transporter, the shark was there, big and menacing, its fins out as it postured. Esther gulped in shock, her air gauge momentarily flashing red until the auxiliary tank gave her curtain a shot of O2.

Subconsciously, she reached to her side, piercing Jim's curtain and taking his hand in hers, comforted by the feel of his warm grip.

"Freeze, divers, freeze," Jojo, their divemaster said.

The big thresher swam to within ten meters of the group of five divers before it gracefully turned and swam along the contour of the reef. At the resort the day before, Kayee, the head divemaster, had briefed them that the local threshers were one of the few breeds of endothermic sharks, that is, they are capable of creating their own body heat. That hadn't meant much to Esther, but seeing how quickly and fluidly the shark moved, she appreciated that biological tidbit.

Esther hadn't been overly keen on making the trip to Malapascua, a tiny island off the coast of Cebu in the Philippines. But Jim, as usual, wanted to explore Earth. Their first official date had been to celebrate the Songkran water festival in Thailand. Their next leave together had been to the Holi Festival in Maharashtra, India (they still said "Holi re Holi puranachi poli" to each other, which meant something like "Holi, Holi, sweet bread," when they went to Sweet Doughnuts for a guilty snack). A year later, it was the rather eye-opening Kanamara Penis Festival in Kawasaki, and Esther had been given the "honor" of being one of the penis riders, straddling the huge wooden phallus as it plummeted down the hill. Two years ago, it had been the Mud Crab Festival in Bali.

The resurgence in traditional festivals throughout human space was part cultural, part money-making, and Jim drank it all in. When he proposed the shark dive for her post-deployment leave, she had hesitated. A spa on Gideon seemed much more relaxing, but he'd been so excited that she'd agreed.

And now, as she watched the shark disappear from sight, she was glad she'd done it.

The tiny island, just two kilometers long, embraced the past. Esther could imagine the Filipinos of the Twenty-second Century living in the exact same way. But the prime draw of Malapascua was the threshers. Very limited numbers of heavily regulated divers were allowed at the shoal each dawn, where, for probably millions of years, thresher sharks swam up from the deep to cleaning stations manned by small fish. Esther had been frustrated by all the rules: don't touch the bottom, keep your hands clasped at all times, don't approach a shark, no flash photography, stay with the divemaster, no venting of the airsuits, no attempts to join the "30-Meter Deep Club," and a hundred other rules. Esther felt that they were being caged in the water for the sharks' pleasure, not the other way around.

Then there was the hullabaloo about her qualifications. At anything over 25 meters, a diver had to be Class C certified. Jim, of course, had ocean diving as one of his many skills, and he was E certified. Esther was a military diver, which was easily as advanced as an E-cert, but she didn't have a civilian qualification. Kayee had to clear Esther with the UAM Environmental Proctor before she was allowed to dive.

Yes, UAM. Malapascua, which was in the Federation, was run by the United Assembly of Man as a "Biological Protection Zone." Here, on Earth, in the Federation, Esther had to get permission from a UAM flunky. It didn't seem right.

As a military diver, her dive gear was designed for long periods underwater. It was basic, sturdy, and foolproof. They didn't use airsuits, which were fine for casual civilian dives but were not robust enough for military use. When given her airsuit the previous afternoon for their check-off dive, she'd no idea how to actually don it. After arguing with the UAM idiot for 30 minutes that she was an experienced diver, she wasn't about to ask for help. By watching the others don their suits, she figured it out. It felt weird, though, as if she was simply wearing her bikini as the four divers and Jojo waded out into the house reef. She'd even held her breath as her head went under, but the suit worked, surrounding her with a layer of air. The suit generator at the small of her back powered the curtain and extracted O2 directly from the water. The tiny high-compression tank supplemented the O2 when needed. The depth control kept her hovering a meter above the bottom—but Jojo had override capability. Bother a shark or break any of the rules, and she'd be rising to the surface whether she wanted to or not.

For the next hour, the five swam along the edge of the shoal. Six other groups from other resorts were in the water as well, but Esther ignored them. Seven more sharks made appearances, swimming in like ancient ghosts before fading away from sight.

"OK, folks," Jojo said at last, "Time to surface. We've bothered the sharks enough for today."

The air suit didn't have private circuits, but she leaned into Jim's face, breaking into his curtain.

"This was amazing, Jim. Thank you for suggesting it."

She gave him a quick peck, then pulled back as he tried to return the kiss with more enthusiasm.

"Surface now, you two," Jojo said, sounding stern.

Feeling like a schoolgirl caught beneath the bleachers with her boyfriend, Esther laughed as she rose, but not before Jim reached through her bubble to pinch her bikini-clad butt. Joining the 30-Meter Deep Club was sounding better and better.

There'll be time for that, Jimmy-boy, she thought. *Jojo's watching.*

They had four hours before their next dive, and their room was only 30 meters from the beach. The two could be in the cabana within a minute of getting ashore.

The sun was barely over the eastern horizon as they climbed out of the water and onto the old-fashion dive boat, complete with bamboo outriggers to each side. Marine divers came out of the water wet, so it felt strange to be sitting chatting with the other two divers, excitedly relating each shark sighting, but completely dry. Maybe there was something to be said for civilian dive equipment after all.

The quiet electric hydrojet (can't have anything loud enough or creating vibrations that could bother the sharks) pushed the boat quickly to the shore. The four divers agreed to meet for breakfast at the in-house resort restaurant, the ancient Craic House (where the tocino was supposed to be delicious, at least according to what Noah had told her before she left).

Kayee was waiting for them as they left the beach; waiting for Esther, that is.

Hell, what have I done now? Kissing your husband scares the sharks?

"Colonel Lysander, I've a message for you. You're to get on your PA immediately. The official one."

As always, Esther was traveling with both her personal PA and her Marine Corps-issued PA. She may be on leave, and probably the only leave she'd have while in command of the battalion, but a commander commanded 24-7. That responsibility never took leave. She was supposed to keep the Marine Corps PA with her at all times, but no electronic devices were allowed at Monad Shoal.

She glanced at Jim. He smiled, but she could see the sudden scrunching of his eyebrows, a sure sign of stress with him.

"You go find out what they want, Ess. I'll get a table at the Craic for us. Tocino, right? Isn't that what Noah said?"

"Yeah, that was it. Don't worry, Jim. It's probably some routine stuff that needs my OK. I'll see you there in a few," she said, leaning to give him another soft kiss on his cheek.

The rooms were old-style cabanas, not luxurious, but still romantic, what with the ocean breezes, swaying palm trees, and blue water just steps away. Esther entered, opened the safe, and took out the PA. She let it read her right eye, and a stream of messages appeared on the display. She read the highest priority message, then slowly lowered the PA as she stared at the wall, a small brown gecko capturing her attention as it bobbed its head up and down.

She stood like that for a few moments, then with a sigh, acknowledged the message. Stepping back outside, she walked over the sand to the Craic House where Jim was chatting with Dierdre and Morgan, their fellow divers. He was laughing at something one of them had said, but Esther knew it was forced.

She caught his eye and motioned him to join her. She could see his entire posture drop for a second before he forced a broad smile on his face as he bounded over to her. Jim was cleared for Level 4 messages, of course, so she simply opened up the recall.

They'd been on the island for less than a day, and now the battalion, just back from deployment, was being recalled. The message didn't say why, only gave her an itinerary back to Last Stop. A water taxi was being sent to pick her up with an ETA in 18 minutes (even the Federation military had to obey the UAM strictures on travel on Malapascua). She was to be taken to the Cebu mainland at Daayanbatan where a shuttle would take her to the Clark Spaceport for further transport back to Last Stop.

"OK, let's go," Jim said, turning to go back to the cabana.

She grabbed his arm and stopped him, saying, "You don't have to go. Your leave is still in place. You stay and enjoy yourself."

"I only enjoy myself when I do these with you. You know that, right?"

She smiled, then gave him a little punch on his upper arm.

"You are so full of it, Jim Aylsworth, but I love you all the more for it."

"We saw the threshers, anyway, and that's what we came for. One more thing checked off our bucket list."

Your bucket list, Jimmy-boy, but yes.

"Besides, we've got 18 minutes. Two minutes to pack, then sixteen to, well . . . ?"

"Oh, that's all you can think of, Colonel Aylsworth?"

"Unless you don't want—"

"Move your ass, Jimmy-boy!" Esther said, darting forward to the cabana. "Time's a-wasting!"

LAST STOP

Chapter 20
Noah

"Seems like I was just leaving you off here," Noah said as Esther came through immigration and out to the passenger pick-up.

"Don't remind me," Esther said with a sour expression on her face.

"Did you at least stare death in the face?"

"If you mean, did I dive with the sharks, then yes. I got the recall right after coming out of the water."

"And you're alive, so I guess that's a good thing, right?"

"You've got such a way with words," she said as he loaded her bag into the trunk of his Fiat-Westerly Avo. She got into the passenger seat, and as Noah pulled out, asked, "What're our numbers?"

"We're at 76%. The XO's arriving in two hours, and all of the company commanders are already on board. We've got six Marines and a corpsman who've not acknowledged the recall. I've got local authorities tracking them all down."

"So, I couldn't pick much up on the transit. Do you have anything more for me?"

Noah hesitated for a moment. His Avo was not a secure space, and much of what he knew was classified.

He didn't think anyone had bugged his old hover, though, so he said, "It's our old friends The Brotherhood sticking their nose where it doesn't belong."

"The Brotherhood? They're getting to be a pain in the ass, Noah, I swear. They're not acting like allies against the Klethos, you know."

Noah did know. When the war with the Klethos had broken out, there had been a groundswell of unity among humanity. It was us against them. But as the war settled into a type of routine, partisanship started to rear its head again. Sure, humanity lost some planets, but they'd regained some and even taken over a few that had been Capy worlds before the Klethos took them. Even when they lost a human world, the UAM Relocation Bureau had the evacuation down to a science. When Kloster was lost, with over 12 billion inhabitants, the UAM managed to remove every man, woman, and child within the allotted three weeks.

The result of this was that the war with the Klethos had almost become routine, a part of the landscape, and without a dire threat, the unity started to pull apart. And as far as the Federation was concerned, The Brotherhood had been the main instigator of friction. For supposed allies, two powers that had never fought a war against each other, The Brotherhood had become a major irritant to the Federation.

"So, what are they doing now?"

"What do you know of Nayi Bharat?" Noah asked her.

"Nayi Bharat? Not much. I mean, I know they're a Hindi world, Class B, I think I remember. They had a referendum a few years back to leave the Federation, but that failed big time. So, what's happening there now?"

"Well, it seems that the Azaad Andolan party, which initiated the referendum, is not taking their defeat lightly. They've evolved into an armed faction that has promised to take over the planet by force, if necessary."

"And . . . ?"

"And they are well-armed. Mostly Gentry weapons—"

"I swear, we should shut down that planet's arms factories," Esther muttered.

Noah ignored the comment and continued, "As I was saying, they've got Gentry weapons and are better armed than the local militia."

"Since you mentioned The Brotherhood, I'm to assume that they're involved with this?"

"Looks like they're funding the AA, as the Azaad Andolan is referring to its military arm, even providing ships to deliver the arms."

"So, let the UAM handle this. That's what they're there for, after all," Esther said.

"I don't think we can afford to wait, and neither does the council. Last week, an FCDC company and a militia regiment were overrun by the AA forces. Intel thinks the AA are going to make a stab at taking Raipur, which is a major industrialized city. We're supposed to stop that."

"So, these AA overran a local regiment and an FCDC company, and we're supposed to go in and stop them?"

"That's basically it in a nutshell, Ess. The powers that be think that if we bloody their noses, we can freeze them in their tracks until the UAM gets off their collective asses and shut off the arms pipeline."

"So, we're not supposed to pacify a planet with . . . how many people?"

"About one-point-two billion. And no. Just stop the advance on Jaipur."

"Well, thank God for small favors. They don't expect the impossible, just the improbable."

"Semper fi, do or die," Noah said.

"Yeah, right. It's the 'die' part that concerns me. This has all the hallmarks of a shit sandwich." She paused a moment, looking out of the hover's window as they got on the expressway to the base. "And we're back on the *Fujiyama*?"

"Roger that. She's the sector's Navy secondary alert force."

The Navy and Marines had been designating returning deployment forces as secondary alert forces for almost 15 years now. On the one hand, it made sense. The ship and Marines units had been certified, and they were used to working together. On the other hand, there was a degree of deployment fatigue that set in after so much time in space, and their abruptly canceled leave had not been nearly enough to rejuvenate the Marines and sailors nor conduct first level maintenance on their gear. Noah had been working hard on that while most of the battalion had started on leave, and they were not in too bad shape, but the *Mount Fuji* was much more maintenance-intensive, and there was no way that the ship was at 100%.

At least the aircon finally works.

"When do we embark?"

"Four days."

"Four freaking days? Oh, I'm so glad they're giving us so much time," she said, sarcasm heavy in her voice.

Noah didn't reply. He knew his sister, and as she became quiet, he knew her brain was going 100 kilometers per hour as she went over what she had to do to get the battalion ready. Four days really wasn't reasonable, but that is what they had, and they'd get it done. Marines have been doing that for centuries, and some things never changed.

NAYI BHARAT

Chapter 21
Esther

"Yea, though I walk through the valley of death, I shall fear no evil—because I'm the fiercest mother-fucker in the valley," Esther muttered the centuries-old adage as she followed the battalion's progress.

Major Kurtzman looked up at her in surprise, then quickly went back to his display as if he hadn't heard her. She was in a foul mood, and everyone around her knew it.

The operations order she and the Three developed took advantage of her battalion's strengths of mobility and fire support, something she thought they needed in facing over 10,000 Azaad Andolan fighters. Her intent had been to focus her battalion's power to strike and crush specific and limited units, then retreat before the mass of enemy could react before doing it all over again. She didn't have numerical superiority, but she could have localized numerical superiority if she could choose the time and place of contact.

As a courtesy, Esther had to brief the local government and militia, and they hadn't liked the plan at all. They wanted to reassure the local populace that things were well in hand, and they wanted a militia presence with the Marines. A complaint had gone up through the Federation Administrator all the way to Earth, and the word had come down from on high. Esther was to comply with Nayi Bharat requests for a more obvious and visible operations plan.

So now, First Battalion, Eight Marines, was marching up the oddly-named Mary Anne Valley, and the AA knew exactly where it was. The battalion had given up the ability to maneuver to choose the time and place of contact.

Jaipur was located at the end of a huge box canyon under which was an almost unlimited supply of geothermal power. There was one major avenue in and out of the city, and that was through the valley. Like Romans leaving the Eternal City to fight the Gauls, the battalion had formed up and marched out, led by a militia company. There had even been a band to play as they passed the provincial center.

Immediately after leaving the city, she had moved the militia to the rear of the column, telling the commander in no uncertain terms that he was to stay out of the way of the Marines. With Charlie Company leading, and the battalion stretched out over a klick, she pushed the pace past the first chokepoint and where she could bring up Alpha Company and move in a modified wedge with two companies up, one back, and the headquarters in the middle. The militia company trailed the battalion and was designated as a reserve force, but Esther didn't plan to engage them unless absolutely necessary.

Colonel Falstaff had been given the unenviable task of telling Esther that her original operations order had to be shit-canned, and he used the phrase "meeting engagement" to describe how the forces would initiate contact. Esther could tell that he didn't believe that any more than she did. The AA would not be marching down the valley to meet the battalion head on. They would ambush the battalion, pure and simple. Esther would commence the coming fight by walking into the opposing commander's kill zone.

All Esther could do was to try and foresee where that kill zone would be and where the ambush would be sprung. She had a fleet of drones spread out before the battalion, and overhead, the *Mount Fuji* was scanning. And there were people in the mountains on either side of her—lots of people. The rocky terrain precluded nice firm numbers, but the Azaad Andolan couldn't evade all of the scanners. Lieutenant Commander Nunez-Kline, the *Mount Fuji's* Intel officer, didn't think the numbers the battalion was passing were enough to be a threat, and Esther tended to agree. They were still close to Jaipur, and if the AA sprang an ambush now, the remaining militia in the city were close enough to come join the fight. Still, she hated to let any enemy get behind her. She had the entire area targeted, and once the fight began, she'd requested that the *Mount Fuji* rain death on the hills. She might not have the mobility she'd originally envisioned, but the *Mount Fuji* was still a powerful resource.

Esther stared at her screen, trying to will it to reveal the AA's ambush site. The battalion's combat AI kept popping up locations, giving probabilities, but nothing struck a chord with her. Displays, even the best of them, just didn't give the same representation as real life.

"Major Kutzman, I'm stepping outside. You run it from in here."

She activated her helmet's display field and stepped between the members of the Alpha Command as they sat at their stations and out the back hatch. The *Hot Shot* slowly lumbered on at a walking pace.

It felt good to be out of the confines of the armored personnel carrier. She'd never felt comfortable inside armor, even the PICS. To her, an Aardvark only represented a target. The enemy spent hundreds of thousands of credits on weapons to take out armor, but as a grunt, a dart or round cost a credit each. By pure economics, that meant they were spending more on armor than on infantry, so that would be their targets.

Intellectually, she knew that logic was faulty, but emotionally, she felt more comfortable on foot. But that wasn't the reason she debarked the command vehicle. She wanted to get a better feel for the terrain, to decide where she would set an ambush if the shoe were on the other foot.

Moments after her boots hit the deck, two of Captain Gill's Bravo Company Marines stepped forward to flank her. A squad had been positioned around the trac to provide close-in security.

"Corporal Spain, how about you and Lance Corporal Thuy step back a few paces. You're making it pretty obvious, don't you think."

"Oh, sorry ma'am," Spain said, falling back and drifting to the side.

Should have brought out a rifle, she thought.

Even without the two Marines on either side of her, if she was spotted, and without a rifle of some sort, it wouldn't take a genius to figure out she was a prime target. The nearest high ground was less than a klick away, and that was well within a sniper's range, even if that sniper hadn't any specified training. She put that thought out of her head and started studying the terrain, referring to her map display, then taking a look at the real thing.

"You OK, Ess?" Noah asked over the P2P.

"Sure. No problem."

"I see you're on foot. Any good reason for that?"

Esther swung around and searched, finally seeing Noah walking behind the *Hot Shot*, about 50 meters back.

"I needed to get the lay of the land."

"Well, get it quick. You're kind of a prime target out there."

"So's the Aardvark. A big one."

She heard him sigh, then he cut the connection. Putting him out of her mind, she went back to her terrain study, trying to put herself into the mind of the AA commander. A good ambush location had a kill zone that could be completely covered with fire and provided cover and concealment for the ambushers. There were several likely locations along the way, but the more obvious, the least likely they'd be chosen. Then, there was the arty back in Jaipur. The militia had a battery-minus of old, but reliable Harrison 105's. The Marines were still barely within the reach of the guns and would be for a little more distance. The ambushers would want to be on the defilade side of the city where the arty couldn't touch them.

She pulled up real-view overlay, superimposing the battalion's position. The lead elements of Charlie and Alpha were 300 meters ahead of her and a few hundred meters short of the second major bend in the highway where it turned left and to the west.

That would be a decent enough ambush site, she thought after checking the arty's fields of fire.

An ambush just around the bend could split the battalion if the AA hit it while it was halfway through, and the lead elements of the battalion would suffer intensive plunging fire. It wasn't perfect, though. It would leave the first ambushing unit vulnerable to flanking. Good, but not good enough, Esther decided.

At that moment, her display indicated possible enemy about where she'd been contemplating where the ambushers might be.

"What are you getting just past Robin," Esther asked Captain Montoya.

"Looks like there could be a good-sized force up there. Nothing clear."

"Spoof or real," she asked the S2.

"I don't know. I don't think their spoofing capabilities are very sophisticated. We know they've got Gentry gear," he said as if that answered her question.

Gentry was the universal depot for cheap military equipment, available to anyone with the credit to buy them. The planet's weaponry was basic, but capable. Their reputation for surveillance and countersurveillance was not nearly so complementary. In most cases, that gear was merely thrown in a deal to sweeten the pot.

"What's your analysis?"

"Somebody's up there, ma'am. How many, I don't know. But there've been people in the hills above us since we left Jaipur."

Esther considered what she'd just said. There were AA fighters up there, but were they spotters or fighters? The site was decent enough for an ambush, but not the best.

But they wouldn't pick the best!

A tsunami of certainty flooded over her.

"Stop the battalion!" she ordered Major Kutzman as she sprinted for the command trac. "Digger-Three," she passed to Charlie Company on the command net, "halt in place and set up a hasty defense. Send a squad forward to check around the bend. I want them visible. Charlie-One, wait two minutes, then I want you to send both PICS platoons up here," she ordered Captain McLamb and swiping a route up the near side of the slope. "I think you'll find a force there oriented to the west. Crush them."

She bolted back inside the *Hot Shot* as all eyes swiveled to her.

"Lieutenant Creighton, can you give me the cannon at 5 megajoules and wide dispersion?" she asked the *Mount Fuji's* naval gunfire liaison officer.

"Uh . . . yes, ma'am. But five megajoules and wide dispersion, that's pretty survivable to protected troops. And, uh, we can't keep it up for long. We've still got the ARG, though."

Esther took a moment to consider that. Creighton was reminding her that atmosphere dissipation was the bane of space-based energy weapons, requiring huge amounts of power to get that energy focused on the target on the ground. The Atmospheric Railgun got around that by sending shells at amazingly high speeds through the atmosphere, each shell being a self-contained pulse generator which energized into a plasma sphere upon detonation. At one kilojoule, though, they didn't have a large effective casualty radius, and the battalion was probably opposing dispersed troops.

"No, I need a wider brush. And I don't think they're too protected. I'll have PICS Marines there, and I can't have you knocking them out or degrading them, so keep it at five megajoules. I want the *Fujiyama* to fire here at my command," she told him, touching the spot on the screen.

"Do you think this is it, Colonel?" Major Kutzman asked.

"Yeah, I do. If I'm wrong, though, no harm, no foul."

"XO," she passed on the P2P. "We're initiating an assault on what I think might be the ambush. Monitor what's happening and keep an eye on the flanks. We know we bypassed AA fighters, and I don't want them converging on us."

She pulled up the overhead and zoomed in. A squad of Charlie Marines was creeping forward as if trying to keep anyone from the west from spotting them. Of course, if Esther were correct, then the "L" in the ambush would be the AA to the east, the ones she wanted Alpha's PICS Marines to take out. Hopefully, when they saw the Charlie squad, they'd focus on them for the few moments it would take the PICS Marines to scale the hill and hit them.

"Let McLamb know we're going to spray his Marines with the *Fujiyama*," she told Creighton.

"And make sure he doesn't send any straight leg grunts, including him, after the PICS," she told Major Kutzman.

Knowing McLamb, he'd run after his two platoons to be able to command them, but without the PICS armor, the *Mount Fuji* would cook him.

Esther scanned the overhead view for a moment before the Three said, "Digger-One's PICS are on the way."

Esther switched her view to one of her dragonflies. The PICS were at full countermeasures, but the combat AI meshed the systems, and she could easily see the PICS as they charged up the near side of the hill, climbing almost 400 meters in 35 seconds, which was a pretty respectable feat. PICS were great on flat ground, but steep terrain was more problematic.

They crested the hill and started down on the other side. For a moment, Esther thought she'd been mistaken, which was not a lethal mistake but might reveal how she intended to fight this battle. But then, a single kinetic round reached out, impacting on one of the Marines. A moment later, the hillside opened up with fire, both energy and kinetics.

"Now, Creighton!" Esther shouted.

A moment later, her display went red as the meson beam hit the hillside. If she'd been at the scene, she might see some wavering in the air as it ionized, but that would be about it. The AI turned the beam red on the battalion monitors, though, for easier identification.

That diminished but did not stop the incoming fire as the Marines rushed the ambushers and started rolling up their flank.

"We've got anti-armor," Sergeant Jeff shouted out.

Esther switched her display just as two missiles slammed into the Marines, taking out one PICS.

"Send Kingery up the west slope as fast as he can and get fire on the far side," Esther told Major Kutzman.

"Creighton, what do you have for me? I need something on the hills."

"We've got a Tungsicle loaded and ready for bear. The standoff is 500 meters, though."

The Gravity Dropped-1905, the "Tungsicle," was a simple, four-meter long column of crystallized ceramic-covered tungsten. It could be boosted with strap-on motors or shot from a modified rail on the *Mount Fuji*, but gravity took over to get the round to the surface. At 80 centimeters wide, it was a hefty 155,000 kg of unstoppable penetration power. It was designed to take out hardened targets, but hitting with the equivalent of 15 tons of TNT, it would wreak havoc on troops as well. It was the very embodiment of the Navy gunners' motto *Velocitas Eradico*, or "I, who am speed, eradicate."

That'll sure get their attention.

She selected one of their pre-planned targets where she guessed AA fighters would be.

"How long for impact?"

"If we rail it, four minutes. If not, ten."

Too long! Alpha's PICS Marines would be within 400 meters of impact, but they were built to take it. Charlie's Marines would still be climbing for the next several minutes, but at four minutes, the first of them would be at the crest and only 300 meters or so from the impact site.

"Canc' the Tungsicle. Just give me whatever the ship can put out all along here," she said, swiping a broad line along both sides of the valley beyond the bend.

"I can give you 30 more seconds before we have to recharge the cannons."

A cruiser could fire in space almost indefinitely, but even a cruiser was more limited firing through an atmosphere. The *Mount Fuji* was a nice firing platform, but she was no cruiser. Her two cannons needed cooling and recharging after sustained fire of any length of time.

"Do it! Then give me the ARG when the cannons are offline."

Esther sat back a moment, gathering her thoughts. Around her, the quiet murmur of the Alpha Command Marines as they subvocalized into their headsets reached her. A strong part of her wanted to jump into each of their comms, to make sure they were doing their jobs, but as Noah was so fond of reminding her, she couldn't let herself get trapped in the weeds. She had the proverbial "big picture" to worry about.

She turned to her command display which offered the same data as her face shield, but over a larger footprint, so it was easier for her to comprehend. McLamb's two PICS platoons were sweeping through the "L" of the ambush. Lieutenant Weisskopf's shielding was down to 82%, which was the lowest of any of them;

whether that was from enemy action or the ship's meson beams, Esther didn't know. Two Marines were down, both WIA. Sergeant Trotter's PICS had initiated shut-down procedures to stabilize him. PFC Corina West was unhurt, but her PICS was down hard.

A moment of panic hit her, but just before she called West, she saw that Weisskopf had already hit her up with a P2P. A quick replay, and she saw that he'd ordered her not to combat molt, to stay inside her ruined PICS until the *Mount Fuji* stopped firing.

Let them do their job, Lysander, she reminded her self. *They know what they're doing.*

Despite her own admonition, she pulled up Weisskopf's feed. She watched for a moment as he pushed over the rough ground, directing his Marines. Twenty meters in front of him, one of his Marines lowered his 20mm and blasted at an unseen enemy. With reluctance, she reduced the feed and sent it to the top right of her display.

The *Mount Fuji's* meson cannon was offline, and the ARG was peppering the hillsides with rounds that bloomed like deadly flowers on her display. She wasn't confident that they'd have any significant effect. They could take out point targets, but against area targets, it was more a matter of luck.

And then, other detonation blooms started appearing on her display, these indicated by the yellow of enemy fire. Intel knew the AA had received tubes, and there'd probably been enough time to get them operational. Most of the rounds were targeting Alpha's PICS Marines, but others were being lofted over the hills to land among Bravo—and the command trac. Major Kutzman immediately gave the order to the *Hot Shot's* commander to move to the left where they could get into defilade.

"Do we have a location on their tubes?" Esther asked Montoya.

"I'm getting it now. Looks to be 32 klicks to the northwest."

Which was well beyond the reach of the militia's artillery back in Jaipur and beyond the reach of any of her organic weapons.

"Lieutenant Creighton, shift fire of the railgun to the target at . . . eight-four-three-six, four-four-seven-nine. Then give me a Tungsicle, railed in, at the same coordinates."

"I can't do both. We've only got the one rail."

Shit, of course. Think, Lysander!

"Tungsicle first, then ARG rounds."

"Roger that. I'm on it."

She didn't bother to shift the targeting for the two cannons. The G-298's the AA received were hardened against energy weapons. A direct hit with an ARG round might have an effect, but not the ship's cannons.

Esther looked over her options. She had three line companies, weapons company, the militia infantry and arty, and the *Mount Fuji*. She could pull up Captain Gill to become the point of main effort, but her distrust of the militia infantry's readiness and willingness to fight held her back. The AA they'd bypassed were maneuvering, and her instincts told her they'd be attacking the battalion's rear. She needed Bravo and the arty to blunt any attack from that direction.

At the base of the L ambush, Alpha's two PICS platoons were advancing readily. Esther didn't know how spread out the AA forces were, but they didn't seem too concentrated, at least those along the high ground. With Charlie now reaching the high ground on the south side of the valley and Alpha on the north side, she could push the battalion forward, sweeping up the flanks of the AA. They might outnumber her, but if they had lined both sides of the valley, they had limited supportability, and Esther could concentrate her forces against relatively smaller numbers of AA at any given time. And if she could get Weapons forward to the bend, then she could start getting heavier weapons to bear.

A blast rocked the Aardvark, but the trac didn't falter. The avatars of two Marines behind the command trac grayed out. She pulled up the names—and felt guilty when she felt relief that neither of them was Noah. Cortez and Willis were still her Marines, and both had just been killed by the incoming arty.

"We need that Tungiscle!" Esther yelled at Lieutenant Creighton.

"Ten seconds," he responded, followed a few moments later by, "Weapon away. Time of impact in two-four-eight seconds."

"Colonel, Charlie is taking fire. Looks like full contact, not a probe," the Three said.

Esther studied her display for a moment, then pulled up Captain Kingery on the P2P to ask, "What's going on, Fred?"

"Third Platoon is in heavy contact," Captain Kingery said. "I think this is part of the main body. I've requested fire support, but they're in close."

"What's the status on Charlie's fire support?" she yelled across the compartment to Top Yunci, her fire support coordinator.

"Can't reach them with arty or mortars, and Lieutenant Creighton's working on the *Fujiyama*," the Top replied.

Esther looked again at her display. "In close" was an understatement. They were almost on top of each other. She understood the AA commander's intent. Despite the AA arty, which was about to be destroyed and knocked out of the equation, the Marines had better weaponry, so he or she was trying to negate the efficacy of those weapons by closing in with the Marines and slugging it out, man-to-man.

If he wants a barroom brawl, I'll give it to him.

The *Hot Shot* dipped down into a streambed, and Esther almost smacked her head against her display. She pushed her feet out under her bench to brace herself. The Aardvark had decent enough stabilization, but it couldn't compensate for everything.

"Ralph, if we catch their tubes, that's going to throw a wrench into their plans. What if we push Alpha forward to take advantage of it?"

Major Kutzman spun 90 degrees in his seat and looked at her for a moment before he shook his head and said, "That'll be 32 klicks away. Yeah, we can take out their tubes, but I don't think it'll do much to shock the ground troops. We'll need something closer."

"Like another Tungsicle, danger close?"

"Exactly."

"OK, do it,"

A wicked smile came over his face as the Three spun all the way around to tap Lieutenant Creighton on the shoulder.

He's right. We need something closer with more immediate shock.

She pulled up Captain McLamb and said, "Wes, we're dropping another Tungsicle, this one much, much closer. We'll give you a heads up, but I'm going to want everyone to take cover. This will be danger close. The moment it hits, I want you in full assault mode. Take advantage of the confusion to push forward. I want you abreast of Charlie and giving him supporting fires."

"Roger that, Colonel. Just give me a head's up."

Major Kutzman swung back to her and said, "The *Fujiyama's* got two Tungsicles left. I'm thinking of dropping one right here." He used his finger to point at the map readout on her display. "We're seeing concentrations of AA moving through here."

"That's about 1300 meters from Alpha's lead elements. That's more than enough."

"And 1200 meters from Charlie."

The impact point he selected was on the north of the valley, same as Alpha. Charlie, while on the south side, was also farther west.

"Do we have a go?"

"Do it. And get word to Alpha and Charlie in time for them to get their heads down."

"We've got movement from the tubes. They're displacing," Captain Montoya said.

"What's the time until impact?" Esther asked as she fed in the Two's display to hers.

"Twenty-six seconds."

Esther watched on her display as the six artillery pieces started to scatter. A Tungsicle hit with a tremendous amount of force, but it was designed for hardened targets. It was not an area weapon. It was going to boil down to whether the Azaad Andolan arty had enough time to get out of the primary blast zone.

The timer ticked down agonizingly slow while the arty pieces moved like ants on meth crystals. Esther gripped the edge of the bench, her knuckles white.

". . . four . . . three . . . two . . . one . . . impact!" Creighton said.

A quick flash lit up the northern horizon.

"I want a BDA," Esther shouted out.

She knew that without people or drones on the scene, she couldn't get anything firm, but she needed to know what happened. The *Mount Fuji* should be able to get something on them.

The ground shook a good ten seconds after impact. Even 32 klicks away, the power of a Tungsicle was awe-inspiring.

"There's too much dust in the air over the impact site to be sure, but it's looking good. Four confirmed kills, and two more look damaged."

Could be worse.

The AA arty had KIA'd four Marines, wounded another ten, and slowed the battalion down. The Cutting Edge needed to regain the momentum. Hopefully, she'd have that momentum after the second Tungiscle hit.

"Where we at, Creighton?"

"About a minute until launch."

Up above them in orbit, Esther knew the gun crews were rushing to get the Tungsicle on the rail, but she needed it now.

"Ralph, let's make sure we're on the same page here. As soon as that big boy hits, I want Alpha to push west along the high ground to the north and provide a base of fire across the valley for Charlie. After Alpha comes abreast, I want them both to push west together providing mutual support. Take it to the AA and roll up their flanks."

"And Bravo?"

"I can't bring Gill into the fight yet. I want Bravo to follow us in trace, but oriented to the rear. I think they're going to have their hands full with probes. We're almost out of arty range, so tell the battery I want them to displace forward in echelon."

"Out of the city? I don't think they'll be too happy with that."

"I don't give a shit if they'll be happy or not. Just get them to do it. They'll still have their infantry between the AA and them to protect their pampered asses.

"And get Creighton to figure out the best use of the ship. I don't want the AA to be able to maneuver and mass. I want the *Fujiyama* to keep their heads down."

"Roger that. I'm on it."

Esther studied her display for a moment, trying not to focus on the two new grayed avatars of Charlie Marines that just popped up and keeping her mind on the bigger picture. She couldn't see anything off-hand that would give the battalion a bigger advantage.

"Wes," she told the Alpha Company commander, "You're really going to need to hit them hard. You've got to relieve pressure on Charlie, then both of you need to kick some ass."

"You can count on me, ma'am."

She knew she didn't need to call him up and tell him the obvious, but it was almost pathologically impossible for her just to sit back and watch things unfold. But sitting back sometimes was what she had to do if she was going to recognize the bigger issues. She promised herself that she was going to stay off the P2P net and let the commanders fight their companies.

She should inform higher headquarters, though, even if they would be monitoring the fight. She reached into her cargo pocket and pulled out the small hadron communicator, the only one in the battalion. She connected with Sector Command, told the duty officer her intentions, then hung up before some admiral could come on the line to grill her.

"We've got increased movement around Bravo," Captain Montoya said. "I'm now estimating 300-400 fighters."

"Three to four hundred?" Esther said, surprised. "I thought it was closer to one hundred."

"That's what our scanners indicated, colonel. But we're getting continual updates."

"Captain Gill already reported increased contact," Major Kutzman added.

Shit, how did I miss that?

She did a data dump, and there was the message.

"AI, increase the priority of company commander messages to level 1."

Her AI prioritized all of the data input flowing across the battalion nets, and she'd been focusing on fire support and enemy disposition, but it should have highlighted Captain Gill's message. She'd been intent on Alpha and Charlie, however, and her AI had that inputted into its algorithm. She needed to look at the entire battalion. Bravo's only casualties had come from the AA arty, but if the 300 to 400 AA fighters were massing on the company, that would soon change.

"Weapon away. Time to impact two-four-seven seconds," the Navy lieutenant announced.

Esther started a timer on her display.

"Let Wes and Fred know the countdown," she told Kutzman.

"Top Yunci, you make sure Captain Gill gets all the fire support she needs. And let me know when the battery starts to displace."

She looked back at her battle board. Charlie was holding firm, which while it didn't surprise her, somehow bothered her. Yes, Captain Kingery had a good position around the knoll, but despite the heavy incoming fire, the AA didn't seem to be advancing.

Maybe they think they Charlie's about to assault them first and they want hasty positions laid?

The Marines had a reputation of aggressive action, so that wasn't a too far-fetched guess. If they were digging in, Captain Kingery was just going to have to deal with it.

The mortars! I've got to move them!

She started to grab Top Yunci, only to see that the half of the tubes were already displacing. She checked the PP overlay, and she saw that Top had them moving north and to the east side of the valley, just short of the bend. This would let them support all three line companies. Charlie already had four fire missions in the queue, and from their new position, the mortars could execute them.

"One hundred seconds until impact," Lieutenant Creighton said.

Esther could feel the tension rising, so she ran through all the Marine and militia positions on her display, noting personnel strength, ammo loads, and PICS power reserves.

Wait, the arty hasn't started displacing, she realized as the data was displayed.

"Top, what's with the arty? I want them to displace now, not tomorrow."

"They've confirmed, ma'am. Just haven't begun yet."

"Keep on them. Bravo's almost out of their range, and we may need them."

Esther's eyes kept straying to the impact point on her display. She felt like she should be doing something, anything, but at the moment, the incoming Tungsicle had her undivided attention.

At 30 seconds, Major Kutzman passed the word to companies for all hands to take cover.

After time almost seemed to hold still, Creighton finally said, "...five...four...three...two...one...impact!"

Not that anyone needed him to let them know the big hunk of tungsten had struck the hillside. There was a flash that momentarily blinded every real-view screen in the command trac, immediately followed by a huge jolt that shook the *Hot Shot*. Three seconds after impact, a low rumble that Esther could feel in her bones swept past them.

Son-of-a-bitch, that's a heavy hand.

If she could feel it inside an Aardvark, it must have felt like a punch in the gut to the straight-leg infantry out there.

She took a quick look at the personnel overlay. Not one Marine had fallen victim to the Tungsicle, which was a relief. She hoped the same wasn't true of the Azaad Andolan. She needed to have taken out a significant chunk of their force.

"Come on, Wes," she muttered when Alpha didn't immediately start pushing ahead, a moment before the rattle of debris hitting the top of the trac brought her up short.

If she was getting pelted in defilade and 1500 meters away, the Alpha Marines had to be getting much more. As if on cue, one of the Alpha Marine's avatars switched to light blue. Still, Alpha had to get moving while the AA were in disarray. She was just about to pull up Captain McLamb on the P2P when Lieutenant Weisskopf and the company's still functioning PICS started forward. A few moments later, the rest of the company began to follow.

On the fire support net, Lieutenant Boston, Alpha's Weapons Platoon commander was calling in fire on targets as they advanced. With the battalion's mortars still displacing, only three of the tubes were available, but they were steadily putting out rounds. Between the mortar platoon, Boston's gun section, and Weisskopf's PICS, that was some serious firepower paving the way for the company. A moment later, two of Charlie's M249's started reaching across the valley to support Alpha as well.

"Keep an eye on ammunition loads," she told Captain Tranh knowing full well that he was doing just that.

At the moment, Alpha needed the fire, but this was only an early phase in the battle. It was going to be a long and bitter fight, and they were going to need the ammo to fight it. She wasn't particularly concerned—she had two hardened commercial hovers with tons of rounds each, one with Bravo and one with the militia company—but she still needed to keep abreast of expenditures.

A battle is never "routine," but for once, things seemed to be progressing as planned. Charlie was holding position, Bravo was in light contact, and Alpha was pushing without serious resistance. Esther wondered where the main concentration of AA was, but by taking the fight to them, she hoped she was keeping the enemy commander back on his or her heels. The Nayi Bharat government wanted to bloody the Azaad Andolan's noses, and Esther began to hope that the battalion could do that without too much more damage to itself.

And the Gods of War took that moment to remind Esther that they controlled the battlefield, not a mere Marine lieutenant colonel.

Esther's alarm went off a split second before Captain Montoya shouted out, "There they are!"

Directly in front of Alpha, her display lit up like a Christmas tree. Hundreds, possibly a thousand, AA fighters were revealed. How so many had evaded surveillance, how so many had survived the Tungsicle strike, she didn't have a clue. For a moment she hoped that the avatars were just a spoof, but from the immediate increase of incoming fire, she knew this was the real deal.

Esther took a couple of deep breaths to calm herself. The forward displacing mortars halted in place and started pumping out rounds, and Creighton was calling for fire from the *Mount Fuji*, but if the numbers on her display were correct, and if the two forces were so close together, then Alpha was going to have to fight their way out of this.

This just keeps getting better and better.

"They've got C20's," Montoya said.

The "Crap 20" was considered a poor-man's combat suit, but despite their nickname, they were pretty decent protection from the lower energy levels of the *Mount Fuji's* meson cannons, and they had the weaponry to take out a PICS if they could hit one. One on one, heck, one on three, a PICS Marine would have the advantage, but there were a lot of Crap 20's out there.

"Increased activity around Bravo," the Two announced.

Patterns were forming to the east of Bravo, and the battalion combat AI gave it an 82% probability that the company was about to get hit.

"XO, take the fight with Bravo," she passed on the P2P. "I've got my hands full up here."

By SOP, a bravo command group bird-dogged the alpha command, ready to take over should the alpha get knocked out. But Esther needed him to focus on Captain Gill and Bravo Company for the moment.

"Roger that," Major Frazier said. "I'm pulling up the militia."

Esther put him out of her mind, confident that he could handle whatever was happening back there. Her attention was riveted on Alpha Company. Already, three more PICS had been knocked out of action by anti-armor missiles. These weren't even high-tech missiles—they were simple rockets, actually, but at such close ranges, they were just as deadly as what the Marines had in their arsenal.

As the fighting intensified, Captain McLamb was coolly giving orders as he maneuvered his company to keep from being enveloped. Even with Charlie diverting more and more of its crew-served weapons to support Alpha, it was becoming clear that there were just too many AA fighters, and they were flowing alongside the company's flanks.

The battalion still had a couple of huge offensive assets. Back on Last Stop, Noah had righteously pointed out that personnel carriers were not just taxis to move Marines around. They were a pretty powerful weapons platform in their own right, and Esther had two of them.

"You ready to rock and roll?" she asked Staff Sergeant Doug Mueller, the armor detachment commander.

The staff sergeant turned from his raised commander's cupula, bent over, and looked Esther in the eye, telling her, "Damned right, I am! About time!"

"Move forward until you can engage."

"Ooh-fucking-rah!" the staff sergeant shouted at her before twisting himself back into position.

"I've just told Mueller to move the *Hot Shot* forward to support Wes," she told the Three who just nodded, holding up a hand to let her know he heard while still speaking to someone on the comms.

With a lurch, the *Hot Shot* started forward. Esther put the Aardvark out of her mind for the moment, trying to figure out how the fight was unfolding. Alpha was taking a pounding, but the company was holding its own. The AA facing Charlie were still applying pressure but didn't seem to be ramping up.

Unless they're holding back and until our focus is only on Alpha . . .

She gave a quick look to Bravo, but the XO and Captain Gill seemed to be handling things for the moment. Not for the first time was she grateful that she had Major Frazier as her XO. It was a blessing to have someone in whom she had 100% confidence.

She checked the time. To her surprise, she saw that 93 minutes had passed since first contact. It seemed more like 15 minutes to her.

The *Hot Shot* came to a stop, and a moment later, the zip of the chain gun sounded above her like an angry wasp. The 25mm gun packed more than enough punch to take out a Crap 20, but Esther waited in suspense inside the trac until a blast reached her. The *Hot Shot's* 70mm smoothbore had spoken. An instant later, on the far side of the valley, an AA Crap 20 ceased to exist, blown to pieces. There was a roar from within the trac—more than a few of the Alpha Command had monitored the shot.

Esther didn't have a clue as to how the bulk of the AA combat suits had evaded detection, and that was something for Fleet and Corps Intel to figure out after the battle. But once they'd engaged Alpha, the low-tech combat suits were readily visible. The *Hot Shot* had forty-five 70mm rounds, both anti-armor and anti-personnel, but even the anti-personnel round could take out a Crap 20 with a direct hit. Unlike on a tank, the trac commander was also the main gunner, and Staff Sergeant Mueller was taking shot after shot, each one a kill. On the chain gun, Lance Corporal Addebe was both racking up Crap 20's as well as stopping in their tracks the AA who were trying to flank Alpha higher up the slope.

"Keep it coming," Captain McLamb passed on the command net.

"Twenty-eight for twenty-eight," Sergeant Jones said, her voice filled with both awe and pride.

Even given their advanced technology, that was pretty awesome shooting. Esther started to feel more confident that they could break the assault . . . until the fickle Gods of War started playing again.

There was a loud, earth-shattering boom, and almost immediately, the *Hot Shot's* fire-suppression foam filled the compartment. The back hatch fell open, and incoming sunlight revealed a mess of what had been a tightly functioning Alpha Command. Directly opposite of her, Sergeant Jones, or what was left of her, slumped in her seat. Next to her, Captain Montoya groaned, right hand clamped to her side. Half of the bank of displays going down the port side had been destroyed.

"Grab your portables and get out!" the Three shouted, and within seconds, the Alpha Command Marines started scrambling.

"Bravo Command, you've got the battalion until further notice," Esther passed.

Staff Sergeant Mueller bent down and asked, "You OK down there?"

"What happened?" Esther asked.

"Took a SASSY on the port side, Colonel. Adedde's gone."

"Can you still fire?"

"I've got a round in the breach, but after that, without power, I can't bring any more up. The chain gun might be OK," though.

"Fire that round, then get out until we can figure out what to do," Esther said before turning to see Major Kutzman on the ramp, waiting for her. After a quick glance at Jones' body, she ran out of the trac.

"Bravo Command's got the fight, but I want us up and running in five minutes," she shouted. "Do it now!"

****

"I'm not sure how much longer we can hold out, Colonel," Captain McLamb passed thirty minutes later. "Anything you can do to help would really be most appreciated."

Esther's mind raced through her options, but they weren't good. Captain Gill and Bravo were locked in combat, and the militia company was slow in supporting them. Charlie Company was in close combat just 200 meters away, which was one of the reasons why she'd ordered Alpha to push forward to put flanking fire on the AA attacking Charlie. It looked like that assault, though, had been more a holding action, with the enemy commander hoping to draw Alpha out and expose it.

And Esther had complied. Not even 300 meters away, on the far side of the valley, Alpha was getting hammered.

Around her, Captain Peaslee and Noah had formed a defensive position, and they were already getting probed by AA fighters coming down the hillside. Her command trac was a ruin. Staff Sergeant Mueller, blood staining his right thigh, was on top of the hulk, trying to salvage the chain gun, but she didn't give that much hope.

"Hang on, Wes. I'll get you something."

She checked her display. Alpha was down to 52 effectives, only 22 being PICS Marines. Weisskopf, Boston, and Germaine were KIA, and First Sergeant Khan was WIA. He had Lieutenants Nueng and Bronstein, then Gunny Keating back with his crew-served. Swarming them still had to be 400 or more AA fighters.

"Do you have comms with the *Fujiyama*, yet?" she shouted at Creighton, who was on the deck ten meters away.

He'd lost his console with the *Hot Shot*, and his portable had been destroyed. He'd been trying to raise him over his PA.

He gave her a thumbs up and said, "I've raised her, and they're patching me through to fire control. Oh, I have them now!"

"Do we have the cannons yet?"

There was a pause, then, "They're up and waiting for a fire mission."

"Wes, we've got the *Fujiyama* back online. Can you break out and pull back? I can light up the area."

"I don't think so, Colonel. We're kind of surrounded." There was a grunt, then "Just took a hit, damn it."

His avatar switched to only light blue, so she knew he was still in the fight. She briefly pulled up his feed, just in time to see him drop two charging AA with his M90.

Fuck, they're all intermixed.

"Look, Wes, you've got to give me some separation. I can fry the entire hillside, but you won't survive it."

There was a pause, then Captain McLamb passed, "I'm not moving. Can't really. Leg's all fucked up."

Esther pulled up the captain's vitals, and her heart fell. His booster had injected him with shock-suppressing nanos, which was why he was still functioning in command with his right leg missing.

"Give me two minutes, Colonel. I'll get some out of the kill zone, and then you bring the wrath of God down on my head."

"I can't. You won't survive."

"I'm not going to survive anyway, Colonel. You and I know that. And there's got to be five hundred of the bastards here. Take them out. Now I've got to give some orders, so if you don't mind."

He switched to his company net. Esther listened in as he gave the command for as many of his Marines to break out down the hillside as possible.

Esther switched to Captain Kingery and ordered, "Give me all your crew served at this point," highlighting the direction Wes McLamb had given his surviving Marines. "Blast a clear path for them."

For Kingery to shift all of his crew-served put his own company at risk, but he never hesitated. Within seconds, all eight M249s started pounding rounds across the valley floor to impact on the far hillside.

"Staff Sergeant Lola, walk a line of mortars along this route. We'll have Alpha following the impacts."

Esther relayed the fire support to McLamb, then brought up the company disposition. Now down to 48, she could see some movement as they started to maneuver. Only some movement, though. At least eight were remaining in place.

"You've got to try, Wes. And what about Khan and Bronstein? And the others?"

"Corporal Ting's got a broken back, but she's still got her arms, and she's covering the rest. I told the others to get out of here, but you know Kahn. Never was much for obeying orders." He paused, and Esther heard the sound of him firing. "You just make sure the *Fujiyama* scours this place."

"Colonel," Major Frazier cut in. "The *Lusty Sara's* still operational. Let me go get McLamb and the rest."

The *Lusty Sara* was the Bravo Command Aardvark, and for a moment, Esther's heart jumped at the thought, but she knew it wouldn't work. There wasn't time, for one, and she doubted the trac could make it through in one piece. Even if she did, there wasn't a way she could climb the hill to McLamb's position.

"Can't do it, Mark. And I need you with Jean to keep the AA from coming up our asses."

"Lieutenant Creighton, on my order, I want 100 megajoules on top of Captain McLamb's position. Give me a spread of 150 meters."

"A hundred, Colonel?" he asked incredulously. "That's . . . I mean, the *Fujiyama* can give it if we twin the cannons, but for five seconds, top, and then she's got to do some serious cooling."

"Just do it," she ordered. "You've got about a minute-and-a-half."

The first crump of the mortars reached her, followed by "Move, move, move!" on the Alpha Company command net.

"Colonel, we've got heavy firing coming from the south," Captain Peaslee passed to her.

"Just take care of it, Captain," Esther said, cutting him off.

Peaslee was surprising her with his, well, competency in battle, but for the moment, she was focused on what remained of the company on the opposite side of the valley. She watched her display as the blue dots flowed together and down the hill. Within a minute, five of them had fallen, yet the intense mortar and automatic fire opened a path so that most of them burst through the first ring of resistance. Could they get far enough, though? In a moment, the AA would figure out that was happening. By closing with the Marines, they had eliminated the threat of the *Mount Fuji* overhead. If the Marines created a gap, the packed-together AA became a prime target.

"Wes, how are you holding out?"

"Not so good, Colonel. Took another two hits. I . . . well, hello, guys. Glad you can join me here on this lovely day. I'd say now, Esther."

Esther turned on the captain's feed, and five AA fighters stood before him, Gentry P40's pointed at his chest.

One of the men said "Esther?"

"Yeah, she can be a real bitch, but I'm damned proud to have served with her," he said to the AA fighters, then to her, "Let it rain!"

Esther's heart fell, and she turned to the waiting Creighton and said, "Fire."

She kept the feed running as one of the other fighters said, "Fuck this asshole" and raised his rifle.

And the feed went blank as a crack of displaced ionized air rolled across the valley, Esther's nostril hair almost standing erect as the tang assaulted her senses. One hundred megajoules were enough to breach a battleship, and even with atmospheric attenuation, it was still a powerful punch. For five long seconds, the air above the far hillside seemed to come alive and immense power passed through it. And then it was over. Nothing looked that different. The trees were undoubtedly dead, but that wouldn't show up for a day or so.

Hesitantly, she brought up the company disposition. The bright blue avatars of thirty-two Marines showed up, thirty-two where this morning were one-hundred-and-twenty-six.

"This is Gunny Keating. I'm assuming command of Alpha Company and am awaiting orders," the new company commander passed on the battalion command net, his AI giving him access.

Esther simply wanted to sink down to the dirt and do nothing. Most of Alpha Company was gone, and she'd not only given the order that put the company in that position, but she'd also given the order to the *Mount Fuji* that directly killed at least twenty of them.

"Ess, the fight's not over," Noah said over the P2P. "Get off your ass and command."

She looked back in his direction but couldn't spot him. He was right, though. She still commanded a powerful fighting force. At the moment, she was strung out in the valley and on the high ground to the west. She was too exposed and had to consolidate her forces.

"I've got it, Noah," she said, energy flowing through her.

This was her battalion, and she was going to wield it like Thor's hammer.

Chapter 22
Noah

"Gunny, take Alpha back along the same route. I do not want you on the valley floor until after you pass the bend. Link up with Bravo," Esther passed on the command net.

Noah let out a deep breath he hadn't realized he was holding. He'd sensed his sister freezing up for a second, and the battalion couldn't afford that. Listening to her now, it seemed she was back on track.

Not that he blamed her. He'd listened in with her comms with Captain McLamb, and he'd been devastated when the *Mount Fuji* had let loose with her cannons. It was bad enough for him, but he hadn't given the orders. He couldn't imagine how she felt. But she didn't have the luxury to dwell on it. The battalion was in a shit sandwich, and they need firm leadership if they were going to get themselves out of it. Esther had a proven track record of tactical prowess, and they needed her focused on the mission.

He'd almost rushed forward when the Alpha Command trac had been hit, but he could see most of the Marines, with Esther being the last one, stumble out. Only the driver and Sergeant Jones had been killed, and while a few of the others were wounded, the rest of the command was still in the fight. They no longer had the full array of their equipment, but they could fight the battalion on foot with their PAs and repeaters.

Esther was issuing orders to consolidate the battalion on Charlie's position. That would reduce their vulnerability, but Noah didn't know how they would then prosecute their mission. He was pretty sure that the powers that be didn't want a defensive standoff.

Should have thought of that when you had us marching out the gates in full view of God and planet.

Noah drummed the Three Musketeers along the stock of his M90, one finger after the other before repeating, a habit he'd recently picked up. It annoyed the heck out of Esther and a couple of his first sergeants, but the soft click-click-click helped steady his thinking. He looked back to where Bravo was engaged with the AA who'd been up on the highlands along their route. The militia arty was gamely trying to support the company, but most of the enemy fighters were just beyond their range. Esther had ordered them to displace forward to where they could better support the battalion, but they were slow in responding.

He hesitated a moment, wondering if he should backtrack and join them, but in the end, he decided to move ahead with the Alpha Command.

"Come on, Coffman," he said to the lance corporal. "We're climbing up there," he said, pointing up the slope.

The young Marine looked up, shrugged up his pack, and started forward.

"Bet you wish you were back on the *Fujiyama*, fixing the aircon."

"I told you, Sergeant Major, that was all well and good, but I'm a Marine, not a squid. This is where I belong."

Noah had been surprised to see Coffman when they landed at the Raipur spaceport, but the young Marine had been right then and was right now. This is where he belonged. Because he'd been out of the loop, though, with Captain Peaslee's security team, Noah had hijacked the young man. Noah didn't have a specific mission other than to advise his sister, and she had the entire Alpha Command for that. So, he'd intended on making himself seen among the troops where needed, and it was better to have Coffman with him than to wander alone through an active battlefield.

He and Coffman started up the hillside. Noah started to feel it after climbing a couple of hundred meters, but with the younger Marine seemingly having no problem, he sucked it up and tried to hide the effort it was taking him. Still, he let out a sigh of relief as the top flattened out a bit.

He took a moment to look back over the valley. The sounds of firing reached up to him, but it looked deceptively peaceful. It seemed surreal to think that down there, 600 meters away, Bravo Company was in contact with the AA fighters. He caught a quick glimpse of a Marine running, then dropping back out of sight. Wondering if the Marine had been hit, he quickly thumbtacked the position on his display, he pulled up a name: PFC Colin Dodderly, who was still in full health.

"OK, Coffman, let's find the Alpha Command," he said, turning away from Bravo and trudging forward.

"Good to see you, Sergeant Major," Captain Peaslee said as the two Marines reached the command's perimeter.

"Always a pleasure to see you, too, sir. What's the situation up here?"

"The CO's over there about 30 meters. She's putting together a frag."

"You know her, sir. We're not going to sit up here and let them bring the battle to us."

"Roger that."

There was an explosion about 150 meters away, and the captain said, "That's in Charlie's area."

"Incoming or outgoing," Noah asked, checking his display as the captain merely shrugged.

No new casualties registered, but that wasn't proof one way or the other.

"You still have that squad from Bravo?"

"Sure do. They came with us when we displaced up here."

"OK, well, I'm going to check in with the CP."

The captain pointed the direction, and the two Marines made their way forward until Noah could see the Marines and sailor from the command group sitting on the ground, backs up against a rock face. Esther nodded to him as he came up but didn't stop what she was doing.

He sunk to the ground and brought up the Alpha Command net.

"You tell me when that probability hits 60%," Esther passed to someone.

Probability for what? Noah wondered.

"If that is them, then we've got to strike. We can cut off the head of the snake."

"What about the militia?" Major Kutzman asked.

"Do you really think they can be counted on?" Esther countered.

"Well enough. But we don't have much choice. Charlie's at eighty-eight percent and Bravo's at ninety-six, but Alpha . . ."

The major didn't need to go further. Alpha Company's 32 remaining effectives, now commanded by Gunny Keating, had linked up with Captain Gill and Bravo, but it was barely above platoon strength.

"I understand that. But I think they would slow down an assault. If we bring Bravo forward, we can leave Weapons to keep the AA from crawling up our asses. Maybe we can bring up the militia to give Weapons some more bodies."

"I think that would be a good idea, Colonel," the Three said. "What about Alpha?"

"Wait one," Esther said, and Noah could see her connect to someone else.

He couldn't hear what she was saying, and if she was on the P2P, he wasn't sure he should break in.

A moment later, she came back on the Alpha Command net and said, "Gunny says Alpha wants to fight. If we bring up the militia, and think we can afford to let the company come forward with Bravo.

"Three, start to displace Bravo to the assembly area we selected. Center peel with enough time for Weapons and the militia to fill in. Then, have Weapons and the militia slowly withdraw as they can to Cardinal. Destiny, you grab me the moment we hit sixty percent. OK. people, we've got work to do."

She cut off the net and sat back. Noah took this as his cue. He got up, his back creaking, and walked over to her, offering her a Zap energy bar he took out of his cargo pocket. With a smile, she took it, popped the wrapper and took a bite.

"Sixty percent probability of what?" he asked.

"You're part of the Alpha Command, Noah. If you'd been here, you'd already know."

"We already discussed this. I think I'm doing more by being seen."

"I know, Noah, I know. It's just . . ."

"You had to call in the strike, Ess. You know that. Wes knew that."

"I know. But that doesn't make it easier." She shook her head quickly, as if trying to jar the memory out of her mind and then said, "The *Fujiyama* thinks they've located the Azaad Andolanalph command."

"Really? They spotted them?"

"No, not that. But by analyzing communications patterns."

"Comms?"

"Yeah, I know. But the more they pick up, the better it looks."

Any command structure, almost by definition, had to communicate with its units. Comms can be scrambled, but the mere presence of the comms could give a wealth of intel simply by existing, never mind its content. To combat that, the Marine Corps comms randomly bounced around hundreds, it not thousands, of relays all around the planet and in orbit. The shifts took place several times a second, unnoticeable by the user, but too short in duration to allow for tracing. This wasn't a particularly high-tech innovation, but somehow, the AAs evidently used an ancient routing system that the *Mount Fuji's* AIs were mapping.

"And if it is them?"

"Then we take them out, of course. We think it's about 250 meters north-northwest from Pelican. If they are there, they're in pretty restricted terrain. I want to send Bravo forward on the far side ridge and down in the opposite canyon while Charlie pushes forward on this side of the slope. Bravo can climb out almost abreast of the AA CP."

Noah pulled up his relief map, studied it for a moment, and then said, "That's some pretty rough terrain there."

"Which is why they won't expect it. I mean, who would try and get through there?"

"Except for us," Noah said, nodding.

Esther had a point. The terrain looked impassable, and sometimes appearances were the reality. He wondered if she was biting off more than the battalion could chew.

"And if Bravo can't cross the terrain?"

"Then they come back over and join Charlie. Together, they sweep the high ground clean."

"That's kind of a narrow frontage for two companies. And do we have the numbers of bad guys between here and Pelican?"

"They're out there, maybe three or four thousand, which is why I want Jean to bypass them."

"And what about you? I mean, the Alpha Command? You've been here for more than an hour. That's a pretty long time to stay in one position."

"We'll be following in trace of Charlie. Look, Noah, I know you think this is risky, and maybe it is. But we can't just sit here and let the AA define the battle. We need to make this on our terms if we're going to get out of this in one piece."

"Colonel? The *Fujiyama* just recalculated. We're at seventy-four percent," Captain Montoya said.

Esther jumped up, shoving the rest of the CCC bar into her mouth and shouted to the Three, "We're on. Let's kick it off!"

Noah was not feeling overly confident. He knew that the AA fighters could not stand up to Marines man-to-man, so Esther was doing her best to diminish the enemy's superiority in numbers by only meeting them at equal numbers or better. Esther had a reputation for tactical innovation, but it hadn't always worked during training. If this worked, she'd be hailed as the second coming of Sun Tzu. If it didn't, they might not survive the coming hours.

****

To Noah's great relief and welcomed surprise, Bravo Company seemed to be up to the task. They'd had mountain warfare training, to be sure, but still, the eight klicks had been hellaciously difficult, taking the company through the short Nayi Bharat night and into the morning. More than a few AA drones had been picked up on the south side of the ridge, but from all indications, the *Mount Fuji* had managed to spoof them.

Shortly before nightfall, Esther had implemented her second frag order. Charlie had encountered stiffer resistance to its advance, and the estimated numbers of AA fighters all along the high ground had continued to rise, to include a sizable force defending the enemy CP. If Bravo was to have a chance in knocking out the AA command cell, some of those forces, at least, had to be drawn away.

Esther's plan, and Noah had to give it mad props, was to have Charlie set up a hasty defense as night fell, then at dawn, begin a feint withdrawal as if trying to link up with the militia. The hope was that as they retreated, the AA would smell victory and follow with the bulk of their forces in the area.

It had been rather hairy during the night. The AA launched three assaults, and Charlie had pushed back each using only half of their forces in an attempt to fool the AA as to how many Marines were still effective. But the ruse seemed to have worked. When Charlie started pulling back this morning, what surveillance they had seemed to indicate the AA was chasing the company.

And now was the moment of truth. Bravo had climbed out of the canyon and was about to crest the ridgeline. They'd be 400 meters from the Azaad Andolanalph command.

"We've got vehicular movement in the valley heading east," Captain Montoya said.

"They're trying to flank Charlie," Gunny Vandervee said.

"Can the mortars hit them?" Esther asked.

"That's a negative," Top Yunci answered.

"Let them come," she said after a moment's consideration.

She could have shifted the fires from the *Mount Fuji*, Noah knew, but the rushing mass of AA troops in the highlands were more of a threat, and the ARG rounds were needed to keep a gap between Charlie and the pursing enemy.

"What's the disposition around Pelican?"

"Lighter, Colonel. What numbers? The estimates are possibly fifty or so," Montoya replied.

Noah was impressed with the S2. She'd been wounded when the *Hot Shot* was lost, with broken ribs and probable internal injuries. Her nano's had done stellar work, but still, it took fortitude to perform over extended periods of time as she'd done. Both Doc Siren, the battalion surgeon, and Chief Higgins, the senior corpsman, wanted her evac'd, but she'd refused.

"OK, then. I think we're there," Esther said as all eyes swiveled towards her. "Execute!"

Immediately, there was a flurry of activity around the clearing as orders were given. Bravo and Alpha were to commence their attack while Charlie came to a halt and reversed course. From orbit, the *Mount Fuji* increased her rate of fire, peppering the area from Pelican to the AA CP, clearing a path down the slope for the Marines.

It took a few minutes for the AA to realize what had happened as several large explosions, courtesy of the two combat engineers attached to Charlie who'd emplaced the mines as the company supposedly retreated, created huge holes in their lines. When Charlie Marines appeared in full assault mode, the AA in the lead units tried to backpedal, creating confusion within their still advancing forces.

While confusion took over near Charlie, it seemed as if Bravo and what was left of Alpha almost had a clear run. Two of the platoons swung to face east, forming a blocking force, and Lieutenant Gaspar's PICS platoon, followed by Gunny Keating and Alpha, continued on to the target.

Noah could watch the displays, but he wanted an actual point of view, so he grabbed the lieutenant's feed. He'd spent his first tour in PICS, and while he'd become a dedicated tanker, the big combat suits still filled him with awe. Lieutenant Gaspar ran his PICS over boulders and scrub pine, his HGL[7] seeking out a target.

But there wasn't a target. There was nothing but more boulders, more scraggly trees. Noah's heart fell. Before they initiated the assault, the *Mount Fuji* had raised the probability that the enemy CP was at that spot to 88%, which was extremely high given the circumstances. Eighty-eight percent was almost a certainty in terms of battlefield probabilities.

The assault started to peter out as the Marines searched for a target, and Noah thought the mission had failed when Sergeant Pawelczak sent an alert. Noah switched to his feed, and something in the rock face of a rise looked odd. The sergeant aimed his HGL

---

[7] HGL: Heavy Grenade Launcher

and fired right into the face, and a hole the size of a hover opened up. He continued to fire round after round as he forced his PICS into the opening, and half crouched, ran down the short passage to a chamber—one filled with thirty or forty AA fighters, including a man with the bright gold epaulets of a First Commander.

Something clanged off of Pawelczak's chest piece, and the sergeant fired off two of his shoulder rockets, demolishing a bank of control equipment along with three of the AA.

"You are now prisoners—"

Pawelczak's feed went white for a split second, then dark. His avatar immediately went gray, as did Corporal Vixen's.

"What happened?" several of the Alpha Command asked in confusion.

Noah switched back to the lieutenant and saw that the man was rushing to the CP, or to the hole that led to the CP and that now had smoke and dust pouring out and up. He started to go inside, but the way was blocked with rubble.

Noah didn't know if the sergeant's shoulder rockets had set off something or if the CP staff had suicided. Probably the latter, he realized, and the battalion had lost two more Marines as a result.

"OK, get your minds back to work. We're not finished here," Esther reminded everyone.

Captain Gill was already ordering Weisskopf and Gunny Keating back to company's hasty line. Bravo was taking fire from AA fighters, and if Esther was going to try and concentrate the enemy, Bravo had not only to stand firm but hold off any other forces arriving from farther west. The Alpha Command had to be ready to support each of the battalion's units.

"Colonel Lysander? The trucks in the valley, they've stopped," Corporal Ikimura said.

"Where?" Esther asked then paused, her body going still.

Noah pulled up the overlay, and it took a moment before he realized that the trucks had stopped directly below them. They had a working dragonfly over the area, and Noah pulled up the feed. Down below, fighters were swarming out of the trucks and up the hill, right at them.

They were the target. Just as the Marines had just cut off the head of the snake, the snake was trying to return the favor. And by staying in one place, they'd made it easy for them.

Noah ran to the edge of the drop-off, trying to spot the attackers, his M90 at the ready. He couldn't see anyone yet, but they'd be well within his range when they came into view.

"Incoming!" someone shouted, and Noah looked up just in time to see several small shapes hurtling at them.

Acting on instinct, he started to whirl when one of the rockets hit him just above the right elbow. The blow spun him around and sent him flat on his face. The shock wave and shrapnel from the rocket, which impacted and detonated just ten meters away, blasted right over him.

He was barely aware of more rockets as he tried to push himself up, only his right arm wasn't gaining any purchase. Confused, he looked at his arm, and to his surprise, it was gone. He held up the stump in wonderment. When the rocket had hit him, his bones hardened, but they could only do so much. The blow shattered his humerus, and then like toothpaste from a tube, tore his arm off and out his sleeve.

"Sergeant Major, are you OK?" Lance Corporal Coffman's voice reached him through a fog.

He held out his stump, still spurting bright red arterial blood, to the Marine and said, "The Three Musketeers, they just issued them to me. I've gone and lost them."

His nanos kicked in, flooding his body with coagulants and meds to fight the shock, and the world shut off.

Chapter 23
Esther

Six . . . seven . . . eight rockets slammed into the small shelf, blanketing the area with shrapnel. Esther was hit several times as she hugged the ground, but her bones did their job and protected her. After the last impact, she raised her head, but dust obscured the area. Pulling up the personnel overlay, she saw—

"Noah!" she shouted, jumping to her feet.

Through the dust, she could see Noah, and too, too much blood. Lance Corporal Coffman reached him, and a moment later, her brother fell back.

"Colonel!" someone shouted, trying to capture her attention.

Before she could respond, Chief Higgins raced up to her and asked, "Are you OK?"

"Yeah, I'm fine. Go help the sergeant major," she said, pulling herself together.

As much as she wanted to rush to Noah, she had a job to do, and the senior corpsman could see to him.

She pulled up the overlay and saw that no one had been killed, thank goodness, but Noah and Sergeant DeMarco were WIA. Esther forced herself to get back into command mode. She knew what had happened. They were on a shelf-like plateau, basically a flat spot on the hillside at the base of a rock wall. The wall gave the CP cover from the west, but it was open to the north. Somehow, despite constant spoofing and shielding, they'd been picked up, and some sort of launcher was on the far side of the valley lobbing rockets at them.

She pulled up the enemy sitmap again, trying to see if the main AA force being pushed by Charlie presented a concentrated enough target to hit yet.

"Incoming!" someone shouted, and Esther hit the deck again.

Another eight rockets slammed into them. Esther hugged the ground again, waiting for the salvo to quit. The moment the last one detonated, she started to shout for Captain Peaslee, but the young officer was already rushing forward with five Marines, two with Hatchets on their shoulders.

"Creighton, can we—" she started on the P2P.

"Lieutenant Creighton is KIA," her AI informed her.

"What?" she asked aloud before pulling back up the personnel overlay.

Creighton's avatar was grayed out, KIA. Lieutenant Poul and Captain Tranh were WIA.

"Colonel, we need to pull back," Major Kutzman told her, taking her by the arm as the Bravo Company squad, which had been providing security slightly downslope and to the east, rushed up and over the crest and onto the shelf. Sergeant Cushman pointed to Esther, and Corporal Spain and Lance Corporal Thuy rushed at her while the rest ran to join Captain Peaslee.

Esther almost balked at the obvious bodyguards, but she had more important things on her mind.

"Get everyone out of the line of fire," she told the Three. "But we can't cede this high ground to whoever is coming up here."

There was a whoop from one of the Hatchet gunners with Peaslee.

"I think we got the launcher," Peaslee passed on the command net.

As if objecting, a string of automatic fire swept the shelf, making Peaslee and his Marine dive for cover.

Esther let herself be led back 30 meters to just past the crown and out of direct fire, but that was about as far as she was going to go. She was relatively secure, and that was good enough.

She pulled up the Bravo Command net and passed, "Gunny Wisteria, Lieutenant Creighton's KIA, so you're the new naval gunfire liaison. Open the link to the *Fujiyama* and then link it to me."

Gunny had some training with naval gunfire during Fire Support Coordinator training, but his experience was with Marine assets, not ships. With the *Mount Fuji* a major player—*the* major player—in her plans, she wanted to make sure there was no room for miscommunication. She and Lieutenant Creighton had come up with the timing, but with Creighton gone, she had to interject herself into the process.

Sorry about getting into the weeds, Noah, but in this case, I've got to do it, she silently told her brother.

"What's the situation up there?" Major Frazier asked over the P2P.

"We took some hits, but we're functional. What about you?"

"Still in contact, but I think some of the AA, at least, are breaking off."

Esther considered that for a moment as automatic fire hit the edge of the shelf just above her, showering her with dirt clods. She could bring the XO and the militia forward, but that could leave their rear vulnerable. The forces opposing the XO and the militia might be falling back, but it wouldn't be the first time a unit seemed to be breaking contact, then turned back and attacked when the defenders had relaxed their vigil. Even if she brought the militia forward, she doubted they'd arrive in time to make a difference. Whatever was going to happen would be within the hour. Any longer, either Bravo would get overrun or the 3,000-plus fighters would turn back and hit Charlie.

"Let's keep the militia where it is for now," she told him. "Uh, look, Mark, you know the plan. You need to make sure that we don't delay with the *Fujiyama*. We need the AA to bunch up, but don't let that keep you from pulling the trigger, or Jean Gill's going to be left high and dry. She can only slow the AA; there's no way she can stop them in their tracks."

"I understand, that, ma'am, but you've got this now, right?"

"Yeah, for now, but we've got AA heading toward us, so, well, I just want to make sure."

"Fall, back, Colonel. We can come up and provide security. No reason to get into a firefight."

"I'm not sure we can. I've got four WIA who can't move, five if you count Destiny. I'm surprised she's still conscious."

"Not to be callous, but leave them. You being there isn't going to make one bit of difference. Take Sergeant Cushman's squad and fall back to us, and I'll send a platoon to meet you."

What the XO was telling her was the book answer. Esther was not going to turn the tide of the battle with her Ruger. She could turn the battle with how she fought the battalion, and things were coming to a head within the next hour.

But she just couldn't. She could not abandon the rest of the Alpha Command. The XO had the plan, and he could execute it, if it came to that.

"I'll let you know if I have to displace," she told him, cutting the contact.

She raised her head half a meter and looked over the shelf. On the far side, Peaslee was in full warrior mode, running the fight with the AA below them. Up against the rock face, Chief had Noah, Poul, Tranh, and DeMarco prone and out of most of the fire. He was bending over Poul, giving him an injection. Beside Noah, a body was ziplocked. Noah was now sitting, his M90 held in his left hand as he faced north.

"What's their condition?" she asked Chief over the P2P.

He looked around, spotted her, gave a thumbs up, and replied, "Lieutenant Creighton's got a pretty good shot at resurrection. Of the rest, Lieutenant Poul's the worst. I've got him under now, but he needs to be CASVAC'd as soon as possible. The rest should recover, but they need medical care. Oh, and the Sergeant Major, he lost his arm."

She ignored the gut shot from his words and said, "OK, thanks for the head's up. We've got a huge evac list, so you do your best until we can get something here for them."

She was relieved to hear about Creighton, but he looked awfully vulnerable in the ziplock. The stasis bag was not designed to offer ballistic protection, and they were still taking fire.

"Corporal Spain—Lee, right? I want you and Thuy to go get Lieutenant Creighton in the ziplock bag. Bring him back here."

The corporal looked like he was going to protest, so she added, "I'll be fine. Just go do it."

She watched for a few moments as Spain and Thuy sprinted over to the WIA and Creighton. Chief seemed to take issue with him, but Spain pointed back at Esther, and Chief nodded. The Two Marines moved to pick up Creighton as Esther slid back to take stock of her Alpha Command. Major Kutzman, her right-hand man, was 20 meters away speaking over his comms. With Captain Tranh down, Top McCurry, with the Bravo Command, had taken over the S4—but the battalion pretty much had what they brought with them. The logistics would come to the forefront after the battle was decided, first and foremost getting their WIA out of there. Doc Siren had set up a temporary field hospital in a commercial hover back with the militia, but the numbers of WIA had her overwhelmed. Lieutenant Poul's loss didn't change much—the heavy comms load had been on the shoulders of Gunny Speckelstein, anyway, and he was with the XO in the Bravo Command. The big loss, at least for the next hour, was Lieutenant Creighton.

And Noah, she thought, her throat tightening.

She looked over at him again, and he seemed to be arguing with the Chief, using his M90 to jab the air. Knowing him, he wanted to fight while the Chief wanted to sedate him. Esther felt a surge of sisterly pride sweep though her.

A fusillade of fire echoed against the rock face. On the other side of the shelf, Captain Peaslee and his Marines were pouring fire down the hillside. Esther pulled up a feed from D6, the Dragonfly that was overhead. Forty or fifty AA infantry were on the slope, advancing relentlessly upwards. A small explosion, probably from a Marine grenade, sent one fighter tumbling back down, but the rest kept coming, using boulders and anything they could find as cover. A few of them were only about 20 meters from the shelf.

"Colonel, we've got more vehicles coming down the valley," the Two passed.

Esther pulled up the *Mount Fuji's* area view, then zoomed in on a line of PTY "Patty" armored personnel carriers running pell mell down the near side of the valley. She ran a quick query, and her AI informed her that together, they could be holding up to 300 fighters. She had a sinking feeling that she knew to where they were heading, and with the added force, there was no way the Alpha

Command could hold on. Their only chance was to end the battle before they could reach her.

"Fred, what's your situation?" she asked the Charlie Company commander, turning her attention way from the oncoming AA. "I can see the readouts, but what's your gut telling you?"

"They're still in retreat mode, but they're getting more organized and putting up some resistance. I think they might be realizing it's just one company chasing them, and I wouldn't be surprised that if they've got some good leadership, they might turn back on us."

One of her father's favorite saying was never to underestimate the enemy, and Esther wasn't about to now. Her plan had been to surprise the AA and force a retreat, but Kingery was right. It would only take a single man or woman of action to turn the force around. Esther couldn't simply assume that the AA leadership was incompetent. Someone could step up for the command that had been killed.

Which meant she couldn't shift some ARG rounds to the slope below her. She had to keep up the pressure to keep the AA fleeing to the west, and she had to give the *Mount Fuji* time to switch the rail to the remaining Tungsicle. She couldn't even shift the mortars—they couldn't reach the northern slope. Captain Peaslee was going to have to handle the AA coming at them.

"Gunny Wisteria," she said to her new naval gunfire liaison, bringing the XO into the loop as well, "I want the *Fujiyama* to begin the salvo to fix the AA in place, then make the switch to the Tungsicle. Keep up the pressure with the cannon, but make sure we've got the power reserves for the linked shot. Either I, or in my absence, the XO, will give the command to fire."

"Roger that. I'm putting in the request now."

"Jean," she said, switching to the P2P with the Bravo Company commander, "Let me know if the pressure gets to be too great. Be ready to break contact downhill."

"Roger that. We're under moderate contact now, but it's building."

And it's going to get worse before it gets better.

The 3,000 or so AA fleeing west had a massive amount of momentum. All Captain Gill could do was to delay them; she could not stop them. If the dam broke, she was to take Bravo and what was left of Alpha and get the hell out of the way.

"Be ready. It could be any minute now."

"Colonel, the Patties will be below us in four minutes," the Two passed, her voice heavy with effort.

Esther looked over to the Three just as the ground around him exploded with multiple impacts. The Major Kutzman rolled to his right, then scrambled to his feet to seek cover. For a split second, she thought Captain Peaslee had been overrun, but like her, the Three was in defilade to the other side of the shelf. Someone had gotten behind them from the southeast side.

"The Bravo Command has debarked. We're on foot," Major Frazier passed to her, something she didn't have time to process at the moment.

She spun around, looking down the slope. Three AA fighters, in their distinctive floppy hats, were charging up the slope. One was still firing his P40 at Major Kutzman, but the other two, armed with Gekos, were focused on Esther and were trying to close the distance.

The Geko was a very short-range carbine that fired a .52 caliber round tipped with a tiny shape charge. It was a close-in self-defense weapon, designed to defeat all known personal armor—including the Marines' skins and bone.

Shit! she thought as she fumbled for her Ruger which hadn't left her holster since she'd stepped foot on the planet.

The fighters were within range, and the first was bringing up his Geko when a someone came rushing by, knocking Esther aside. A quick burst cut down one of the fighters, but the second shifted his aim and fired.

The heavy round hit Corporal Spain in mid-chest, the shape-charge burning through his bones, a small flash of fire and blood exiting through the armor on his back. He dropped face first in front of Esther, sliding down towards the AA gunman.

The fighter took an instant too long to look at Spain, and that was all the time Esther needed. She took him out with two quick rounds.

"Give me your Ruger," someone shouted beside her.

Esther looked up as Noah grabbed her by the arm and pulled her back up over the edge of the slope and into the flat shelf.

"What are you doing?" she asked, her eyes drawn to his missing arm.

"Told the Doc to give me a BOOST. I'm good for a couple of hours. Give me your Ruger," he repeated.

"Why?"

"Because I can't fire this very well one-handed," he said, letting his slung M90 slide off his shoulder.

He looked like a maniac, his eyes, glowing, and Esther didn't know if she should trust his judgement. BOOST affected people differently, and it was a huge drain on the human body. Coupled with his shock and the anti-shock meds, Esther didn't even know the consequences, which she imagined could cause a complete shutdown, even death. But what was done was done, and he was right. He couldn't manage the M90 well, and she could. Without a word, she took the carbine and handed him her handgun.

The rest of the Alpha Command who'd taken shelter over the edge were scrambling back. Lance Corporal Thuy was pulling Lieutenant Creighton's body with him.

"Captain Peaslee!" Major Kutzman was shouting, and Esther put their defense out of her mind for the moment.

"What's the status of the *Fujiyama*?" she asked Gunny Wisteria.

"Doing switch-out now. Estimated time until ready is a little over two minutes."

"Stand by," she told him as she brought up the battle overlay.

Bravo was in heavier contact. She had her AI run an analysis, and from the volume of fire, at least 1,000 AA fighters were bunching up in front of the company. Captain Gill couldn't hold out much longer. To the east of her, Charlie was still pushing, but the push had slowed down. The situation wasn't perfect, but she was afraid it wasn't going to get any better.

"*Mount Fuji*," she passed. "Fire when the rail is loaded. Confirm."

"Confirmed. Will let you know when the G-1905 is fired."

An explosion broke off chips from the rock face, sending them raining down on them. The AA on the south-eastern slope evidently had grenade launchers. As they climbed a little higher on the slope and had a better angle, those grenades would start impacting among them.

Then something the XO had said hit her.

Bravo Command debarked?

"Mark, why did you debark your command trac?"

"I sent the *Lusty Sara* forward."

"Why?" she asked as she pulled up the vehicle overlay for the first time during the battle.

And it immediately became clear. The *Lusty Sara* had reached the bend and was heading west, straight towards the oncoming Patties.

"Are you getting this?" she asked Noah. "Check the vehicle overlay."

"I—" started the Major before Esther told him she could see why he'd sent it forward.

The *Lusty Sara* fired once, and the lead Tabitha, which was slowing down to debark its troops, erupted in a fireball.

"Get some, *Sara!*" Noah said with remarkable enthusiasm for someone who'd just had an arm torn off.

Esther turned to her brother, surprised that he sounded so, well, *normal.*

The *Lusty Sara*, still rushing forward, fired again, and the second Patty was destroyed. The rest of the vehicles came to haphazard stops, their nice column disrupted, and that made them easier targets. Within ten seconds, three more Patties were destroyed, and the rest were trying to turn around and retreat.

Esther wanted to watch, but while the threat from the Patties was broken, things were still getting dicey on the shelf, and the Tungsicle hadn't been launched yet.

Five AA fighters rushed over the lip and into the shelf, weapons firing. Esther fired Noah's M90 and maybe hit one as Captain Peaslee and three Marines rushed back to close the gap in their perimeter. The five were cut down, but not before one of Peaslee's Marines fell as well.

"GD-1905 launched. Impact in 247 seconds," the sailor on the other side of their comms said.

Esther immediately forwarded that to all hands. The remaining PICS Marines, with their added protection, were to stay and try to hold the AA in place, but the straight-leg infantry had to get cover. Bravo and Alpha's Marines were to get downslope as far as possible before going to ground, and Charlie's Marines were to retreat for 200 seconds before doing the same. Particularly for the more exposed Charlie Marines, this was danger close.

"It's done," she told Noah. "Now we have to wait to see what we've trapped."

"If the AA lets us," Noah said as another burst of concentrated Marine fire echoed against the rock face.

Noah had led Esther back towards the WIA, Chief, and Lance Corporal Coffman. This gave her a full view of the small plateau they were on. Now that the Tungsicle had been launched, she had time to really look around her.

Including the remaining members of the Alpha Command, they had Captain Peaslee and ten of his security element, eight Marines from Sergeant Cushman's squad, and Chief Higgins. Facing them was an unknown, but certainly larger number of AA fighters.

What was going to happen with regards to the bigger picture had already been put into motion, and it would proceed or not even without her input. She could be killed, and Major Frazier would take command. That didn't mean she didn't care, of course. What had been until now a more pragmatic outlook on the battle had changed, and her warrior spirit was rising. If the AA wanted to take them out, she was going to make them pay dearly in the attempt.

She lampreyed into Captain Peaslee's limited command net.

" . . . right below you. We're tossing grenades, and when they detonate, I want you three to pop up and light them up. No more than three seconds, though. I don't want you exposed longer than that."

Esther knew the problem with grenades and slope. In the battle on Mount Zeus on Elysium, her teams' grenades were somewhat ineffectual as the bounded past or fell short of the enemy before detonating.

Peaslee and two Marines rose to their knees and tossed their grenades over the edge. Esther barely heard the detonations when they went off three seconds later, but four Marines, led Sergeant Tyre, jumped up and blasted away downhill before falling back.

"One hundred seconds until impact," Gunny Wisteria passed.

More rifle grenades hit the rock face, and Esther instinctively ducked as rubble rained on them.

"Chief, should we move them?" Esther asked, pointing at the WIA.

"Except for Lieutenant Creighton, I'd rather keep them here, but as for him," he said, pointing at the lieutenant's ziplocked body, "I don't know where would be any better."

Esther pulled up the main battle display with enemy and friendly positions highlighted, the count-down timer tucked in the corner. She could see the non-PICS Marines retreating, but it looked like the enemy was on the move as well. A force of what looked to be almost 200 was pushing at the thinned Bravo lines, possibly sensing most of the Marine's withdrawal. Two PICS Marines—Corporal Hickson and Lance Corporal Dennis Bird—were standing firm, expending enormous firepower to hold the AA back. The AA were returning the fire, however, and Hickson's PICS was redlining while Bird had lost his HGL.

"Gunny Wisteria, I want mortars to put rounds here," she said, indicating a position 100 meters in front of the two Marines. "And now."

It might be too late, but hitting the main body as they were doing at the moment might be moot once the Tungsicle impacted, and Corporal Hickson could use all the help they could provide.

There was a huge blast at the edge of the shelf taking two Marines out. A moment later, half-a-dozen fighters appeared, scrambling over the rubble, firing wildly while the Marines picked them off. Noah stepped in front of Esther as rounds impacted on either side of her. She joined Noah in firing at the AA, dropping at least one of the attackers. As soon as the last one of the initial wave fell, another dozen came over the edge. The fighters seemed to be focused straight ahead, which put Esther and the WIA in their crosshairs. Esther, Chief, and Noah fired back while Captain Peaslee and two Marines rushed from the side, dropping fighter after fighter. PFC Vanmeter, rushing forward with the captain, was hit with a Geko round in the leg and went down.

One of the last AA fighters had a grenade, and as he pulled his arm back to throw, Peaslee or one of the other's dropped him. The grenade fell to the side towards the captain and up against Vanmeter. Esther started to shout out, but with a pivot, Captain Peaslee picked up the grenade and gave it a shovel pass to clear the shelf—except that it detonated centimeters past his fingertips, shredding the captain's arm and face. The force of the blast sent him over backwards, and Esther didn't have to check his avatar to know that he was gone.

"Thirty seconds," Gunny Wisteria passed.

"Keep fighting!" Major Kutzman passed over the Alpha Command net, beating Esther to the punch.

Down below the rock face, they were pretty well protected from the Tungsicle, and if they starting kissing the dirt, the AA assaulting them would rush the shelf. They had to keep fighting.

Two AA fighters emerged through the hole created with Peaslee down. One of them saw Esther and charged, Geko held up and ready. Before he'd covered three steps, she shot him in the chest, then as the second came to a halt and tried to engage her, Vanmeter, still on the ground and in obvious pain, took him out with a string of darts.

" . . . five . . . four . . . three . . . two . . . one . . . impact!" Gunny Wisteria passed as a huge flash of light lit up the area, so bright Esther could swear she could see the bones—her actual bones, not the armor inserts—in her hands. The shockwave hit a moment later, knocking off some rather large boulders in the rock face to come crashing down among them. Four seconds later, the boom reached them as it rolled out.

Esther felt as if the air had been sucked from her, but she quickly blinked up the battlefield display again. The *Mount Fuji's* scanners were almost useless when trying to pierce the 100 megajoules of death that were now sweeping the area between

Charlie and Bravo. The ship couldn't keep that up for more than five or six seconds, though, and the moment the twinned cannons ceased firing, Esther's display lit up with data.

She immediately noted 21 friendly WIA and one KIA. Pushing that aside for the moment, she tried to analyze the enemy situation. The Tungsicle had hit right in the center of the largest concentration of fighters, and death and destruction radiated out from the impact site. The ship's powerful AI was trying to calculate the casualty rate, but it looked to be upwards of 75% with numbers over 3,000.

"It's not over, Ess," Noah reminded her.

"You look like shit, Noah. Sit down, at least."

"I'm still high on BOOST, Ess, we've still got bad guys with ill intentions, and they were just as protected as we were," he said, tilting his head to indicate the AA just downhill of them.

Which was true. Esther was hoping that losing their command, losing so many of their comrades above would take the fight out of them. It was true that there were still 6,000 or more of the fighters in the area, but the losses so far had to have been a huge, huge shock. They could either decide to fight on or simply break contact.

Unfortunately, they decided to fight on. There was a roar of anger, and then the sounds of what had to be chants reached them.

Noah jumped up and ran to where Captain Pealee's body lay in the dirt. He immediately started to take charge, shifting Marines' positions to cover the gaps.

Oh, hell, Noah. You're hyped up on BOOST, she thought as she chased him down.

BOOST pushed past pain, it pushed past shock, but it could affect rationality, and her brother was not in shape to command his home holo, much less Marines in combat.

"Major Kutzman!" she shouted as she ran after her brother, "Take the southeast. They're still coming!"

She reached Noah, who was exposing himself to the AA below as he fired one well-aimed shot after the other, grabbed him by the shoulder, and said, "Stick by my side."

She could hear battle cries from below as she and Noah hastily started rearranging their positions. She told Corporal Ikimura and Sergeant Bore to start tossing grenades, more to remind the AA below that there were Marines on top waiting for them than anything else.

She almost ordered Captain Kingery to send a platoon her way, but she still didn't know what the company faced. Sure, lots of AA had died up there, but even if 3,000 had been killed, at 75%, that could mean there was still 1,000 fighters on the high ground, and if they were as angry and looking for revenge as the AA facing the Alpha Command, he'd need every available Marine. Even if she had sent the order, she doubted a platoon could get there in time to be of use.

"Thank God the *Lusty Sara* took out that Patty column," Noah muttered as he dropped an AA fighter who was scrambling over the edge of the shelf. "That makes this easy-peasy."

Esther tried not to roll her eyes. They might hold the high ground, but they were still outnumbered by some pretty pissed off fighters.

"Yeah, Noah, 'easy-peasy.'"

"OK, Marines," she passed, turning away from Noah, "They're angry, and angry fighters are not good fighters. Keep your heads on your shoulders, and we'll throw them back to join their brothers and sisters in whatever hell spawned them."

And the assault began.

With disciplined fire, the Marines wiped out almost all of the first wave, but that contracted the Marines' fields of fire and left a corridor, if it could be called that, where the first dozen fighters reached the shelf. The next fighter appeared 20 meters in front of her, Geko held high as he screamed out in wordless rage. He should have fired instead of screamed. Esther raised her M90, but Noah beat her to it, and the man fell back and disappeared from sight. And then there were more targets for her—many more.

She engaged at least six fighters when she felt a hand tugging at her waist. She spun around, but it was Noah, trying to pull out another mag for her Ruger, which was on the deck at his feet. She popped out all four mags, put one of them in the handgun for him, and left him with the other three.

With a few of her Marines falling, more gaps were appearing in the perimeter, and more AA fighters were reaching the shelf, then spreading out. Fighting had devolved into hand-to-hand combat in places, and the Marines weren't always coming out on top. She caught a glimpse of Chief, standing over the wounded while blasting an AA almost in half with his Grayson combat shotgun before falling to a fighter who came up behind him. Esther shot that fighter and dropped him.

As soon as she fired, she felt more than saw one of the fighters aim a grenade launcher at her. A launcher was not designed to hit a person, but at this range, he could hardly miss, and her bones wouldn't do much against a point-blank detonation. Noah shoved her out of the way and faced the fighter calmly, as if on the pistol range back on base. Whether it was the sight of a one-armed Marine standing resolutely in front of him or if he just had buck fever, the fighter somehow pulled his shot high, sending the grenade bouncing off the very top of Noah's shoulder. Her brother faltered a moment, raised his upper lip in a sneer, and took out the fighter with two well-aimed shots.

"Your still in the fight, Ess," he said as he helped her back up.

One after another, Marines were falling, always taking out more of the Azaad Andolanalph, but falling nonetheless. They had broken down into small groups, no longer fighting as a unit, and because of that, Esther knew they'd lost.

"Mark, I'm passing command to you," she said.

Whatever he had to say in response was lost as something big hit Esther in the head, knocking her to her knees. She was dazed, but still functional. Her helmet wasn't though. It had shattered, and her display was down.

With a shrug, she pulled off the remnants and dropped them. She'd shifted the command to the XO, so she didn't need the display. She was no longer a commander but now a Marine warrior, fighting with her brother at her side, just trying to take as many of the bastards out with her.

Esther still had her warrior on, but a sense of calm determination swept over her. As the CO, she'd been required to try and keep herself safe. It had always grated on her that she had to put her own safety above that of her Marines, but that was the way it was. Now, command had been passed, and that restriction was no longer in place. It freed her, and despite what was going to happen to her, she was happy. If she had to fall, it would be like this, fighting to the end with Noah beside her instead of huddling in a CP somewhere when an enemy round found her.

"You ready to do this, Noah?" she shouted as she backed up almost into him.

"Sure am, Ess. Let's make dad proud of us," he said as he dropped another fighter.

Suddenly, she had to say something, despite the gravity of the situation—or maybe *because* of it.

"I haven't always treated you right, Noah, ever since boot camp. But I—"

Several rounds pinged off of her back, her bones hardening on cue as she spun around and shot one of the AA and made the other bolt out of the way.

"But I love you, little bro. Dad would be proud of you, and *I'm* proud of you."

"I know that. I love you, too, and I've got your back," he said, grunting as something hit him.

Esther felt him slump against her for a moment, then struggle back to his feet.

"You've always had my back."

"So, let's do this," Noah said, in obvious pain despite the BOOST. "Together."

And together they did, firing measured round out of measured round. Ten, twelve, maybe more AA fell to them. Esther lost count. She had only one thing to do, and that was to kill the enemy.

She was hit half a dozen times, but never with a Geko round, and she kept on her feet. Noah collapsed, however. Esther took a step to her right, and astride her prone brother, kept up a steady fire.

Other Marines were still alive, still in the fight. She caught glimpses of Corporal Ikimura, Lance Corporal Coffman, and Major Kutzman, but it was down to man-to-man by this time. AA bodies littered the shelf, but still more appeared, at least to the north. To the southeast, the flood of AA had stopped. Major Kutzman hesitated when there was nobody left to fight there before he began to sprint towards Esther and the few Marines left on the north side.

Two more AA charged her. She managed to hit one, who stumbled, and the fighter following him vaulted over his comrade, intent on closing in with Esther. She fired, but after a single dart, her magazine was empty. Her training took over, and she swung the carbine up in an attempt to break the fighter's jaw, but he swerved to the side, taking the blow to his upper chest. The follow-through exposed Esther, and the man crashed into her. She staggered, but kept her feet, trying to push him away, but the man was like a bulldog.

And suddenly, her opponent was going over backwards. Noah had somehow gained enough consciousness to wrap his arms around the man's feet, tripping him. Esther reversed her M90 and drove the barrel with all her strength at the base of the fighter's neck. He started gurgling in panic as the muzzle penetrated his skin and hit the neck bones before sliding off to the side.

"Thanks, Noah," she said as her brother slipped back into unconsciousness.

Esther got back to her feet and started to shout for the Three when figures appeared again on the southeast side. She raised Noah's M90 to engage, but it hit her: they weren't wearing the floppy hats of the AA.

Hell, it's the Nayi Bharat militia, she realized with wonderment.

Within moments, the few became a flood as more and more of them crested the shoulder and rushed into the battle, sweeping the AA before them. Esther turned to join them, but the battle was over. Several AA, shocked by the sudden appearance of the militia, stood with hands raised over their heads. Others turned and bolted down the sides of the hill to the north with the militia in hot pursuit.

"Colonel, are you OK?"

Esther turned back around to see Major Frazier standing before her.

"I've been trying to reach you," he said through his external speaker.

She held up her finger to her bare head, and shrugged before realizing that he could hear her even if she couldn't hear him on any of the nets.

"Lost my helmet," she told him.

"Do you want command back?"

"Not now. Do you have any corpsmen?" she asked as she knelt to check Noah.

"No, but we've got three militia medics. They know their stuff."

"Get them up here. We've got a lot of Marines who need care."

She checked Noah's neck. He had a pulse, but it was quick and reedy. Besides his arm, he'd been hit at least three times that she could see. His bones, which were tied into his skin's circuits, had evidently been knocked out of whack somehow. Two of the hits looked to be darts, which his bones should have stopped.

"What's happening with Bravo and Charlie?" she asked, looking up from where she had her brother's head in her lap.

"The surviving AA are in full retreat. I told Jean to let them go, not to engage."

"Good call," she said, almost absent-mindedly. "We're here to bloody their noses, not exterminate them."

"Well, you did that, Colonel."

"*We* did that, Mark, All of us did."

She looked around the shelf. Most of her Marines were down. Chief Higgins was down. Most of Alpha Company was lost. They may have done the AA damage, but the AA had dished it out as well.

One of the militia medics rushed up and started evaluating Noah. Esther stepped back and let him get to work.

"Don't worry ma'am, he's going to be OK," the medic assured her, but his voice sounding doubtful.

She turned back to Major Frazier, but from his posture and the way his hands were moving, she knew he was intensely into conversation with someone else. Esther knew she could grab his helmet and take command again, but the fight was essentially over, and the battle-lust that had been coursing through her veins had dissipated, leaving her . . . not calm, but spent.

She took the hadron communicator out of her pocket and inputted Admiral Jallaby's code. He answered immediately, as she'd expected. He'd been good at keeping out of her hair, but she knew he'd been monitoring everything he could.

"You wanted to bloody their noses. I think you've got that, Admiral. Now it's up to the politicians to take care of this mess," she said before she cut the circuit.

FS MOUNT FUJI

Chapter 24
Noah

Noah opened his eyes to see Esther nodding off in a chair beside him.

"Ess?" he said, or more accurately, croaked out.

She woke up with a start, jumped to her feet, and took his left hand in hers.

"How are you feeling?" she asked.

"Grubbing awful, like I've been run over with a tank a couple of times."

She smiled at him and said, "It's going to be a while. The ship's surgeon said that taking BOOST after the anti-shock meds was dangerous, very dangerous. You're lucky to be alive."

"Chief Higgins said the same thing. I kind of forced him to do it, Ess. Don't worry, I'll heartily slap his wrist, if you want me to."

He saw the cloud immediately come over her face, and his heart fell.

"Chief?"

"In stasis. Not a good chance for resurrection," she said in a subdued voice.

"Um . . . what's was the butcher's bill?"

"Pretty heavy, Noah. I'll let you know later when you've regained some strength."

"Come on, Ess. Tell me."

She looked up as if checking for medical staff before turning back to him and saying, "Ninety-six KIA, two hundred and fourteen WIA. Forty-one of the KIA have no chance at resurrection, and another twelve have little chance."

The blow hit Noah hard, and he had trouble catching his breath. Esther looked worried and started to call for help when he reached out with his left hand and stopped her.

"I'm OK," he said, lying through his teeth.

Three hundred and ten casualties? That hasn't happened since the Evolution!

Where . . . I mean . . . the ship's sick bay isn't that big."

"The dead are in one of the hangars. The wounded, well, only the seriously wounded got beds on the ship. The rest are back on Nayi Bharat or in their berthing spaces here."

"So, I'm one of the seriously wounded ones?" Noah asked, more to give him time to process the information than anything else.

"Noah, I almost lost you. It was pretty close. Forget about your arm, forget about the three rounds you took, one just a millimeter from severing your spine. The BOOST could have been enough to kill you. What ever possessed you to do that?" she asked, her emotions playing out across her face.

"You needed me. I had to have your back."

"You couldn't take my back if you were dead!" she shouted, leaning over him.

"But I didn't die, Ess."

"But you could have," she said, only slightly quieter.

"And you could have died when you chose to stay on that shelf, Ess, when the XO told you to leave," Noah said with a little more venom than he intended.

"My place was with the Alpha Command," she said. "I had to fight the battalion."

"And my place was with you," he answered.

She looked down at him for a moment, then bent over until her head was on his chest.

"I know now why father said it was a mistake for him to have Uncle Joshua in his platoon. And I know why it was a mistake to have you as my sergeant major."

"It was always a mistake, Ess."

She raised her head and looked at him, asking, "You've known that? Why did you agree, then?"

"Because you asked me too, Ess. And you're my sister. I've always been there for you. You know that."

Esther put her head back on his chest, and Noah could feel her hot tears drip onto him.

"Uh, by the way, what happened? I mean, why are we here instead of, well, dead? Or were we captured by the AA?"

"No, we weren't captured. The cavalry arrived. Major Frazier and the militia came just in the nick of time like in the best Hollybolly flick."

"Really? The militia? The Navi Bharat militia?"

"That's the only militia on the planet, to the best of my knowledge, so yes, the very same."

"I'm guessing I owe the good major a big thanks."

"We owe him a big thanks."

"And the war?"

"There's still at least 7,000 Azaad Andolanalph hiding in the outback. We broke them at the Battle of the Mary Anne Valley—"

"The what? The Battle of the Mary Anne Valley?"

"That's where the battle was fought, Noah."

"Yeah, but that's hardly . . . that's hardly an awe-inspiring name."

Esther shrugged and continued, saying, "Anyway, after the Tungiscle strike, the surviving AA simply ran. They're calling it a tactical withdrawal, but they ran like whipped dogs," she said, and Noah could hear the pride creeping back into her voice. "We let them go, not that I had too much choice. We were beat-up pretty bad, and it took us a day just to get everyone trucked back to Jaipur.

"But within another day, while we were embarking, the AA heads were contacting the Navy Bharat leadership to arrange for talks. Our Council thought that if we bloodied their noses—and damned if I'm not getting tired of that phrase—that would bring the AA to the negotiating table. And I guess the Council was right, at least this time."

"So, we did what they needed us to do, and we took the punishment. Uh . . . so what's going to happen to you?" he asked hesitantly.

"What do you mean?"

"I mean, well, we lost a lot of Marines. Who's going to take the blame?"

"No one's taking the blame, Noah, at least not officially. We're freaking heroes, and that's the official stand," she said.

Noah could hear the bitterness in her voice.

"We're heroes? I know we fought hard, but the losses, Ess. Aren't they going to blame us?"

"No blame. The commandant specifically told me that. No, we're being held up as everything the Marines are supposed to be. They've even conveniently leaked more than a dozen recordings of the battle. Hell, I heard that Corporal Hickson has already received a couple thousand proposals of marriage."

"Hickson? From Bravo?"

"Yeah. He and Lance Corporal Bird stood tall and kept a couple hundred AA from escaping the kill zone. Both were WIA and left back in Jaipur, and when the recording came out, the press found them. Hickson—"

"Who's a good-lucking young man . . ." Noah said.

"Exactly. He's gone viral, he and Bird."

"Good for them. Good for us, Ess."

"I know, but . . . I mean, I'm proud of the battalion. I still can't believe that they pulled it off—"

"We pulled it off, not they. You're the commanding officer."

"OK, OK, 'we' pulled it off. But I've got the feeling that we're being paraded around like dancing bears, ready to perform."

"And you don't like that, Ess."

"Of course not. We have a job, and performing for the public is not in our job description."

"But it is, Ess. We perform every time we take a mission. It just isn't broadcast as much as you're telling me this is."

"Maybe. I just feel uncomfortable about it," she said, not sounding convinced.

"And if Hickson can get some attention, all the more power to him. Better him than me, though."

"Don't speak so soon, brother of mine."

"What do you mean?" he asked.

"We've gone viral, too. You and I. On the shelf, fighting back-to-back at the end. Public Affairs is going to town with it."

"Oh, grubbing hell!"

"Grubbing hell is right. We've got more than a few press junkets after we return."

Noah needed time to take all this in. His head was pounding, and he wasn't sure if that was from his brush with death or from the news. He just wanted a few minutes alone to digest the news.

"I'm glad to see you, Ess, but I'm a little tired, and I'm sure you need to get in your reports."

"All done, at least the ones I could send."

"Already? How could you do them so quickly?"

"Quickly? Noah, you've been out for five days. We're only a day out from Last Stop."

Five days?

"But the doc said you'd probably be tired, so I'll let you be. You get some rest, and I'll stop by."

Five days? he asked himself again.

She stood over him for a moment, took a step as if to leave, then leaned over again to give him a hug. Noah instinctively brought his left stump around to hug her back, giving him a jolt of pain that got through the meds.

Esther jumped back, and Noah said, "It's OK."

He looked at the stump for a moment, the first time he'd seen it when not in shock or on BOOST.

"I was getting used to the Three Musketeers. I'm going to miss them," he said.

"They'll get you into regen. You need it for the nerve and cardiac damage anyway.

Cardiac damage? Maybe the BOOST wasn't such a great idea after all.

"Maybe. We'll see."

"Well, OK. I guess I'll go," she said. "Got to go command or something, you know."

"Yeah, you go command, Ess."

She nodded, then turned away to leave.

"I heard you say you love me, Ess. Back on the mountainside."

She stopped in her tracks still facing away.

"It's on the record now, so you can't deny it," he said as a smile crept over his face.

Noah had always known Esther loved him, even during the time that she wasn't on speaking terms with him, but now he wasn't going to let her forget it.

"Little brothers can be a pain in the ass, you know that?" she asked.

"That's part of the job description."

She turned around a smile on her face as well, reaching down to squeeze his foot under the blanket and saying, "I wouldn't have it any other way, Noah. And yeah, I do love you."

"And I love you too, Ess."

TARAWA

Epilogue
Esther

Two Years Later . . .

Esther walked through the open double doors and into the auditorium. To her no surprise, the place was packed with officials, Marines, friends, and of course, the press. One of the handlers spotted her and came rushing up.

"Colonel Lysander, can you come with me please?" the young captain asked, her arm out pointing the way to the stage.

She started to follow, but a familiar face caught her eye, and she held up a hand to forestall the captain.

"It's good to see you, Miriam," Esther said as she approached the family. "Hannah and Shiloh, you, too. Where's Chance? Is he coming?"

"He's here. He was talking to his dad a few minutes ago."

"Ryan, good to see you, too," she said to Miriam's husband.

"Thank you, Esther. And congratulations, I might add."

"Well, thank you."

Lieutenant Colonel Howard seemed like a good man, and he was treating the kids well, but Esther always felt a little awkward around him.

"Well, I'm glad you could come, all of you," Esther told them.

"We're all still family, Ess," Miriam said.

"Well, I've got a captain about ready to pee in her pants if I don't get down to the stage. We all have to be seated in place before the great man comes."

Miriam leaned in to give Esther a peck on the cheek, then quietly said, "Come over some time. Shiloh keeps talking about you, but she hardly knows you."

"Oh, mom!" the young girl said, clearly embarrassed.

"I'd love to. I'll give you a call."

She let the captain escort her down the side aisle to the front. A couple of people called out to her, but she kept her head straight ahead. There'd be time for mixing with friends later, which she looked forward to, and with the press, which she didn't. Noah kept making fun of her for her continual attempts to duck the media while quiet, shy Noah, had become readily available for each and every request.

"Please take the fourth seat, ma'am," the captain said, and Esther climbed onto the stage and sat down, taking the seat next to Major General Lace-Reimer, now the Chief of Weapons Development here at HQMC. Applause broke out as more people noticed her.

"Colonel," he said as she sat. "Quite a big day, isn't it?"

"Yes, sir, it is. Maybe after today, things will finally get back to normal," she said, nodding at the still clapping crowd.

"You grew up with your father. Do you really think things are ever going to be normal? Will you ever be out of the public eye?"

"Probably not, General, probably not."

Esther took a moment to look over the crowd, most of who were already seated. In the front, right in the middle, was Lieutenant Colonel James Aylsworth. He was looking up at her, and he gave her a wink which she returned.

I'm so lucky to have him.

He'd been a pillar of support over the last two years, giving her an anchor in reality. From the moment the battalion had returned to Last Stop, she'd needed it. For two weeks, the battalion had been the flavor of the month for not only the Federation media, but from all over human space, all pushed by an aggressive Marine Corps Public Affairs Division. And then after the attention moved onto the next big things, there were still dinners, symposiums, several documentaries, and of course, the award ceremonies.

First Battalion, Eight Marines, now held the record as the most decorated battalion for any single action since Third Battalion, Seventeenth Marines during the War of the Far Reaches. If you went by upper-level awards, 1/8 could be considered the most decorated battalion overall since the forming of the Corps.

The battalion landed on Navi Bharat with 783 Marines and sailors. A total of 186 battlefield commendations of all three classes were awarded, 32 Bronze Stars, 18 Silver Stars, 1 Legion of Merit with Combat V, and five Navy Crosses. The battalion itself was awarded the Chairman's Unit Commendation. And of course, there was today's ceremony as well. A week prior, Captain Wes McLamb's Federation Nova was presented to his wife on his home planet of San Gabriel. Today was different. The public loved living Nova recipients, and the press was here to milk it for all it was worth.

Esther at first balked when General Lace-Reimer had personally told her upon their return that her first job was to determine awards. She didn't believe in quotas for awards, and she thought the commandant might be pushing her in that direction. However, she had gone over each and every one of the BC3's and above, and they were all deserving. Not just Hickson and Bird, or Lieutenant Eikbush, for that matter, for their Navy Crosses. Not just Major, now Lieutenant Colonel, Frazier's Legion of Merit, not just the higher awards, but right on down the line to the last BC3 she recommended, given to PFC Islington, who'd rushed into fire to pull back a wounded Marine to safety.

She'd been proud to award the battlefield commendations, and she'd attended every other award ceremony. She'd cried for the 68 recipients who'd died earning their awards, but she was proud to have served with them.

More applause broke out, and Esther looked up to see Noah come out of the wings of the stage. He gave the crowd a little wave, then sat beside her.

"Glad to see you can make it, little bro," she whispered about of the side of her mouth.

"Wouldn't miss it if I could," he whispered back. "And oh, you weren't going to mention something to me? I just saw the selection list, Colonel (Select) Lysander."

"You've been a real sergeant major for eight months now, so don't you think you should have checked the list by now?" Esther countered.

"I don't bother with officer stuff. Too political and all, you know."

"That's the pot calling the kettle black, Sergeant Major."

Noah merely let out a grunt.

"I talked to Miriam a few minutes ago. She invited me over to the house sometime," she asked, waiting for Noah's reaction.

"Do it. The kids need to get to know you, the real you, not just what they say on the holos."

"So, they can see I'm not a stuffed-shirt prig?"

"You've kind of got it 'bass-ackwards,' Ess. I want them to see the warts, and you sure have a lot of them."

Without turning her head, she flung out an arm and punched him in the left arm. Laughs rang out from the crowd.

"Grubbing hell, Ess. You should be sitting on my other side."

"What, and punch D'Artagnan? Fat chance of that. I'd break my fist."

Noah never did go through regen for his arm, choosing a prosthetic instead. Not only did he refuse a lifelike arm, but he chose one of a highly polished titanium alloy.

"Would serve you right."

General Lace-Reimer gave an exaggerated cough, his way of telling them to quit playing around. Like chastised school children, they sat back in their chairs.

Not for long, though.

"Miriam said you were talking to Chance?"

"Fatherly duties. He needed some, well, guidance."

"You like doing that, don't you?"

"Yeah, I do. You'll love it too, being a parent, when the time comes."

She took another look to Jim, who was speaking with Ryan Howard. The rest of Noah's family, to include Chance, were now sitting next to Jim in the front row.

She was saved from a response when someone announced, "Ladies and Gentlemen, the Chairman of the Council of the United

Federation, Dexter Tse Won, and the Commandant of the Marine Corps, General Peter Joseph Rzeminski."

The entire auditorium rose to their feet applauding. The three Marines on stage rose as well, although they stood at attention.

The chairman waved at the crowd, then shook each of the three Marines' hands. Esther knew the man was the ultimate politician, but still, she felt as if the man was talking to her like an old friend for the ten seconds he spent with her. He even took Noah's titanium hand without pausing, pumping it vigorously. Finally, he and the commandant took their seats.

"Ladies and gentlemen," the announcer started, "Welcome to the awards ceremony for the United Federation Nova."

There was cheers and applause.

"On February 20, 343, First Battalion, Eighth Marines, Third Marine Division marched into history. Before we begin, we'd like to honor the entire battalion, so would all members of the battalion on that date who are here with us today, please stand?"

Over 200 Marines and sailors rose to their feet to the thunderous applause of the rest of the audience.

"That's you, too, Ess," Noah said standing up.

She hurriedly joined him. She caught a few faces: Bill Keating, Jack Hilborn, Dewaine McCurry. Jean Gill. She saw Steven Anderson and motioned for him to stand up as well. They could not have won without the *Mount Fuji*.

But there were faces she didn't see: Chief Higgins, Lee Spain, Jeff Peaslee, Wes McLamb, and many, many more. She'd come to grips with those who were gone; she was done with second guessing herself on what she could have done differently. She'd commanded the best she could, and she was comfortable with that.

The unseen announcer went over the battalion's actions for those two fateful days, a story everyone in the auditorium undoubtedly knew, but they all listened. Not many Federation Novas were ever awarded, and those lucky enough to attend wanted to remember every single moment. Esther knew what had happened, though, and her mind wandered.

She'd always been driven to succeed, in school and in the Corps. When she enlisted, she knew she'd achieve two things: she'd become half of the first father-daughter recipients of the Federation Nova, and she'd become half of the first father-daughter Commandants of the Marine Corps. At times, she'd been a real asshole about it, putting career before humanity. And she'd done well, the first of her NOTC class to be selected for colonel. On her chest were three Navy Crosses, something no living Marine or sailor had achieved.

She stole a glance at Noah. She'd been surprised when he'd enlisted, and she'd been even more surprised that he'd climbed the ranks. He didn't have the same drive she had, at least not obviously. His main motivation had been to gain the respect of their father, even after his death. Working for that had cost him his marriage. She gave him a little nudge with her shoulder, and he pressed back.

Looking back down to the front row, her eyes locked onto Jim as he listened to the announcer. For the thousandth time, she wondered how she, the driven one, had been so lucky in love while Noah, the personable one of the two, had a broken marriage.

The announcer finished his narrative, and the chairman looked around. In the wings, a young suit motioned for him to approach the lectern. For a moment, he looked like an old man, somewhat confused, but the minute he reached the lectern and looked out at the holocorders and the crowd, he transformed. He immediately went into a history lesson, mentioning their father and what he'd done for the Federation. When he remarked that blood ran true, Esther's thoughts wandered again.

Does it really run true? What would she have accomplished if she was Esther Smith or Esther Hernandez? Would she be sitting up here on the stage without Ryck Lysander as her father? She'd like to think she would, but she decided that for a "what if" question like that, it was probably better just to believe.

Suddenly, she realized that the chairman had stopped speaking. She managed to stand up with the other three Marines as the chairman walked back to stand facing them.

"Would the audience please rise?" the announcer's voice filled the auditorium.

"The Chairman of the United Federation of States takes great pride in presenting the United Federation of States Nova to Sergeant Major Noah Lysander, United States Marine Corps, for service as set forth in the following citation . . ."

Esther heart filled with joy, true joy. She didn't care that she wasn't receiving the award herself, and she was proud to bursting that her little brother was. She'd received the Navy Cross for leading the battalion, and her military career was more than on track. Noah, after losing an arm, had insisted on a life-threatening BOOST injection in order to protect her, and he done so until he'd been cut down.

He stood tall and proud as the chairman put the medal around his neck, and tears streamed down his eyes. Esther knew that the tears were for those lost in the battle, but also for their father.

Esther was sure, beyond a shadow of a doubt, then somewhere up there, General Ryck Lysander was looking down on them and was absolutely proud of his son.

Jonathan P. Brazee

Thank you for reading *Blood United,* the final novel in the Lysander Twins series. The series will conclude with *Coda,* a novelette which will be released in late August. I hope you enjoyed this book, and I welcome a review on Amazon, Goodreads, or any other outlet.

If you would like updates on new books releases, news, or special offers, please consider signing up for my mailing list. Your email will not be sold, rented, or in any other way disseminated. If you are interested, please sign up at the link below:

http://eepurl.com/bnFSHH

Other Books by Jonathan Brazee

The United Federation Marine Corps' Lysander Twins
Legacy Marines
Esther's Story: Recon Marine
Noah's Story: Marine Tanker
Esther's Story: Special Duty
Blood United

Coda

The United Federation Marine Corps
Recruit
Sergeant
Lieutenant
Captain
Major
Lieutenant Colonel
Colonel
Commandant

Rebel
(Set in the UFMC universe.)

Behind Enemy Lines
(A UFMC Prequel)

Women of the United Federation Marine Corps
Gladiator
Sniper
Corpsman

High Value Target (A Gracie Medicine Crow Short Story)
BOLO Mission (A Gracie Medicine Crow Short Story)

The Return of the Marines Trilogy
The Few
The Proud
The Marines

The Al Anbar Chronicles: First Marine Expeditionary Force--Iraq
Prisoner of Fallujah
Combat Corpsman
Sniper

Werewolf of Marines
Werewolf of Marines: Semper Lycanus
Werewolf of Marines: Patria Lycanus
Werewolf of Marines: Pax Lycanus

To The Shores of Tripoli

Wererat

Darwin's Quest: The Search for the Ultimate Survivor

Venus: A Paleolithic Short Story

Secession

Duty

Non-Fiction

Exercise for a Longer Life

Author Website
http://www.jonathanbrazee.com

Made in the USA
San Bernardino,
CA